WHO WILL FIND HER?

PRAISE FOR
WHO WILL FIND HER?

"A harrowing crime novel that will leave even the bravest of readers double-checking the locks at night. **Ryan Young** has written the binge-read Southern thriller of the year."
-**C.W. Blackwell**, author of
Hard Mountain Clay

"...has some serious *The Body* by **Stephen King** vibes. The mystery kept me guessing and the last forty pages had me racing to the finish to find out the fates of our young heroes."
-**Alexander Nader**, author of
Absolution Blues

"A tension fueled page turner that will keep you guessing until the last word. Character-driven dialogue and the mounting horror will keep you captivated until the end."
-**Candace Nola**, author of
Bishop

"...weaves an enthralling web of narratives. From the lies we tell ourselves to get by, to the lengths we'll go for the ones we love, *Who Will Find Her?* will rivet you from start to finish with a story that's both new and terrifyingly familiar. This is a thrill you don't want to miss!"
-**Brett Allen**, author of
Sly Fox Hollow and *Kilroy Was Here*

WHO WILL FIND HER?

A Novel

RYAN YOUNG

Published in the United States by Puree Publishing,
an imprint of Falling Pear, LLC.

ISBN (paperback): 979-8-9862212-2-9
ISBN (ebook): 979-8-9862212-3-6
ISBN (hardcover): 979-8-9862212-4-3

Cover design by Ryan Young
www.pureepublishing.com

For my girls, this one and every one.

ONE

"Two counts of aggravated sexual assault of a minor. One count each of robbery, child abuse, possession of child pornography, kidnapping, stalking, drug possession, and harassment. Those were the charges you pleaded no contest to during your initial arraignment. Does it sound like I missed anything, Mr. Finely?" The judge looks over the rim of the reading glasses that cling to the tip of his nose. The defendant, in full orange, absorbs the stare from across the courtroom with a bowed head. A court-appointed attorney sits next to him. The man places a hand on the defendant's chair which seems to draw out a voice.

"FIN-LAY."

"Excuse me?"

"It's pronounced FIN-LAY, your excellency." The defendant doesn't bother to look up from his lap where his wrists are bound.

"I will not tolerate your mockery, Mr. FIN-LAY." The judge pushes his glasses further up the bridge of his nose and scans the documents in front of him.

Outside of the courtroom, Erin Heart watches the camera feed, unblinking. "Jesus, this guy is as nuts as they say he is." Her camera operator shrugs. She holds her HBN-branded microphone against her low-cut dress. The angel pendant around her neck bounces against the wired dome of the mic and she is quick to stash it into her cleavage so it won't make noise once she goes live.

On the monitor, Finely stirs in his seat and lets out an audible exhale. The judge licks a thumb before leafing through the stack of papers. He taps them on his bench and places them neatly in front, straightening the edges to perfect ninety-degree angles.

"As Mr. Bartlow here should have already informed you, the family members have elected not to speak, aside from the letter that has been submitted and provided to you. Can you confirm receipt of this letter, Mr. Finely?"

"Who? Oh, him?" Finely nods to the rotund man sitting to his left in a well-pressed but poorly-fit gray suit. Sweat pours from the man's brow, just under what fine gray hair has chosen to remain and fight the battle against baldness. The last Spartans in a receding phalanx of slicked-back monochrome.

The judge's stare is ice cold and Finely straightens in his seat.

"Yes, your honor. But I'm sorry to say I've been a bit busy. Haven't had quite the time to give it a read, seems a little long-winded."

The attorney leans over and whispers to the defendant who levels his head to look at the judge, a crooked, ugly smile in the middle of white and gray stubble. Thin, white hair sprouts from the liver-spotted skin that is stretched too tight across his scalp.

"Here we go." Erin stands from her seated position outside of the courtroom. "Get up!"

The cameraman juggles the camera to his shoulder with a noticeable lack of agility and adjusts his earpiece. "The desk is ready. They'll throw to you on his way out, either way."

Erin leans back into the courtroom monitor, laser-focused on the unfolding drama. This Finely was a nobody forty-eight hours ago, but all it took was the Florida Republican Governor calling out the newly elected Democratic Governor of North Carolina for being soft on crime and suddenly everyone cares about the fate of one old, perverted man. As soon as the feud went nuclear on social media, Erin knew it would all be gold and she's perfectly positioned to reap the benefits of the public's outrage.

The judge clears his throat. "Well, decisions like these are never easy, or are they made in haste." The people seated in the gallery can be heard as they anticipate the judge's ruling. A raised palm brings quiet. "It is the opinion of this court that the time served, six years of a thirty-year sentence, is sufficient to meet the criteria set forth in the initial ruling. I hereby grant your request for parole, Mr. Finely, and sentence you to two years probation."

An audible gasp carries over those inside. A shriek pierces the air and a woman is escorted from the room. Once calm has been restored, the judge glances down at his watch and then back to the defendant. "This ruling is effective today, July the 30th at 12:07 p.m. Court is adjourned."

Finely scoffs but shows no sign of surprise, it's as if the parole is a grave injustice worth protesting to the fullest measure of discontent. He waits for the bailiff to arrive behind him before standing and offering his arms to be uncuffed.

"Oh and Mr. FINE-LY."

The defendant turns back to the judge, but his decrepit smile has vanished. An emotionless, empty look causes the tired judge, who appears to be sinking under the weight of his robe, to stutter before continuing.

"I'll-I'll…warn you now, one slip up, you so much as forget to signal while pulling into whatever Podunk bar you'll stain with your presence and I'll have you locked up faster than you can say Fin-LAY."

Finely doesn't respond for a beat. His attorney adjusts his tie knot amid a painful gulp. The bailiff steps closer. That awful, nightmarish smile returns.

"Mighty kind advice of you, your excel—your honor." Finely raises his fingers to his forehead in a mock salute and as he turns to walk away, drags them across his unshaven throat.

Nobody in the courtroom, save the judge, seems to notice. In a flash of black fabric, he retreats to his quarters without so much as looking back at the defendant.

"Fuck me. You see that, Marcus?" Erin says to the voice in her ear.

She can't make out what the producer is saying in response so she adjusts the IFB, forcing it deep into her ear, and stares straight into the lens of the camera, waiting for her cue. Adrenaline courses through her veins, her heart rate increasing along with her breathing. She can feel a deep pressure in her throat. This is what she lives for, this exact moment. The anticipation, those two words that are like a drug. Time slows, maybe stops. A bomb could detonate and it would be but a distant interruption while her entire attention is listening for the cue.

The cameraman wags a finger at her and then she hears it. "You're live." The words make her body tremble as she imagines being with the man who is commanding her through the IFB. Before anyone can notice, she's back and going full speed.

"I'm Erin Heart live outside the courtroom where the now infamous child predator, James Finely, has just been granted his petition for parole and is now a free man." She speaks his name correctly, ad-libbing the new information like a true professional. "Originally sentenced almost seven years ago, Finely has resurfaced a number of times while appealing his conviction. Each time causing fresh anguish to the victims and their families. It would appear that the sixty-five-year-old Finely is to some an example of the system working as intended, and to others another glaring example of lax criminal policies that endanger the public."

The courtroom door swings open to a commotion of reporters and spectators that echo off of the marble floor. Police officers surround the defendant, leading him out and toward the exit. Erin is in hot pursuit. She's no amateur and as her last location assignment before her debut on the desk, she will not screw this up.

When the hallway of bodies compresses and she sees that she'll be cut off from Finely, she turns to the cameraman and points to a side door. "This way!"

"Erin, we're staying on you," says the voice.

She flashes a subtle OK sign to the camera as they burst into a stairwell and go down a half-flight of stairs. The image bounces and shakes as her cameraman tries to keep up with her. Sunlight flares white as she barrels through the emergency exit and moves to the front of the courthouse.

Erin makes it to the landing as the escort brings Finely out the set of double doors.

"Mr. Finely, Mr. Finely." Erin runs up to meet him, the camera still right behind her, all live for the world to see.

"Mr. Finely, how do you feel now that you're a free man?" She shoves the HBN microphone in front of his hanging head with no expectation of a response. They rarely do, at least the smart ones.

A chuckle takes her by surprise. It even scares her a bit. She presses.

"If you've been granted parole, why are you still being escorted?"

Finely turns his murky eyes to her as he's led down the sidewalk.

"Well, shit, honey. Aren't you a sight?"

She offers a faint, charming smile and pushes the microphone closer to him. Flirting goes a long way in this business and her wardrobe choice was no accident.

"You see, the man in the black dress with the banging stick didn't want a bunch of hubbub on his precious front yard, so these fine gentlemen are giving me one last ride."

"And you feel you've been rehabilitated? That ordinary citizens have nothing to fear with your reintegration into society?"

"Big words don't always mean big brain, honey. Plus, I'm innocent, always will be. Doesn't matter what no one says."

"But you pleaded guilty to the original charges."

"Ah! No contest. But you knew that. We get the TV on the inside, ya know. I've watched you many, many times. And I also know you don't ask questions you don't already know the answer to."

The thought of this man watching her, and doing Lord knows what else, makes her skin crawl, but she fights to hide any tell in her body language.

"So, you're sticking to your recanting that your original confession we coerced?"

"I'm saying I took the damn plea. I was guilty in their eyes before they even put cuffs on me. Just the right white trash at the right moment."

Erin pushes back, it won't be said she didn't do her research. "There were hundreds of documents, eye-witness testimony, DNA even!"

"You try mounting a defense with one of these dropouts they give you for an attorney." Finely's lawyer takes it in stride along the path to the road that seems endless. "You ever hear of discovery, chain of custody for evidence? Maybe look into how they got my DNA in the first place."

With that, she's stumped. She read the file but didn't dig deep enough into the court filings to understand the semantics. She has a moment of panic, trying to fill the dead air, but the officers come to her rescue by stopping to hold back the media as the door to the transport van is opened from the inside. Still, she can't let it end without leaving her mark.

"James Finely, did you or did you not molest those two children?"

He stops, taking his police escort off guard. Everyone goes tense, including Erin. Before the detail can put themselves between the defendant and the reporter, Finely steps to her and plants a forceful, wet kiss on her cheek. He protrudes his tongue to make contact as he's dragged back by an officer.

"Oh, I like you," he whispers.

Finely is pulled off his feet and placed into the van. The sliding door slams closed and the van accelerates away from the courthouse.

Erin accepts a rag from the cameraman who is focused on the van and quickly wipes her cheek, careful not to smudge her makeup in the process. When she sees the camera pan from the transport back in her direction, she throws down the rag and paints a wide smile, adding a hint of brave trauma survivor for good measure.

"Well, that wasn't quite what any of us here expected but I'm thankful to have brought it all to you firsthand on HBN. Now I'm sure this story is not over. In fact, I see the Florida Governor has already weighed in." Erin gestures with her phone and then lowers it out of frame. She listens to her earpiece as the desk correspondents wrap up the coverage. She nods, beaming that million-dollar expression into the lens.

"That's right, Jason. Definitely the feeling on the ground here as well."

One last nod and a head tilt of gratitude.

"Thank you, it's been an amazing experience. One last time, I'm Erin Heart and I'll see you all in primetime! Back to you!"

She waits for her cameraman to give the all-clear. He rests the camera on his leg as if he's about to collapse from exhaustion.

"Wow. Incredible right?" Erin now realizes she's short of breath and fans herself.

The cameraman nods. "It was, something."

Erin removes her IFB and hands it and her microphone to the cameraman. She looks around, gauging if any public eyes are on her. An officer places a hand on her elbow and asks if she's okay. She acknowledges the courtesy and retrieves the pendant from its hiding place. The officer tries to avert his glance but fails. He's quick to join the others heading back to the courthouse.

"Hey good luck to you Erin, it's been a hell of a ride." Her cameraman goes in for a hug.

She blocks him with a handshake. "You too, Leonard."

After a short and sweaty exchange, he shoulders his camera bag and heads in the direction of the news van. "Bitch."

Erin hears what was intended to be silent but she won't let anything ruin her mood. Soon she'll be the face of primetime at HBN. And she'll have everything she's ever wanted. The time slot, the office, the advertisements with her face and name. Everything she deserves. She waves her hands at her eyes as they burn with tears of anticipation and ecstasy.

TWO

THREE MONTHS LATER

Hawksboro is the kind of small town with a single stop light. Where residents still leave their doors unlocked and send their kids out to play until dark. Granted, they might have phones in hand instead of baseball cards and motorized scooters instead of Huffys, but the spirit is the same. If not for the turn-of-the-century cars, many still a decade old at that, the quaint North Carolina town looks the same as it did in the '80s. Both '80s, as a matter of fact.

The town was incorporated post-Civil War by Colonel Jeffrey Hawkes after returning from his time in a Union prison camp where he lost an arm and a leg. His descendants claim that's where the phrase originated, but no proof could substantiate the attribution. The statue of Hawke's pre-injury pose was removed a few years ago and replaced with that of a regional Cherokee Chief named Black Hawk. Town members now argue which man represents their namesake.

Melody's thoughts are pulled from her senior thesis on the history of Hawksboro when an old pickup truck shifts gears as that sole light changes from red to green. Scrap wood hangs over the tailgate. The driver slows and honks a friendly hello to the kids in soccer jerseys piling into Gio's Pizza & Bar, their coach herding from behind with a polished trophy. Yellow and orange leaves drift from the treelined sidewalks and swirl into the parking spaces, finally resting in small piles against the curb.

With a dream-like stride, she jogs along the Main Street sidewalk. She's 17, though she could pass for a woman a few years older. Sometimes it has its perks, but most of the time it's a curse. With all of the pressures of transitioning to adulthood, can't she just be a kid for a while longer?

Her perfectly straight blonde hair, pulled back in a tight ponytail, bounces with every strike of her unblemished, white trail runners. Her phone is in a waist pouch, like a sleek fanny pack for runners, but she doesn't wear headphones. Music would be a distraction, making the run easier, and she runs for one reason: to be the best in the 10,000m in the state. That's how she'll get out of Hawksboro. That's how she'll pay for college.

Another honk echoes along Main Street as a different truck slows next to Melody. She can't help the feeling of being watched. No stranger to drive-by stares, she decides to force a smile before turning her attention to the driver. It's a boy her age in a high school football jersey. Jimmy Atkins, she thinks judging by the make and color, but it's hard to see through the glare in the windshield. Indulging out of kindness, she gives a quick wave and then sees the freckled number 8 who almost hits a parked car as he waves back. He swerves into his lane and the quarterback accelerates out of view, undoubtedly to avoid further embarrassment.

She's used to the attention. Since she was a young girl, Melody has been aware that people find her attractive. Though she can't seem to see it in the mirror herself, she doesn't lack confidence and has mastered the art of using her gifted beauty to her advantage, but never at the expense of humility or honor. Before she excelled at running, grades and character were going to be her ticket out. Now they're just bargaining chips for the colleges that have already begun courting her for next year. With that thought, Melody realizes a year from now she'll be on campus somewhere, far from here. It puts an extra kick in her stride.

"Hiya, Melody!" A man's voice calls out.

She's startled for only a moment. Now on the edge of town and beyond earshot of Main Street, Melody turns to see her teacher working in his yard. A rusted lawnmower sits upturned at his feet, he wields a flathead screwdriver in one hand and an oiled cloth in the other.

"Hi, Mr. Alexander!" Not allowing the greeting to alter her pace.

"Keep up the hard work! You better get a move on it, some nasty clouds rolling in." He gestures with the screwdriver to the sky above the towering and colorful mountains that surround the town.

She glances up, already aware, but considering them as a courtesy to his advice. "You got it. Tell Dorothy I say hello!" Melody quickens her tempo once again, not only for the storm but to politely put an end to the exchange.

"Will do, see you Monday!" Mr. Alexander calls out, nearly yelling as she's already passing the end of his yard.

After a few minutes of pushing up a slight incline in the road, Melody takes a sharp right turn onto a trailhead in the trees on the side of the road. UPPER TRAIL 2.3 Mi. She reads the sign, as she has done dozens of times before with her set training schedule. Her dad would prefer she run the track at the high school instead and has asked as much since that's the event she's training for, but being among nature and the uneven earth feels like another obstacle to overcome. Not something a flat, repetitious oval can offer. She tells herself it will make her better, faster. And most of all she's able to avoid the small talk of a bustling practice field. *Focus.*

A light sprinkle drops between the branches and dampens the dusty path before her feet. She can see the growing dark orbs of water among the lighter, dry dirt. A rumble of thunder makes her think twice about continuing. Melody has run plenty of times in the rain, in fact, she finds it to be a refreshing and exhilarating experience, but she knows enough to not mess around with lightning. She can always turn back.

Fifteen minutes down the trail and the thunder has grown louder and the flashes more frequent. Melody is getting nervous but can see the turnaround loop up ahead. There's a small bench with a roof and a worn, faded map of connecting trails above it. As she makes it to the dead end, lightning explodes around her. The instant crack of thunder rattles her wet and shivering body. Her socks are saturated but haven't started to rub to the point of blisters. She wonders if she should wait under the small roof for the storm to pass or run through it and get back before sundown. The clouds have sucked the majority of the light out of the forest, advancing the darkness by an hour or more.

Melody feels for her phone and digs it out of the waist pouch. She rests her back against the upright log that serves as the support for the wood-shingle roof. Another terrifying explosion of lighting causes her to wince and cower. She fumbles with her phone, trying to bring up the call list. Scrolling through the RECENTS, she searches for DAD. He won't be happy but she should be able to get back to the trailhead by the time he can get there to pick her up.

Her hair stands on end and she cowers, waiting for the boom of thunder but realizes there was no lightning, but a cough. Or someone clearing their throat. Melody whips around and peers into the thick growth, water running over her eyes and reddened cheeks.

"Hello?" Her lips quiver as the dampness extracts the heat from her core. "I'm on the phone with my Dad, do you need a ride?" She calls out, bluffing.

A shape moves among the depth of the trees. She can't tell if it's a shadow or a coat, or nothing at all. It's obscured by sheets of falling water. Melody releases a long exhale to try to calm herself. Her thumbs slide over the phone to wake it up. Water has dripped onto the screen and she can't get it unlocked. It vibrates with each failed attempt. She thinks about hitting the EMERGENCY CALL option but decides against it. She's never done it and doesn't even know what it would do. Does it open the call app? Does it call 911 immediately? She doesn't want that, how embarrassing that would be.

"Shit!" She wipes the water from her forehead and tries to dry her hand on her shorts.

Branches crack or settle, in the downpour. Melody can't be sure. The woods and storm are playing with her mind. She'll laugh about this once she's in the warm cab of her dad's truck.

"Come on, come on." Melody finally gets the phone to open and scrolls once more to see DAD on the list. She presses down on the name and the CALL, TEXT, VIDEO options appear.

"Pssst."

The sound is distinct and horrifying. But it can't be real. She's alone. Until she realizes that she's not.

She pushes her thumb down on the CALL button but it doesn't register. Before she can try again, a gloved hand covers her mouth and yanks her into the darkness. The phone falls into a muddy puddle at the base of the bench, accumulating raindrops on the still-active screen. One drip hits above the CALL button and slides down the glass. As she fights, grabbing and kicking while being pulled backward, her eyes never leave the phone. She prays the call will go through. Wills the water to make the selection. Then the screen goes to sleep and the number is left undialed. Her hope and consciousness fade as one.

THREE

rip. Drip.

Cheyenne stirs in her soft, white blanket ordained with galloping horses. She's first aware of the light rain outside before hearing that someone is at the bedroom door.

"Chey, wake up. It's Jason. Chey!" As loud of a whisper as the young boy's voice outside can manage.

She bats her eyes and turns them toward the alarm clock on her bedside table. It's still early, just a little past 10 p.m. The rain must have lulled her to sleep. Cheyenne feels for the book that she was reading an hour before.

"Chey, come on open up or I'm barging in!"

"I'm coming, Jason. What is it?" She rolls herself out of bed and places a foot on the cover of the book. Careful not to crease any pages, she smooths it out and returns it to the bedside table next to the clock.

Only now does she see the lights dancing off of the walls and ceiling from outside her window. Alternating blue and red, soft and distant. Otherwise, it's still dark in her room. Gram must have checked on her before going to bed and turned off the reading light.

Her steps cause the boards to creak as she makes her way to the door. As the handle clears the latch, Jason pushes into the room and moves right to her window, peering through the raindrops that cascade down the surface of the glass. The same colored lights now reflect off of his face. He brushes his eye-length bangs of dark brown hair toward his ear. She expected him to be in PJs but he still wears the same clothes he wore all day at school.

"What are you doing, weirdo?" Cheyenne turns to him, still half asleep at her door.

"There's something going on over at the high school."

She shakes her head as if this was not an acceptable reason to wake her. "And?"

"Maybe there's a fire! We could miss school tomorrow!"

"Tomorrow's Saturday, genius."

He looks at her as if she crushed a dream and returns his attention to the lights.

"Well, maybe it's a big fire."

Cheyenne crosses the room and throws her weight down on the bed. Jason jumps to her closet and tosses her a pair of shoes.

"Come on."

With minimal effort raising her head, Cheyenne looks at Jason's feet, which are already clad in tight-laced sneakers. She rolls over, burying her head in her pillow.

"Fine. I'll go without you."

With a groan, Cheyenne tosses her pillow at Jason and picks herself back up to the edge of the bed. Acting as somewhat of a stand-in mom for three years now—since the accident just before her 12th birthday—has been surreal at times with just one year between their ages. Sometimes 14 feels more like 34, she imagines. A sense of guilt comes with the self-loathing as her grandparents have done more than enough to care for them, but she can't avoid the burden of responsibility for the clear blind spots they have when it comes to kids. The thought of Gram and Grampa worrying about him, when she could have made sure he was alright, is all the motivation she needs to slide her feet into her slip-on shoes.

"Yes!"

"Just to the school and right back. If Gram checks either of our rooms and we're not here she'll have a heart attack."

"I just wanna see!"

"Hand me my jacket, numbskull."

Jason hops around the room, unable to contain his excitement.

"Shhhh. Let's go."

It takes less than ten minutes to walk the couple of blocks from their house to the back side of the high school. The rain has stopped and the shine on the asphalt reflects the lights of the police vehicles across town in every direction. The ground looks aflame with bright blues, reds, and whites.

A crowd has gathered at the steps of the gymnasium and three Hawksboro police SUVs line the sidewalk that curves with the bus loop out front. A man in uniform is at the top of the steps on the wide landing with faded railings on both sides, boxing him in and he appears trapped as he stands with a few other deputies. A man in dress clothes, like something someone would wear to church, hovers behind the officers as they address the group of people that have pushed to the base of the stairs. Cheyenne recognizes most of them as parents of kids from her school.

"Hey isn't that the sheriff?" Jason points from their concealment behind the school sign at the center of the roundabout.

They're not hidden as the entire oval is well-lit. Ever since they put in the new halogen lights after a string of spray painters and trash tossers ransacked the school, the whole place has been as bright as daylight. It stands out in stark contrast to the older tungsten lights that still line the dim streets of the town.

Maybe thirty feet away, they could probably join the group without much notice but Cheyenne would rather not be that much closer when it's time to leave.

"I think so. And the mayor too. Now quiet and maybe we can hear," she says.

The sheriff finishes speaking with one of his deputies and then holds up his hands to silence the grumbling parents. They shush to an eerie silence and he coughs into his hand, either clearing his throat or stalling to find words.

"I'm sorry to keep you all waiting, I know you've been out here for some time. First, thank you for migrating from the station to the school as this will help keep the flow of our officers uninhibited as they do their jobs."

Cheyenne can just barely make out the words. Even though the people have stopped murmuring, the running vehicles and sounds of the night make them hard to decipher.

"Sheriff, have you found anything?" asks who Cheyenne thinks is Dora Jenkins.

"Yeah, Rodney, does anyone even know who saw her last?" A man she doesn't recognize chimes in.

"Folks, please. I don't have a lot of information but I'm going to share what I can. OK?"

The sheriff scans the faces of the crowd before continuing.

"We got a call this evening just before seven from Molly Anderson, Melody's mother, that she hadn't returned home from a run. I've had a few people confirm they saw her going through town a bit before the storm came through and spoke with Jack Anderson on the phone about an hour ago. He mentioned she was most likely running the Upper Trail Loop, which is where he's at now with Officers Rodgers, Harlow, and Delnado."

"I saw her running along Main Street around five, I think." Cheyenne sees Mr. Flowers speak up and looks around for his daughter, Rachel, but as far as she can tell they're the only children. More of a reason to stay back a distance.

"Thanks, Glenn. Now I appreciate everyone coming down out of concern, there's just not a lot anyone can do right now that we aren't already doing. I know you're eager to form a search party and I can promise you as soon as the time comes for that we'll have organizers spread the word. I'd like to wrap it up here so you can all get home, if nobody has anything further to share that could help us in our efforts."

The crowd turns their attention to the roar of a large white pickup truck speeding into the bus loop. Cheyenne and Jason move around the sign to try to hide them from the view of the oncoming truck. Rodney pushes his way through the people on the stairs and out into the road. The truck slides to a stop and several football players hop out of the open truck bed. Jack Anderson leaves the driver's door open and darts around the hood where Rodney shields his eyes from the headlights.

"Tell me you found her, Jack."

Jack wipes his square, hairless jawline. "Rodney, I need you to call in some backup. We gotta get back up there."

"Slow down. Tell me what you found." The sheriff places his hand on Jack's shoulder and leans forward to look him in the eyes.

"This was on the ground about 3 miles out, just off the path." Jack's voice cracks as he reveals Melody's phone. He puts both hands behind his head and draws in a large breath.

"Don't jump to any scenarios just yet, okay? This doesn't necessarily mean anything other than she's just without a phone."

"We tried following some tracks in the mud, but there was more than one set. It was a mess. Oh, God. I don't know what to do. You gotta call someone."

"I got it, Jack. I got it. I'm calling in state and park services. Go home. Tell Molly only what you absolutely need to. No point of her and Simone getting worked up until we know more."

Jack looks around at nothing in particular then down to his hand. He holds the phone as if seeing one for the first time. An object of unfathomable capabilities.

"Just hold on to it for now, keep it charged. If anyone other than Melody calls or texts I want to know, understand?"

Nodding in agreement, Jack slides the phone into his front pocket.

As the sheriff steps away, he presses the push-to-talk button on his radio. "Zero one to zero seven, over."

"Go for zero seven, over." A voice crackles over the shoulder radio.

"Hey Darren, I'm headed up your way. Meet me at the trail-head, going to call in support while I'm en route, over." Rodney moves to his flashing SUV.

"10-4. Hey uh Rodney, we did find something, over."

"Copy that, Jack has her phone for now, over."

"Negative. We found some clothing, and there's blo—"

Rodney is quick to cover the radio with his hand and side of his face, pinning it between his cheek and shoulder. Jack's eyes flare and he bolts back to his truck.

"Goddmannit. Jack! Wait, Jack!"

The truck screeches as it fishtails and accelerates the wrong way out of the bus loop. Rodney hops into his SUV and chirps the siren before shifting into drive.

Cheyenne motions for Jason to stay down as there's nowhere to hide out of sight. She's just hoping that by not moving they won't look in their direction. The sheriff's window is down and she can hear him even clearer than before as he flies past their hiding spot.

"Copy. Darren, Jack's beelining it to your 20. Until we can get some assistance I don't care if Christ Himself shows up, nobody else goes on that trail!"

"10-4."

Rodney steers the SUV out of the bus loop and accelerates to try to catch up to Jack's truck which is already making its way out of town.

Cheyenne turns to Jason who stares off, a stunned expression hanging over his face as colorful lights cast harsh shadows under his eyes and nose. She can see his fear and confusion so she pulls him back away from the sign.

"Everything's going to be fine, let's get back."

She can hear the mayor trying to calm the parents at the steps as the kids sneak across the wet grass. They aren't even out of the bus loop when a paneled station wagon rolls up beside them, wet brakes squealing as it slows.

"Uh-oh." Jason tugs on Cheyenne's sleeve and gestures to the road.

"Get in." The passenger window is down. Inside the vehicle Grampa sits behind the wheel with only a stern and forward-facing expression.

Cheyenne opens the front door and Jason takes the backseat. "How did you know we were here?" she says.

"I was up to the bathroom when I heard you both sneak out. Wasn't going to say anything to Gram but then the phone started ringing with the news, which I suspect you're now aware of."

They apologize in unison. "Don't apologize to me. Gram's waiting for you at the house."

FOUR

When the wagon pulls into the driveway and she hears all three doors close, Cynthia releases her grip from around the edges of her flower pattern nightgown. Her knuckles ache from clenching her fingers shut while she awaited Rick's return with the kids. When the phone first rang, she figured it was probably a wrong number or maybe even a spam call despite the hour, but once she realized the children had snuck out all of her fears and worries came crashing down on her.

Cynthia places her glasses on the kitchen table as Jason is the first through the door. Cheyenne is close behind. A moment later, Rick closes and locks the door and makes a point to leave the room so it's just the three of them. She examines both carefully, not angry but curious. They're wonderful children and she's sure their motive was harmless, but the dangers of sneaking out can't be excused away, especially not now.

"Well, Cheyenne, do you have something to say?"

"What, Gram, me? Why me?"

Jason looks to his feet. She already knows it was likely his idea and he wears the worry of being tattled on all over his face.

"You're the oldest, you should know better."

"I'm sorry, okay. We just woke up because of the commotion and lights and wanted to see what was going on at the school. Figured since the police were there it had to be safe."

"Why didn't you ask us? You can't just be sneaking out of the house like that. That's not like you at all."

"It was my fault, Gram. I asked her."

"Well that's nice of you to say Jason, and you're not off the hook either. You understand how worried I was when I started getting calls about a missing girl from the school and you two aren't in your beds or anywhere to be found?" Her voice trembles with a gravel-like interference.

"We didn't know about that at the time, just wanted to see," says Jason.

"So you heard?" Cynthia leans back in her chair, allowing her momentary displeasure to pass and show she's thankful that they're home safe.

"Yeah. A little. I'm worried about her," says Cheyenne.

"Me too, dear. I'm sure we'll know more in the morning. We'll keep Melody and her family in our prayers tonight, okay?"

Both children nod and wait for their Gram to give the order.

"Alright, shoes off. Back up to bed. I don't want to see your lights on when I come up."

They kick off their shoes and carry them up the stairs, one after the other.

"And no phone or computer, I mean it!" She calls out after they've left the room.

A moment later, Rick pops his head into the kitchen.

"All clear?"

Cynthia forces a smile and pushes herself to her feet, the metal discs of the chair grating on the floor.

"You should really be more upset, I think." She moves to the counter where her tea has been cooling and retrieves the bag, placing it on the spoon.

"They're kids, dear. Not so much different than you or I at that age I reckon."

"No, I spose not, but it's a different time, not like it used to be."

Rick takes her place at the table as she sips her still-hot tea, the steam fogging her glasses for just a moment as it's raised to her mouth. It clears as soon as she brings the mug to rest in front of her nightgown.

"Anyone else call while I was out? Quite the gathering down at the school, word seems to have traveled pretty fast."

"The usual callers, no news other than the first call about Melody not coming home. So sad, you think I should call Molly in the morning?"

"I think that's a bit premature, let them handle this the best they see fit and you can reach out when the time is right. They know you care, but can't imagine they can think clearly right now, anyhow. I don't know what I'd do—"

He doesn't need to finish as they both fill in the gaps, remembering their daughter and son-in-law and the way they pop up for uncountable reasons unknown.

"If she isn't lost and was…taken…who could have done such a thing? In this town? Everyone knows everyone. I can't stomach the thought that a person like that walks among us."

"All we can do is hope for the best, and if the time comes, lift up their family any way we can. It'll be hard on everyone though, the kids especially. They don't understand things like this."

"You'll have to tell them. I don't think I'll have the heart to speak of such horror." She places her half-finished tea in the sink as if the very thought of the conversation has ruined her taste.

Rick rests his elbows on the table and leans into his clasped hands. He looks to Cynthia whose eyes beg for reassurance, or at least it's her desire to convey. He clears his throat and speaks with a soft and comforting tone that makes his words that much more terrifying.

"It's a sad day, having to tell a child that monsters are real. That they don't live under their bed but far, far worse. That they're often among us, in plain sight, and that the days of naïve strolls and false comfort are not only gone but were never real." Rick's mind is somewhere far away but his careful words always feel as if they're being gifted rather than spoken.

"Watching that light go out in their eyes—the veil of deniability that is adolescence—is as sad in its own right as anything else I can think of. They won't be our children any longer, at least as much as they ever were. They'll be our responsibility, and for an old man that is a fear I was not prepared to face."

Cynthia tips the mug toward the drain and watches the dark brown tea swirl the sink before disappearing. She rinses it and the spoon under the faucet and places them in the otherwise empty drying rack. She dares not make eye contact not knowing what emotions it might bring, but more out of respect for his own that may be on display. She keeps her eyes on her slippers as she shuffles across the kitchen, placing a hand on his shoulder as she passes. His calloused touch acknowledging hers, and the years gone by saying everything else that needs to be said.

"I'm off to bed," says Cynthia.

FIVE

Within five minutes of leaving the school, Rodney had called the state police as well as the park service agent on duty as the trailhead is part of the North Carolina State Park system. It was more of a courtesy than a request for backup as he had embellished to Jack, who he followed at a safe distance not wanting to make the distraught man drive any faster or more dangerously than he was already.

After twenty-some agonizing minutes of driving the speed limit and several radio calls to the officers on scene to be ready for Jack's arrival, Rodney pulls his sheriff's SUV into the parking loop directly behind Darren's patrol truck, the lights on top flashing their reds and blues into the abyss of trees that surround them. Two other police SUVs are up ahead, their lights adding to the raucous display of unsynchronized color. Jack's truck is parked on the grass and his abrupt stop kicked up trenches of mud. The door is open and he can see the man move through the truck's windshield, crossing the headlights.

Rodney takes a long swig from his metal cup before exiting the vehicle. The coffee long cold but the whiskey warming his chest and belly as he steps into the crisp air. Jack is just ahead, lumbering toward Darren who holds firm behind yellow caution tape with a hand up. Rain has saturated his uniform and he looks like a wet dog left out in the cold.

"Darren, get out of my way. Nobody is keeping me from my little girl."

"Take it easy. I can't allow anyone to go out there until we can get some help to preserve the scene, alright?" Darren's trembling shakes the yellow tape in his grip.

"Scene, what scene?" Jack yells.

The sound of his raised voice combines with the patter of rain and the squish of Rodney's boots as they displace the mud that meets the grass along the lot. He feels like he's walking in slow motion, sliding his hand across the bed cover of Darren's patrol truck, feeling the texture of the liner and the wetness between his fingers. They instinctively roll tap producing a dull echo.

When his eyes travel from the trail of water left behind by his fingers on the black surface, they don't find Jack, Darren, or a single tree. Instead, the familiar flash of emergency lights bounces off of dark red brick. Walls of an alley. A fire escape ladder. Police cars from another decade. His hand rests on the lid of a dumpster and the sudden smell of rancid oil fills his nostrils. Cardboard and trash bags litter the area.

Up ahead, police tape forms a square around a body covered in a sheet. He's confused until the side of a police cruiser that blocks the adjacent alley comes into focus. Baltimore PD scrawled across the side of the door. Now he knows what's happening. He's lost in his purgatory. At least that's his name for it. The occasional call back to the worst day of his life that he's forced to relive. He listens for the sounds of the scene but they're muted as if heard through a cheap pair of headphones.

A detective leans over the body and lifts the sheet. Another officer, maybe his partner but the face always a blur, shakes his arm. He can't feel the touch but somehow the vibration travels up his arm into his shoulder.

"I said, did you see a gun?" The unknown man says.

"Huh? A what?" Rodney understood the words but can't discern their meaning.

"Did he have a gun? A knife? What the fuck happened?"

Rodney looks at the shape beneath the blanket. It could be anyone, he pretends, pushing the image of the boy's face out of his mind. The feeling of cold steel at his fingertips makes him look down at his other hand. The service pistol hangs loosely and is scooped away by the man asking him incoherent questions. He has a sense of guilt, of wrongdoing, but he doesn't know what for. It comes not as a condemnation of malice, but of failure. Of fucking up and having to pay the price. He feels like he's waiting for his dad to loosen the belt and point to the chair.

Who's under the sheet? he wonders, pressing his memory to clear the fog and get this detour from reality over with. That's how it ends, he sees the face and everything clicks. Cold sweat and heart racing reaffirm that he's out. But when he leaves early, it hangs over him for days, until it can resurface and run its course to completion. This time, he's due for torture as the real world regains its grasp.

"Please, I don't want to restrain you," a hollow voice pleads.

"Try me, asshole!" This voice is louder, clearer and the man holding his arm is gone.

Fresh, damp pine replaces the sour smell and the sounds of the city become a forest in the dead of night. Rodney bats his eyes to take in the towering man about to pummel his deputy.

"Hey, Jack. Jack." Rodney catches up and holds him back a step.

"Back off, Rodney. You can lock me up but I'm getting to my girl!"

Rodney releases his restraint and puts both hands up to signal he's giving up. Jack takes a step away but sizes him up and contemplates his position.

"I get it. But think about it, Jack. If something did happen here, we need to preserve any evidence that can help us find her. Do you want to be the reason we miss something?"

The man puffs out his cheeks and the redness flushes from his face, the vein on his forehead collapsing like a garden hose gone dry. Jack breaks down and slides to his knees on the wet earth, grass and dirt clinging to his pants as if wanting no part of where they rested. Rodney places a hand on his shoulder and nods to Darren. "I got this. Catch up with Delnado."

"Where's my baby? Please, God. You gotta find her. You gotta——-"

The sheriff does his best to console the grown man who is covered in mud and bawling at his feet. He looks around the cold, empty blackness that is the woods with the distinct feeling that he's not prepared for whatever comes next.

SIX

Erin straightens her dress, pulling it down and closer to her knees before tapping on the door of the producer's office. The Monday morning summons could mean anything. It will be her first show on primetime so perhaps they'll just talk rundown. Ideas flood her mind, ready to pitch several news stories, especially the missing girl. Yes, that's her lead for tonight.

"Come in," a man's voice calls from within.

Her stomach flutters, but she's not nervous. It's the same voice she's had in her ear at every live broadcast. Erin pushes down on the handle, leaving only enough space to squeeze between the door and the frame before latching it softly behind her. She already has her phone in her hand ready for diligent notetaking.

Across the small office, with blinds drawn and only a corner lamp lighting the space, her producer sits on the edge of the desk facing the door. She's taken aback as she realizes the man is fully exposed.

"You're late." The man looks her directly in the eyes while adjusting himself.

Erin holds a poker face. She could snap a photo with her phone and use it for leverage. She could scream and end his career.

Or she could do what she's done countless times over the past three years with Marcus, the married, father of three.

"You're lucky I didn't make you wait longer." It takes her only a second to close the distance between the door and the desk.

They wreck the office, shushing one another and laughing while they push over photos of his family and award statues alike. First, they're on top of the desk, then he's in the chair while she tries not to tip them both over, and finally that itchy, decades-old carpet scrapes at her back as he finishes. The sex isn't even that great, he's not particularly endowed and a bit clumsy, but the thrill. It's always been about the thrill. Erin knows she's playing with fire but she's not the victim here. She holds the power. It's why Marcus will go along with whatever story she chooses to lead. A little carrot, much like his own, that she'll dangle in front of him. So simple, so predictable.

Once they've redressed in silence and are settled in to talk business, Marcus spins his computer monitor so Erin can read the text on his screen.

"You see this?"

Erin leans in, composed despite the romp.

"Is that Finely? It pinged my phone over the weekend, what about it?"

Marcus raises his eyebrows and points to the date listed on the article.

"Look at the timing."

She leans in closer, finally reading more than the headline. "Not the first guy to skip parole but his face was everywhere this summer, just a matter of time before someone recognizes that ugly mug."

"Maybe, and you're going to help because ya gotta run it tonight. At least a five-block."

"Five? One-minute tops and that's if you can get me a remote of anyone that knows him. You know I'm running the girl tonight."

"The hot one?"

"Fuck off. And gross. She's 17."

Marcus laughs and taps the screen. "What if I said you could do both? Keep reading."

As Erin makes her way through the article, it's as if the light in the room pulses and grows. Everything is brighter as a story forms in her mind. This could work. It's plausible Finely could make it to Hawksboro and as far as she could tell no other theories on the girl's disappearance were compelling. She visualizes the segment and the excitement grows.

"I want half the program. Friends, family of the girl. I still want someone who knows Finely, maybe a guard, just not that fat fuck lawyer. And get the parents of one of the kids he molested, the dopey pair from the hearing." Her thumbs can't keep up with the notes she's typing into her phone.

"You're a cold bitch, you know that? Haven't they been through enough?" The tone suggests that Marcus doesn't even try to fake sincerity. "We still need to do your intro in the first half. Try to make people like you before you go conjuring the boogeyman."

Erin stands and leans across the desk. She bites his lip hard. Enough to leave a sore he'll need to explain to his wife. Her toes curl at the thought.

"Like me, hate me, they can put my face on a blow-up doll or target practice. As long as they're engaged, I'm winning."

She opens the door and plays a submissive demeanor. "Anything else, sir?"

"Damn, your narcissism makes me so hard." Marcus rubs himself playfully.

"Hmm. Looks the same to me," she says, squinting, before turning and closing the door behind her. Erin can hear him mutter "fuck you" through the door. Maybe later, if he can book the parents for the show.

The story begins forming in her mind as she continues reading articles about Finely's case on her phone, ignoring the various good morning and congratulatory greetings from around the newsroom. So Finely misses parole last week and the alert goes out. Assuming he can find a ride, it's a few hours to Hawksboro. What kind of fuck town name is that? She prays she won't have to go on location. This girl, Melody, seems a bit old for his demographic. None of his previous victims were even teenagers let alone basically an adult. Erin curses away the rationale. Viewers just need to see a sex predator and if he's in the same state then it's a fair assumption. She'll look for a parachute angle later, just in case the story falls through.

"Hey, Erin!"

Fuck. Gerrard. She spins from her phone with a beaming smile. "Gerrard, hey!" Erin throws her arms around his thick, soft neck.

Her new co-anchor is an installation around here. She has no idea how since he's not particularly charming and definitely not handsome. Would hair plugs kill him? His half-crop of balding scalp must be a nightmare for the lighting guy. And hugging him feels like wrestling a man-sized Vienna sausage.

"Ready for tonight?" Gerrard asks.

"I think so! It'll be exciting."

"Well if you need anything don't be afraid to lean on me. I won't leave you hanging."

Of course, he's already pissing in his corner under a veil of kindness. "Aw, that's sweet."

"Did Marcus—"

"Hey Gerrard, I gotta take this. I'll catch you at the pre-pro meeting this afternoon." There's no one on the phone as she presses it to her ear and walks down the hall.

"Sure thing, bye!" he says, or something inconsequential.

The introductions for Erin were almost unbearable. She felt like she did as a kid when everyone would sing happy birthday and she just had to sit there, forcing a smile, unsure if she should sing along or clap when it was over. Nearly half the show was spent bellowing her accomplishments and manufactured history. Then, after what seemed like the longest commercial break, the time had come. She spent the entire day getting the segment perfect. Worked the angles and rehearsed her opening monologue to be as polished as Marcus' trophies.

The three months prior, since her last day as a location reporter, were meant to be a well-earned vacation but she spent it obsessing over this very moment, usually in a pharmaceutical-induced frenzy of over-preparation and self-neglect. She has no regrets.

Lights dim. The floor director steps to the side of camera one and makes eye contact. She holds up a hand to Erin. The countdown begins. Erin's focus is on the light. Red. Oh, sweet red. She almost doesn't wait for the cue. Don't fuck this up.

"Tonight, our coverage takes a turn for the worst. With a heavy heart, I must report on the horrific case of Melody Anderson." In her peripheral, Erin can see the broadcast feed. A beautiful, school photo of the girl appears on screen.

"Last week, she went out on a jog, part of her daily routine. A budding track star for Hawksboro High School. Her entire future ahead of her. Honor student. Loving daughter and sister. Gone!"

She takes a breath for effect, selling her irritation that such a tragedy could befall a young woman with so much promise.

"Police have been searching for clues of her disappearance but very little has turned up so far. Could it be someone she knew? A friend or boyfriend perhaps?" Now she's getting to it. Let the show begin.

"Or could it be James Finely? Convicted sexual predator who skipped parole and his whereabouts are unknown. His last location was just a couple hundred miles away from the small, scenic town." She can sense Finely's conviction photo onscreen. The heightened narrative is arousing. Bring it home.

"Our thoughts and prayers are with this girl and her family and all those who live in Hawksboro who are in mourning. We hope for her safe return and a breakthrough in this chilling case. Could it really be James Finely behind it all? Given his history, there's every reason to expect he's armed and dangerous. Undoubtedly capable and pure evil."

The floor director signals the upcoming break and she tingles with raised flesh as she can see the last line of her opening script scroll up the teleprompter.

"We'll be back with our panel and an exclusive with the parents of one of his previous victims."

She holds for the all clear and exhales a quivering breath. He may be an inadequate lover, but he's a hell of a producer. Well done, Marcus.

SEVEN

Cheyenne kicks at the dried leaves that scatter the sidewalk. Next to her, Jason and two other kids walk in a line down Main Street carrying backpacks and wearing autumn jackets. It's cool out, she would say, but not cold. Breezy but not blustering. A typical afternoon for the time of year that ushers in the feelings of the season. Halloween, Thanksgiving, school break, it's the fastest time of the year. It is both exciting in its pace and depressing in its departures. The leaves, the green, the warmth, and the sunlight all retract until spring. Maybe they've all got the right idea.

"I can't believe Mrs. Turner gave us homework on the first day back," says Manny. He's the closest to the street and dances on and off the curb. His curly brown hair bounces on the tips of his ears as he's up and down.

"We were only out for three days, Manny. Besides, I like Mrs. T. and the homework is easy," says Jason.

"Haha, you called her Mrs. T. She your girlfriend or something?"

"Whatever, at least I can read. M-m-m Manny."

Manny turns red and Cheyenne slaps Jason on the shoulder.

"Jason, that's enough! Tell him you're sorry." She looks at

Manny. "He didn't mean it."

"She's right. I'm sorry." Jason seems embarrassed. "So what if I am Mrs. T's boyfriend, how do you think I get straight A's!"

Cheyenne rolls her eyes but it gets a laugh out of Manny.

"Careful, I'm getting jealous," Rachel says. She's soft-spoken and her addition to the conversation is uncharacteristic of her shy demeanor. Her auburn hair and freckles match the surrounding colors of fall.

Jason blushes as Cheyenne and Manny tease him. Shoes on concrete interrupt the banter. Heavy panting approaches from behind them. The paces slow down as the person catches up next to Cheyenne.

"Hey, guys. Can I walk with you?" The boy, around her age she thinks, looks over his shoulder as they walk.

"Wait up." He jogs again to keep in line with them.

Cheyenne recognizes him from school, having seen him for the first time earlier that day.

"Aren't you the new kid?"

"Yeah, my parents just moved here last week."

"Picked a hell of a time for that," says Jason.

"No joke," the boy says, still checking over his shoulder.

"Sorry man. This is kind of an exclusive group we have here. You have to receive an official invitation letter—"

"Shut up, Manny." Cheyenne reinforces the command with her gaze. She then turns back to the boy. "It's okay, you can walk with us. I'm Cheyenne, by the way."

"Thanks, I'm Donovan." His smile fades as he checks the sidewalk behind them.

"What's wrong?"

"Nothing, just some guys giving me a hard time."

Manny hustles around the front of the group and takes up

position next to Donovan, putting his arm over his shoulder. "At least we've got another minority!"

"I'd like to think they're doing it because I'm the new kid, but who knows."

Jason elbows Rachel. "Hey, we're the minorities now!"

Cheyenne places a hand on her brow.

"I thought you and Chey were part Ind—Native, Native American?" asks Manny.

"You should tell someone," Rachel adds, ignoring Jason and Manny.

"No, it's okay. My dad was in the military. He's taught me a lot of cool things. I'm not afraid," says Donovan.

"Then why do you keep looking back?" asks Manny.

A rumble of tires rolls past them down Main Street. Then another set, and another. News vans. First, a few local channels and then two major networks in a parade with an apparent pre-determined path.

"My dad was talking about this. He says things are going to change for a while," says Rachel as the vans turn onto the next street, one after the other.

Cheyenne feels a pit of discomfort. Change has never been welcome and every time it's come in her life it's meant pain. She can't put a finger on it, but it feels heavy. Like the weight of something smothering her. As the news vans pull away, she takes a deep breath.

The kids walk past the diner and Manny peels off, fist-bumping Jason on the way.

"Nice to meet you," Donovan calls after him.

Manny looks back from the door. "Yeah, you too." The bell jingles as the door opens and closes behind him. Only a few patrons can be seen on the inside through the large glass windows facing the street.

"His dad is a cook or manager or something," Cheyenne says.

Donovan acknowledges with a head bob, reading the sign overhead.

As they get to the next corner, Rachel crosses the street heading in the opposite direction.

"Bye Jason," she calls out without looking back.

"Uh, bye. Bye! See you tomorrow!" He winces.

"That's our grandparents' house over there." Cheyenne points just down a side street to the two-story, aging house with cracked blue siding and faded white shutters that hang on the windows to both sides of the sagging front porch.

Jason doesn't linger but jogs ahead to the front steps.

"You live there?"

Cheyenne watches her brother for a moment before answering.

"Yeah, just the four of us."

"Oh."

Cheyenne can feel the awkwardness of Donovan not knowing what to say. "Well, it was nice meeting you, Donovan. If you want to walk with us in the morning, we meet at the corner at 8:15. Unless the weather is bad then Rachel's dad picks us up. Do you live close?"

"Not really. But it's no biggie. I'll be here in the morning." Donovan waves as he speed-walks down the side street. He passes a group of girls walking in Cheyenne's direction.

She starts walking to the porch but notices Melody's sister among the girls. She hadn't seen her in school but maybe she missed her. Cheyenne looks between the house and the girls, wondering if she should say something.

The four girls pass by, ignoring her at first. Two have their arms around Simone who is in the middle and looks to be sobbing.

"Hey, Simone," Cheyenne says, quieter than she intended.

Simone sniffles and looks her over. "Do I know you?"

"I think so. We have homeroom together but I wanted to say I'm sorry about what you're going through. I hope they find her."

The girls collectively scoff. The tall one furthest away puts a protective arm over Simone. "Ugh, what's wrong with you? Can't you see she doesn't want to think about that?"

"I'm sorry. I didn't mean—"

Simone's tears have disappeared. "Oh, you're sorry? Thanks. I feel so much better."

Confused and hurt, Cheyenne retreats toward the house.

"Gross, you live there?" Another girl adds.

"You know what, I'm sorry too," Simone says.

Maybe there was some misunderstanding. Cheyenne pauses, believing her apology sincere. She tries to offer a smile but Simone's bark may as well have been a punch.

"I'm sorry your jumbo ass has to live with your ancient grandparents because your drunk Indian dad got himself and your mom killed."

The tears well like a dam breaking but she musters everything inside her to hold them back, refusing to let them flow in front of them. It feels like her eyes will pop out of her head. With a single inhale through her nose to hold back the mucus, she steps close to Simone. Cheyenne is almost a foot taller than her. The other girls back up.

"I hope she comes home soon." Cheyenne doesn't wait for a reaction, only turns and walks as fast as she can without appearing to hurry. The curtain in her living room shifts as Gram tries to hide from view.

"Let's go before we're attacked by a stray dog or something."

Cheyenne's tears finally let loose as she walks up the rickety steps and opens the screen door. She can't get inside fast enough.

Gram is already in the kitchen. She must have hurried there from the living room. Her back is turned to the door as Cheyenne kicks off her shoes and goes for the stairs.

"Hey hon, hungry? Can I make you a sandwich?"

"I'm fine, Gram. Got a lot of homework, I'll be down for dinner," Cheyenne calls out while climbing the steep, carpeted steps.

"Okay, dear. Tell Jason to turn off his video game and come down to help Grampa."

As she walks past Jason's room, Cheyenne pounds a couple of times on the open door. She doesn't look to see where he is or if he's listening.

"Go help Grampa."

Jason nearly bumps into her as he bounces into the hallway.

"What happened to you?"

"Nothing. Go downstairs." Cheyenne slams her door and dives onto her bed.

"Sheesh."

She can hear Jason taking heavy steps down the stairs.

Cheyenne buries her face into her pillow and bawls. After the tears stop coming and her whole face hurts, she rolls over, her blurry eyes finding the picture on her nightstand. A photo of her parents, in a cheap metal frame with dusty corners. Her father and mother stand behind Cheyenne and Jason, both kids much younger.

Of his two children, she is the one who looks most like her father. Darker skin and straight black hair. Jason, more like his mother, with fair skin and light brown hair. She can't help but feel jealous, and then a wave of guilt overcomes her with the desire to disassociate from her father. Hatred for Simone fills her thoughts but those are replaced with empathy. She can't imagine what it would be like if Jason went missing and tries to convince herself her words were because of that pain. *Hurt people, hurt people.* She can still hear her mom's voice, though it's a little softer every day. The thought of it going away entirely brings a cloud of dread.

The pep talk does little to numb the pain and so she turns her attention to her backpack. Cheyenne retrieves her books and notes and dives into her homework. Losing herself in math and English, she works to repair the damage of the words through distraction. This is how she's survived her first years of high school and what keeps her going is the thought that *it has to get easier, right?*

EIGHT

"What's up her butt?" Jason said to no one in particular after hearing Cheyenne slam her door. He dragged his feet down the stairs to see what Grampa needed help with and was surprised to find out he was working on the shutters on the porch. Jason didn't ask questions for fear of being drawn into more chores and more work which meant less time on his computer and talking to Rachel. So, he held the nails and handed Grampa whatever he asked for and helped put everything away as fast as he could move the business along.

When Jason was asked, "How's Cheyenne doing in school? Not her classes I don't expect you to know that, but friends and all that?" His grandpa tried to play it off, not even looking up from straightening the bottom of the loose-hanging shutter and pounding a nail to pin it in place.

"Okay, I guess. Why? Is something wrong?" All Jason could think about was how weird it seemed. Maybe it was just the normal awkwardness of his grandparents trying to play guardian but they rarely poke into their personal lives so the question took him off guard.

"No, no. I'm sure she's doing fine. Whaddya think?" Grampa stood back admiring his work and leaning in to double-check the straightness of the shutter.

"Looks great, brand new even."

An unusual side-eye suggested he didn't appreciate Jason's sarcasm to which Jason couldn't help but draw back the sides of his mouth, exposing his teeth in a nervous smile. Grampa cracked a smle and rubbed his hair.

"Alright, smarty-pants. You're free."

Jason lept to his feet from his cross-legged spectator spot and was ready to barrel through the door when the rattle of the nail screamed as if to say, "Not so fast!"

His eyes moved from the rusted coffee can to the raised brow of his grandpa who gestured both the can and the hammer in his direction. Jason stomps back and grabs both.

"Back in the shed where you found them, please."

He hates the shed. The backyard is more of a mud lot than a lawn and the 20 or so yards to the back corner of the sagging wooden fence is poorly lit. Even though it was late afternoon, the towering oak trees shaded the area with untimely darkness. Every time Jason walks under them he thinks that they must be hundreds of years old and this will be the exact moment they decide to drop a large branch, crushing him like a cockroach.

While he walked around the house the jingle of the nail can echoed off of the chipped siding and developed a ringing in his right ear. As he rounded the back corner and through the opening where the fence door used to be, he stopped in his tracks. He knows he latched the shed, Grampa insisted on it for fear of leaves or wild animals making their way inside. Both of the doors were wide open, swaying in the autumn breeze.

From where he stood, he couldn't see anything among the

stack of boxes, lawn equipment, and Christmas decorations. The sound of the front screen door slamming shut made him jump and half the nails flew up and landed in the dirt all around his feet.

"Shit," he said, first afraid Grampa may have heard him then actually afraid when he realized the sound that made him jump meant he was all alone outside. Jason locked eyes on the void within the shed while he carefully scooped up the nails. Jason couldn't say why, but he blew on them before dropping them into the can in an attempt to make sure no dirt was along for the ride.

The one moment he let his attention fall from the shed to the very last nail sticking up out of the ground he could swear he heard a sound come from somewhere within. His hair stood as vertical as the last nail and a chill swept over him. Jason stared forward for several moments looking for any sign of movement, for so long that his mind played tricks on him in the darkness that filled the shed.

He finally mustered the courage to stand and take several steps across the backyard. The drifting of the doors as they moved in and out looked as if they were two hands beckoning him to come closer for an embrace as his grandma would do. But instead of a flour-dusted apron where he'd place a warm hug, only a black square awaited him.

"This is so fucking dumb," he said to himself. It was enough to put some speed in his feet and he crossed the rest of the yard in a brisk trot until his shoes touched the wooden ramp.

Certain nothing was inside as he hadn't heard or seen anything since that first whatever it was, he purposefully stomped up the worn tread, secretly hoping Gram could hear him from inside. Jason made his way to the exact spot on the built-in shelving where the nail can sat and deposited it as instructed. When he turned to the opposite wall to hang the hammer on its marked hook on the water-logged pegboard, that same feeling he felt a moment ago returned.

"Pssst."

He didn't believe his ears as he let go of the hammer, allowing it to bounce in place on the hook before his brain could tell him to draw it back as a weapon. Jason didn't look to the rear of the shed from where the voice came and he wasn't sure how he found himself on the outside of it with the doors firmly shut and latched. He expected an animal or criminal or something horrific to pound and squeal on the other side, but it never came.

Now in the safety of his room upstairs and having just told Rachel the entire story, possibly embellishing the amount of danger he was in as well as the bravery he displayed, he takes a breath and gives her a moment to get a word in.

"Wow, that's something." Rachel's face pixelates on the computer monitor that sits on the rear of his small desk.

"You don't believe me!" Jason leans back in his chair.

"I'm sure it was just an animal. Hey, did you do your Ecology homework yet?"

He flips open a book on the corner of the desk and the notebook that is tucked inside.

"No, but I will tonight before bed. Looks pretty easy." Jason closes it just as fast.

"Why are all invertebrates so gross?" Rachel quivers and closes her book.

Jason laughs and pretends his hand is a spider crawling across the screen.

"Eww, no. Stop it!" Her laugh is infectious. "Hey, you know what I heard today? Oh my God, it's so scary."

He shakes his head no.

"Okay, well I heard some of the older kids, juniors and seniors, talking about Melody today. You can't tell anyone but do you want to know what they said?'

Jason looks around the room, knowing nobody is listening but checking to make sure Gram or Grampa didn't peek their head in. No more close calls. Satisfied it's clear he nods to indicate she should continue.

"So the kids were mainly exchanging theories of who they think did it. Took her I mean. One girl says it's the science teacher, Mr. Alexander—"

"What! He seems nice, no way!" Jason feels bad for interrupting and hopes she won't stop telling the story.

"Well, supposedly he was the last person to see her and he doesn't live far from where she went missing. PLUS, he's always talking about bodies and stuff. Kinda creepy."

"Doesn't he teach anatomy? Doesn't sound strange to me."

"I guess, another boy said the same thing basically, and then guess who he said did it?"

Jason pretends to think but just wants her to say it. After a beat, he raises his arms.

"No idea, who?"

"The janitor!"

"Whoa, now that I can see. He's always lurking around in the dark and is the only one who is allowed to go down to the boiler room area."

"Right? And he drives that old busted car, basically looks like a hearse."

He laughs at the thought.

"I don't know, seriously though I bet it's someone she knew. Ex-boyfriend or something," says Jason.

"Oooh, maybe. That's scary though, to think one of the kids we go to school with could do something like that."

A moment of silence threatens to become an awkward pause but Rachel is quick to offer a theory of her own.

"You want to hear who I think it was?"

"Yes, of course!"

"That Finely guy, from the news. I heard my dads talking about him and looked him up online. I bet he's hiding out somewhere in town just waiting for his next victim. Maybe in your shed!"

He knows she's trying to be funny, and normally he would laugh, but something doesn't feel right–like a hint of truth getting in the way of a joke. The way a rotten strawberry ruins the whole container. A little cloud of mold and you could toss just the one fruit, but you'll wonder if the rest are tainted by unseen spores.

"Ha, yeah. Could be," he manages to respond.

A door opens on her side of the call and her head turns off-camera. She nods and looks back to Jason.

"I gotta go. Dinner time. See you tomorrow." She waves an innocent arc of an open hand and smiles.

"Okay, bye Rachel!" Jason waves vigorously and tries to slow it down once he realizes it probably looks stupid on her end. Her screen disconnects and he's left staring at the chat window.

He minimizes the program and thinks about digging into the homework but figures Gram will be calling up for dinner soon also, so no point in starting it. He moves the mouse to the internet app and opens a new browser. First, Jason snoops Cheyenne's social media since he doesn't have any of his own. "When you get a phone," has been the answer for some time. Maybe for Christmas, he hopes.

Jason scrolls and scrolls. It's the usual fare, dumb girl stuff he doesn't care about mixed with reshared videos he has either already seen or cares nothing about like the dancing bits. He hates that everyone thinks people want to watch themselves dance. Then he comes across some newer stuff on her page from that very day.

It's a video from right outside of their house and a girl is recording Cheyenne talking to Simone. He can't make out what's said but the comments are horrible. Jason feels sorry for his sister and hopes she hasn't seen it, though it's inevitable. When he's had enough doomscrolling he jumps over to a search engine and types in JAMES FINELY. The results that come back are all local news articles.

They range from the short, repetitive headlines that many outlets seem to regurgitate, to the speculative ones that beg for his attention. Jason can't help but click one and goes deep into a rabbit hole on the man's criminal history. There are crime scene photos, courtroom videos, vivid descriptions that should come with an MA rating. The photo of Finely at his first court appearance, dressed in orange and looking over his shoulder into the audience behind him, is as tall as his monitor will allow.

Finely stares into the lens of the photographer's camera. The eyes capture Jason. The slender cheekbones are covered in thin, gray fuzz. Red and brown splotches on leathery skin. He feels drawn into the image and while the thought of the teacher, the janitor, or even a kid he's bumped into in the hall all seem scary, it's in a fictional way. Too close to home that it feels like a book or show. But this monster that smiles a crooked grin to a room full of people who hate him, feels terrifyingly real.

As Jason's stomach tightens, the man in the picture opens his mouth and whispers, "Pssst."

He exits the browser as fast as he can and nearly falls out of his chair as he bounds for the door. Jason opens it just in time to hear Gram calling up the stairs.

"Kids, dinner!"

She can barely finish as his feet hit the treads, already thundering their way down toward the kitchen. "Coming down!" He yells, hoping the sound of his voice will chase out the other one before it can spread spores in his mind.

NINE

ONE YEAR LATER

Rodney sits in his torn, faux leather recliner. A lukewarm, unfinished beer bottle dangles from his fingers, precariously hovering over the other five empties on the floor below. It's night but the only light in the small living room is from the large television. A memorial program running on HTN has his undivided attention.

Elegant graphics accompany Melody's photo. A montage edit of news coverage from different outlets and programs.

"We're here live in Hawksboro—"

"Tragedy and misery have fallen on this quiet town as authorities continue to search—"

"With a population of only twenty-four hundred, Melody was no stranger in this community that is just heartbroken—"

More photos fill the screen. Of Melody. Of the search. Of the family. It might as well be a damn music video, he thinks. The emotional tugs feel superficial and forced. Overly cinematic music enhances the cheapness of it all. Christ, it's horrific enough on its own it doesn't need this pomp and flare. He raises the beer to take a sip but pauses as he now sees himself on screen.

"There's some speculation that police have uncovered important evidence and are looking to contact a person of interest, though they have yet to officially name a suspect."

Rodney gulps the last of his beer and lets the bottle fall among the others, crashing them like pins at Hawksboro Bowl & Darts. He wipes his mustache with a rolled-up sleeve, still in his sheriff's uniform. He adjusts the volume louder with the remote as the show continues.

"It's been almost a month but police have finally identified James Finely as the primary suspect in the case of missing teenage beauty, Melody Anderson." It's now Erin Heart speaking during one of her newscasts that propelled her to fame. One couldn't think of the name Melody Anderson without hearing Erin Heart's voice draw out the syllables. A chilling photo of Finely fades onscreen next to his rap sheet.

"Bullshit," Rodney says to the empty room. If he had to put a finger on when things took a turn it was then. He doesn't know if Finely had anything to do with it but they should have been the ones to make the call, not the media. Instead, they were left chasing the news every single night. The entire department felt like their hands were tied and being led in one direction. It didn't help that the mayor took it hook, line, and sinker and was practically towing the rope that bound them. The program displays a flash of white signifying a dramatic passage of time.

"James Finely, a convicted sex offender and child predator, has been off the radar nearly four months after he skipped parole and just three months after being named the lead suspect. He was first incarcerated in 1992 for sexually assaulting a waitress outside of a bar. In 1998 he was arrested again, this time for possession of child pornography, but those charges were later dropped on account of lost evidence."

Rodney kicks down his recliner footrest and groans as he lumbers into the kitchen, the coverage still playing more than loud enough to hear a room away. He can see the TV but the same white transition lights the entire space like a lightning bolt. He can only imagine what it looks like from the street outside.

"Then, seven years ago he was tried for the molestation of a young autistic boy and his brother for which he plead no contest, presumably as part of a plea deal with the DA."

He glances at the TV as he reaches into the fridge, knowing exactly where to find the next beer. Footage of news vans and reporters swarming Hawksboro. The mayor gesturing some bloviated speech in front of flashes and microphones with the sheriff cowering just over his shoulder. Rodney cracks a can this time as he makes his way back into the living room and collapses back into his chair.

"A press conference will be held tonight and the family is expected to make a statement."

Video plays of the family huddled around a podium while Rodney is speaking into a microphone. He watches himself. He can't believe how much his physical appearance has changed. His eyes leave the TV looking for anything else. Hearing his voice makes him cringe. He takes a large gulp to drown out the sound.

"Now Melody's sister Simone would like to say a few words on behalf of the family. They will not be taking questions."

On the screen, Rodney steps away and Simone approaches and adjusts the microphone to meet her face. She unfolds a note and lays it flat in front of her.

"Thank you all for coming out in support of my sister. Melody. She would be upset that so much trouble is being had for her, but that's one reason why we're all here. She was, is, so humble and such a great big sister. I miss her so much and we haven't given up hope that she's still out there. Please help us bring her home."

His last beer is vanishing too quickly.

"Whoever has her, if you're watching this, please don't hurt her. Just look at her, talk to her, get to know her. There's nobody else like her. Please don't take Melody away from us and this world. I don't know what I would do without my big sister, she means everything to me. Who will I talk to about boys or college—"

Simone breaks down mid-speech. Jack steps in and pulls her close while adjusting the microphone to his level. He still has to lean down and speaks too loud at first.

"Uh, thank you all again for being here in support of our daughter. We miss her and are still working day and night to find Melody. We appreciate your prayers and kindness and respectfully ask the media to honor our privacy at this time. Thank you."

Rodney returns to the podium but a new clip in the montage cuts over him. He tensed at the prospect of hearing himself again but isn't any more thrilled with his replacement. Erin appears onscreen behind her primetime news desk. At least no flash of white this time.

"It's been exactly six months since the disappearance and suspected abduction of Melody Anderson and authorities are no closer to solving the mystery of her whereabouts. The main suspect, James Finely, is still at large as the search continues."

Footage of a candlelight vigil at the high school. It was late winter, February he thinks, as a rare dusting of snow covers the ground as the group carries candles and photos. He remembers that night with clarity. At least most of it, the ending is a typical blur. Erin talks over the imagery from a later news program.

"As the winter snow has melted in this early spring heatwave, some new evidence has been discovered in the missing person's case of Melody Anderson. A bracelet that the family has identified as Melody's was found in a storm drain filter by a county worker who turned it over to the police. DNA and fingerprint testing were inconclusive and no further clues have been found."

Rodney recalls the bracelet and what a shit show that was. The county worker put it in a sandwich bag. It was handed off to Darren at the station who handled it for an entire day, not realizing it had any connection to the case. He blamed it on a language barrier and said he thought the man was turning it in to lost and found. By the time it got to testing, the chain of custody was non-existent and the bracelet itself had traces of mayonnaise, the worker, the deputy, Melody, and several other contaminants.

The one thing it did bring was some closure. After that, most people seemed to believe she was gone for good, though every few weeks a resurgence in attention or passion would stem from a news program mentioning her case. At least the internet sleuths have mostly stopped dropping into town. Hard enough to do his job with a national spotlight without these soccer moms and their ten subscribers somehow making their way to Hawksboro with a $200 audio recorder and begging for an interview. Fucking podcasts.

He can't understand the obsession with murders, probably because most people have never seen a real body. The worms. The maggots. The contorted limbs bent and angled in unnatural ways. Grey eyes, if they haven't been plucked out by birds. No, it all sounds like fiction when it's through the ears or on the page.

Rodney nods off in his chair as a weather report takes over the TV. His thoughts are a muddy entanglement of the past year, what he could and should have done. Regret. His desire to resign. The prospects that will get him out of this town and out from under this cloud. Then to Melody, and the dozens of different ways that she could have perished that haunt him every night. These violent images usher him into a light, drunken sleep.

His incoherent dreams cease, sometime in the middle of the night, and it feels like a curtain is pulled back revealing a towering brick wall. Police lights bounce off the alley. The fire escape. Even in his inebriated sleep state, he understands he's back in Baltimore. Rodney has had many of these moments since the disappearance and this one is picking up where the last one left off, his feet moving toward the body.

Rodney is aware of the surroundings but his memory is looking down on his wet shoes. They navigate the cracked asphalt that is damp with oil-slicked water. No, not just water. The reflection is different. Large splotches of crimson, thick and raised off of the street's surface. A voice calls to him from behind but it's far away and he knows it's the man with the blurry face, but somehow, he still feels confused by it.

As he makes his way to the sheet-covered body, which now has a large red stain in the midsection, he slows his gait and kneels next to the hand that sticks out from the covering. The voice behind him grows louder and though he's aware there are several other police officers on-scene, he is alone; or feels alone. Rodney extends his hand to the fabric, trying to complete the flashback so he can get the ending over with. Just as his fingers are about to make contact with the sheet, he's jolted awake.

It takes a moment to realize that he's in his chair, the TV still playing, an infomercial he thinks, but he doesn't look as his head is throbbing and the light will only inflame the crushing pain. Rodney recalls the beers, every one of them, and settles in to try to fall back to sleep. As each time before, the hangover is an intended penance for his failure in this case. Every pound of his splitting headache a tap on the shoulder from Melody's cold, outstretched hand. Before returning to the land of obscurities, which takes only a few seconds in his current state, Rodney makes a mental note. *I'm going to need more beer.*

TEN

Cheyenne makes her way down the stairs, rubbing her eyes. She runs her hand through her tangled mess of hair, still not used to it being several inches shorter. The smell of breakfast wafts from the kitchen the way warmth travels upstairs. It's the aroma of pancakes and maple syrup. Well, fake syrup. She hopes it's pancakes, anyway. Jason is horizontal on the flower pattern couch watching anime or something weird.

"Good morning, sweetie. Grab some juice, it's almost ready." Gram is already dressed and done up for the day, she notices, with a full head of permed, white curls, as she tends the stove. It's an old gas appliance that somehow works flawlessly despite it being made sometime last century.

"Morning, Gram." Cheyenne yawns as she pours a full glass of orange juice from a faded plastic pitcher.

"Jason, come to the table please!" Gram turns off the burner and prepares a wide, ceramic serving platter.

Cheyenne retrieves her phone from her pajama pants pocket. The screen is cracked but it works by the smallest of standards. They couldn't afford anything fancy so Jason helped her find a used one online. Since she shares a plan with her grandparents' "old people service" as she's heard it called, her minutes and data are limited so she's always conscious of her use, though it's not like anyone calls her. The majority of use is on Wi-Fi at home and at school.

"No phones at the table," Jason hollers as he skips into the kitchen, plopping himself down at the table. He also pours a full glass of orange juice.

"Is this no pulp?"

Cheyenne nods as she exits the app of photos that she was scrolling. The phone goes back into her pocket much slower than it was retrieved.

The door whines as it opens inward, the screen door slamming behind it.

"Am I late?" Grampa wipes his wet boots on the floor mat and kicks them off next to the radiator that juts up from the linoleum floor and pulls double-duty as an entry table for keys and clutter. His hunch has gotten worse but he is still tall and the signs of muscular tone under his spotted skin haven't diminished one bit. The hair above his brass-rimmed glasses, including the caterpillar eyebrows, is now more white than it is gray, which enhances his bright blue eyes behind the split focal lenses.

"Just in time, Rick. Get yourself a plate, there's juice already on the table." Gram places the platter in the center. Steam billows from a stack of pancakes.

She's met with a kiss on the forehead as Grampa passes her while retrieving a plate. Gram takes out a stick of margarine and the artificial syrup from the fridge. The sticky ring on the shelf clings to the bottom of the translucent plastic jug, stretching out arms of high-fructose corn syrup that thin and break. Even their slow drop back to the shelf ring seems sad.

The kids pile their plates with the pancakes and pour an

abundance of syrup over the stacks. The jug makes a kissing noise every time it's picked up off of the plastic tablecloth. White strands of the cotton liner stick up through the tears in the cloth as if hoping for their own chance to join the bottom of the container. Grampa and Gram sit across from one another, first adding a slice of margarine then a modest drizzle of syrup.

"Thanks for breakfast. Right, kids?" Grampa says, smiling.

"Thanks, Gram."

"Yeah. Thanks, Gram." Cheyenne forgets the ills brought on by her brief time on her phone and basks in the warmth of the pancakes. The sweet lather of the syrup that she would defend as better than the real thing. Another wall, another piece of armor.

"Save some for everyone else. Maybe you shouldn't eat so much before practice!"

Cheyenne scowls at Jason. "Maybe you should eat more so you're not smaller than your girlfriend!"

"Rachel is not my girlfriend!"

"Settle down you two. Chey, dear, you have as much as you like." Gram pushes the platter closer to her.

"Looks like it's drying up out there. They still may have it in the gymnasium, though," adds Rick. "Might be a bit cool in those uniforms."

"Can't. Cheerleaders aren't allowed in there during basketball," Jason says with a mouthful of pancake.

"Good. I don't want to go anyway." Cheyenne stabs her breakfast with a fork but doesn't take a bite.

"We talked about this. It's good for you. You don't have to play sports but you need to do something. You're not going to sit in your room on that phone all day."

"Your Gram's right. What's the problem? I thought you liked cheerleading?" asks Grampa.

Jason cleans his plate and chugs the rest of his juice.

"I hate it. And I can't stand the girls there. Especially Simone. I hate her, too." The fork dissects the last piece of pancake in a pool of syrup. She stabs both halves and savors the bite.

"Hey now, you don't hate anyone," says Grampa.

"Okay well, very much dislike then."

"Can I be excused?" Jason is already to his feet.

"Go ahead, clean up please," Gram points to the sink.

Grampa pats Jason on the shoulder as he leaves the table and then leans in closer to Cheyenne. "She's had a rough year. Try not to take it to heart, dear. And trust me, your Gram has made me do a few things in my day that I didn't want to do but it all worked out for the best. She's no fool."

Jason dumps his plate in the sink, blasts it with a quick shot of the faucet, and runs into the living room. The awful music of the dumb show he watches, returns. Either her grandparents can't hear or they don't mind. Must be nice.

"Like what?" Cheyenne asks.

"Well, let's just say I eventually saw the wisdom in her thinking. And Cheyenne, don't you worry about those other girls. They're just jealous of the light that shines in you." Grampa sits back and cuts a pancake on his plate.

The phone on the wall rings. Cheyenne picks up her plate and empty glass as Gram answers the corded yellow phone. By the time she's cleaned her plate and is headed back to the stairs, Gram has already finished the call.

"Alright. Yes, thank you, Glenn. Thanks. Buh-bye now."

"Who was that?" Cheyenne expects Glenn means Rachel's dad but she asks anyway.

"Rachel's dad. Just checking in to see about picking the two of you up tonight for the memorial," Gram says.

Jason appears at the doorway, sticking his head into the kitchen. The silence indicating that he paused the show.

"Ugh, I forgot that was tonight." Cheyenne loathes the idea.

"Yes, it's been quite a year. Not easy for you kids either, I'm sure. I did hear that they might forego the Trunk-or-Treat event and let everyone go back to going house to house. So that's something," says Gram.

"I heard Jimmy say that he overheard Simone say that Melody probably just ran away because she got a tattoo last year and her parents were super mad and grounded her. Probably has a new name and everything."

"Jason, you forget you heard that and don't you repeat it." Grampa says, stern but gentle. "Something very terrible and tragic happened and people like to make things up because they like the attention they get from having information, whether it's true or not."

"Yeah, genius. I don't get what Rachel sees in you." Cheyenne hustles up the stairs not wanting to stick around for a drawn-out bickering match with her brother. From the kitchen she can hear Grampa chuckle.

"So, Rachel, huh?"

Jason's footsteps bound back into the living room.

"Have fun cheerleading, jerk!"

The music picks up at full volume and she closes her bedroom door. Cheyenne laughs to herself having gotten under his skin. She swipes open her phone and falls to her bed. The brief moment of levity is soured by the instant onslaught of images on the app. The tight, sharp words that perfectly caption each.

Why can't she ever sound so clever? Even as remnants of the fake syrup try to stop her fingers, she keeps scrolling.

ELEVEN

The dimly lit basement has the scent of sweat and mothballs. It's half-finished with one interior wall consisting of studs. An Army Ranger banner is draped on the block wall next to the small egress window. It's weathered and adorned with the regiment and dates along with a province location in Afghanistan. As Donovan descends the stairs, his father Kenneth reps out bench presses in the far corner. Music plays just loud enough to hear from the steps.

"Are you almost finished?" Donovan puts a hand against the metal support column in the center of the room.

The cylindrical beam spans from the concrete floor to the wood above. Flat, square plates on both ends push in both directions under the weight of the first story. A single iron pin sits in a hole that centers the column. He rubs his thumb over it, wondering what would happen if he were to push it out.

Kenneth racks the weight, sits up, and wipes his face with a towel. The veins on his bald head and neck are thick as snakes. The water droplets traveling along their backs all the way to the collar of his gray Army PT shirt. Thankfully he's wearing sweats and not those awful Ranger panties he sometimes wears,

Donovan thinks. Kenneth walks over to another bar in front of a floor-to-ceiling mirror and begins doing curls. If his veins are snakes, Donovan understands why people call biceps pythons. He rubs his own arm, curious where they even come from.

"Grab those." Kenneth gestures with his head to a pair of small dumbbells on the floor. "And like I showed you."

With a sigh, Donovan picks them up and performs curls in the same mirror as his dad.

"Back tight. Imagine there's a quarter stuck back there and you can't let it fall."

Donovan pinches his shoulder blades as he lifts the weight. It's only 15 pounds but it feels heavier. He keeps going, hoping his persistence will buy him some favor for what he's about to ask.

"Can I hang out with Manny today?"

Kenneth resets the curl bar and examines the reflection of his arms before making eye contact with Donovan in the mirror. "What'd your mom say?"

"To ask you."

Donovan sets the weights at his feet. He shakes his wrists and rubs each forearm. The swell in his biceps is hard and immediate.

"Tell you what. Do a few more sets with me and I'll drive you over there for lunch."

Donovan nods, trying not to look too eager, or disclose that he was willing to go as high as agreeing to rake the leaves. As the two finish the workout together, Kenneth's attention travels from his own workout to the boy's. Donovan catches his dad watching him in the reflection of the mirror and instinctively pulls his shoulders back.

"What?"

"Nothing." Kenneth smiles. "Keep your elbows in!"

A sign on the door of the diner, which is really just a piece of paper written in marker, is new since the last time Donovan was there. He stops to read it before going inside.

"What's it say?" asks Kenneth a few feet back on the sidewalk. "Uh, it says 'we will be closing at 4:00 p.m. to attend tonight's event. Thank you, MGMT' What's MGMT?" He asks. He tries to think of Manny's dad's initials or anyone else it might represent.

"Management, just an abbreviation."

"Why not just write it out? Seems like it takes more time to explain it than writing a few extra letters."

"Sure, son. Go on." Kenneth laughs as he points to the handle.

Donovan opens the door and the bell rings. He and his dad step into the quaint restaurant. Large windows let all the light in from the street. It's on a corner so a third window spans the entire side of the far wall. A half dozen patrons sit at the counter and only two tables have customers. Even though it's late-morning on a Saturday, it's not very busy. Hasn't been since they built that drive-thru coffee shop over by the Ingles, Manny's dad has said on more than one occasion.

A waitress approaches them. It's the one with the pretty face but he still can't quite tell how old she is. Could be 30, could be 50. He knows enough that if asked to go low.

"Hello again. Is it Kenneth?"

"Kenneth, Ken, hey you over there, any work."

She looks from the towering man down to the boy who is nearly her height. "And let me see…Dominic?"

"Donovan, ma'am."

"Ah shoot, well I'll get it right next time, promise." She pulls out a notepad. "What can I get you handsome fellas? Counter or table?"

"Actually, ma'am, is Miguel here today?"

"Well, I sure hope so. Don't think we could be open without him!" She darts off, going around the cash register and into the kitchen.

A minute later the heavy set, Hispanic man leans to look out of the serving window of the kitchen. Tickets hang in front of his face and he moves to get a clear view.

"Ken, Donovan! Good to see you!" He's gone as fast as he appeared.

The kitchen door barrels open and Miguel steps into the diner. He's wearing all white with a stained apron. He wipes his hands on his front before extending his right one to Kenneth.

They share a handshake and does the same with Donovan. "Can I get you guys anything? Wonderful lunch special today. Fried fish. Let me get you some. Hey Mary—"

"No, no, Miguel, it's fine. Thank you," Kenneth insists.

"You sure?" Miguel makes an okay sign and pouts his lips.

"Yes, thank you. I've gotta get back to the house. Ton of yard work to get done this weekend or I'll be kicked to the curb. Donovan was hoping to spend some time with Manny before the memorial tonight, if that'd be okay?"

"Of course! Will be a somber event but it's great to have such a close community. I've been busy all morning preparing some light refreshments. Are you sure you don't want to try something? I know Donovan enjoys the Dulce de Leche cake."

The boy's eyes light up. As long as he doesn't have to ask for it by name, he always gets it wrong. Kenneth answers for them both.

"No thank you, I'll save the surprise for tonight. Please, give me a call if he overstays his welcome. I'm happy to come back and pick him up."

"No, no, no. He is a pleasure. If only Manny could be more

like him maybe I wouldn't need to ground him so much."

Donovan looks to his feet as Kenneth puts a hand on his nearest shoulder.

"Alright, well we'll see you tonight. And if we can ever watch Manny, we're happy to have him at the house. He's a good kid."

"Thank you, Ken. Please, take at least some pie to go!"

Kenneth laughs as he backtracks to the door. "Thank you, but next time. Give Gloria my best!"

"Sure thing!" As Kenneth exits the diner, Miguel guides Donovan to the counter. "Manny's out back. Don't get too dirty. Come in if you get hungry."

"Thanks, Mr. Rosales." Donovan jogs through the back area of the diner and out through the rear exit.

Wooden steps lead down into the dirt lot behind the restaurant. A few sprouts of brown grass cling to the trampled area. Against the back of an adjacent building, an old, rusty delivery truck is being reclaimed by the weeds and vines that grow around it. The front and grill area look nothing like any other vehicles driving today. The headlights are inset, round tubes and the whole face is void of sharp angles, instead they're rolling and smooth curves. The once shiny bumper has little gleam left but has fared better than the rest of the painted surfaces.

A pale gray cloud has created an overcast midday sky. The lack of sunshine drops the temperature by quite a few degrees. Donovan looks around the yard with apprehension. There's nothing to be scared of, middle of a Saturday and dozens of people within earshot, he tells himself. He thinks about the older kids at school. They give him less of a hard time since his growth spurt, all but one. Greg Pullman. That son of a bitch would probably hide somewhere out here just to get the jump on him. He imagines Manny with his arm bent behind his back and that stupid camo blade that Greg likes to show off held against his skin, a crooked finger signaling to stay quiet.

"Manny? Quit messing around, man. You always do this shit." He moves to the far building and walks along the basement windows that sit just above the dirt surface. Most have broken glass or none at all. Donovan tries to see down into the basement but it's too dark and his eyes are adjusted to the daylight, despite the clouds. He also doesn't want to linger at any since his imagination conjures every sort of horror reaching out and dragging him down into the nothing.

He walks over to the truck, deflated tires spread flat under the weight. Donovan places a foot onto the driver's side step and elevates on his tip toes to try to get a look inside. The glass is fogged and dirty. Grime and smudges make it all but impossible to see inside. The details he can see are the high contrast ones. The yellow cracks in the black seats where the foam pushes through, the glare on the shiny shifter nob, the flash of a smile.

As he recognizes the whites as teeth, a loud crash sends Donovan back onto his ass in the dirt. Manny pops up from inside the truck and presses his face against the window, distorting his nose and lips while blowing out his cheeks. Manny then bursts out laughing as he opens the truck's door. It screams with the twisting of the metal hinge.

"God, you're such a child." Donovan wipes his hands on his jeans, still seated on the ground.

"You're too easy, that's all," Manny says as he extends a hand out.

As Donovan grabs on to it, Manny lets go and Donovan falls back to the dirt. Manny again laughs out loud but is immediately pummeled. The two wrestle and laugh with each other in the dirt.

Down the alley, a trash can knocks over and glass shatters.

The boys quit horsing around and look that way.

"Raccoon?" Manny asks.

"Hope not. If so, it's probably got rabies."

"Sweet!" Manny is up and running down the alley.

Donovan is swarmed by a wave of discomfort once again, like he's being watched. He can't help but look to the closest basement window, a single shard of glass the sole tooth in a black smile. The darkness inside beckons him to return and have another look, a pull he has trouble resisting. A whisper calls to him from within and the piece of glass wiggles ever so slightly, like a child pushing on a loose incisor with their tongue.

"Hey, wait up!" He pulls himself to his feet and swears. "Idiot."

TWELVE

A light pattering of rain trickles down the window of the office in the police station. Outside, a sheriff's SUV is parked along the curb. It's dirty with caked mud and signs of rust. At his desk, Rodney drifts in and out of sleep, face down on a stack of papers. An empty bottle sits next to him.

"Heya, boss."

Rodney snaps out of his daze and looks to the door, a page stuck to his face that he quickly peels away and returns to the stack in front of him. A deputy stands waiting and the sheriff removes the bottle from the desk and tucks it into a lower file cabinet.

"Sorry, Rodney. Didn't mean to disturb you. Just thought you were going over something."

"What? I was." Rodney straightens up his desk and the clutter of papers. "What is it, Darren?"

"May I?" The deputy points to the lone chair across from the desk.

"Have a seat."

With some hesitation, Darren shuffles his feet and sits on the front edge of the chair and leans forward placing his elbows on the desk. He pauses as if he's waiting for Rodney to begin.

"Go on," Rodney says.

"Sure. Of course. I was just thinking I could take the last patrol tonight. I know you're on the calendar but I just thought, since you've been pulling so many hours, that maybe the memorial thing would be a bit much."

Rodney discontinues cleaning and tilts his head.

"I mean, I just thought you may not want the reminder, or all the commotion. You know what, it's fine. Forget it." Darren stands up from his seat.

"Look, Darren. I appreciate what you're trying to do—"

"It's nothing, sir—"

"BUT. I am still the sheriff of this town and I can handle a memorial gathering in a park just fine." When Darren doesn't respond Rodney expresses some agitation. "Is there something you'd like to say?"

"Sir, the drinking. The missed calls. I'm not saying you're not doing a good job or that you're not a good sheriff or anything like that. This town is lucky to have you, and after what happened anyone else woulda run outta here, but you stuck around. The people know that, we know that. That doesn't mean it hasn't affected you. It's only human."

The compressed area of Rodney's face that was white from lying face down has now turned dark red. His eyes pierce Darren's.

"Do you think I'm incapable of dealing with the responsibilities of this position? Maybe you'd like to take a crack at it, is that it?" He pulls off his badge and slams it on the desk. Darren jumps in his seat. "And reminder of what, exactly? Is this some PTSD intervention? You've got some nerve."

"You're right. I'm sorry." Darren is up and retreats to the door.

"I've been holding this post since you were chasing skirts in junior high. I don't need my deputy coming in here and questioning my fitness!"

Darren drops his head and steps out of the office. A wave the only farewell.

"Damn it. Darren, hold on." Rodney rubs his eyes as if to push them back into his head. The headache, hangover, lack of well, everything, is taking its toll.

The young deputy, tall and slender with signs of some muscle tone under his black uniform, places a hand on the frame and looks back into the office. His brownish blonde hair waving just above his eyes. A baby face. Naive, but sincere.

"I was out of line. I apologize. Thank you for your concern."

"It's not your fault, sir. Melody, I mean. You've done everything you could and put in more hours than frankly I would have guessed possible. Nobody thinks any different. That's all I wanted to say." Darren pats the door frame.

Rodney rocks in his seat and dances his fingers on the papers in front of him. "I hear you. But you're to leave on time today, get home to Cindy and the baby." He does his best to demonstrate his regret at the outburst.

Darren crosses the office again and retrieves a paper from the floor. He looks at the heading as he hands it to the sheriff.

"Yes, sir. Goodnight, sir."

He leaves the office and Rodney waits for his footsteps to fade down the hall. The paper in his hand goes on top of the stack that he neatly piled in front of him. Rodney rereads the top line of the security job application form. With an audible sigh, he evens the edges of the papers and places them in the same cabinet as the bottle.

Families enter and exit the large park in the center of town that has been transformed for the memorial event. Ribbons decorate tables that are covered with photos and mementos of Melody. Candles and paper lanterns line the sidewalks. Music plays over a pair of large speakers on stands. It's dark already this time of year and from the outside it looks like it could be a fun event, a fall festival. Instead, it may as well be a beacon to the failure of the unsolved case.

Rodney sits in his police SUV across the street with the windows down. Water remains on the windshield and pavement but the rain had stopped several hours ago. He drinks from a stainless thermos that rides in the cupholder. Just enough coffee to hide the scent of the whiskey. He's people watching. Rodney follows the visitors that come and go with a focused stare. He daydreams of seeing a clue on a stranger who's come to canvas the memorial. A sick game of cat and mouse where he would finally catch the missing piece and end the pain that's occurred on his watch.

In the nearest corner of the park, Jack, Molly, and Simone huddle around a table and are surrounded by well-wishers, hugging and shaking hands and receiving cards and sympathies. Rodney takes another long drink. Cars whoosh by on the wet road, slowing at the sight of his SUV. Children play on the sidewalk under the streetlights. It could be Halloween come early if it wasn't so somber. He dreads the holiday that's a little less than a month ahead. The mayor, having gone out in front of him with the least bit of consideration, announced a return to normal festivities. All those kids in costume, adults in masks, trouble makers and pranksters. And that looming darkness without a face. A real-life boogeyman who's far scarier unknown.

A knock on the hood startles him, spilling a splash of liquid on the front of his vest.

"Sheriff." Speak of the devil. The mayor leans against the door and observes the turnout with a wave here and there.

"Mayor Adams," Rodney says while wiping himself with a napkin from the console.

"Hell of a crowd tonight. Of course, that's no surprise. A little rain won't keep this community from showing up to support a family in need." The mayor's tone always sounds like he's on the election circuit.

It's painstaking and Rodney is already looking for a way out. Where's a high-speed chase when you need one? "Yes, looks to be a success as far as something like this can be considered in a positive light."

The mayor turns his attention from the park and gives Rodney a confused look with his wrinkled crow's feet. You'd think Rodney shit in his cereal.

"This again?" The mayor finally asks.

"Look, mayor, you know where I stand. I'm not going to pretend like we're winning here somehow. That's delusional."

"You'd better watch your tone, Sheriff. There's nothing delusional about helping a town cope with the tragedy of losing someone like Melody."

"She's not lost. Someone took her."

"On that we agree, so why don't you give me someone? It is your job, isn't it?"

Rodney could pull him through the window and bash his head off the steering wheel yet he's able to keep his cool.

"And who would you like me to bring in this time? We've already ruined the teacher's life just by us questioning him."

The mayor scoffs.

"And the county worker, who we owe for the only evidence

we have, is no better off. Marriage fell apart, quit his job, and last anyone saw he was holding a sign at the light down by the Ingles."

"You cast a wide net, you're bound to catch a tortoise or a dolphin or some innocent thing you don't intend, and everyone's heart breaks for the poor dead animal." The mayor motions with his hands as if he's performing some monologue that he's rehearsed in front of a mirror. Maybe his nightly mantra to help him sleep at night. Unfortunately, he's not done.

"But if you catch the shark that's been killing children on the beach in the same net, suddenly nobody gives a flying fuck about the collateral damage. In fact, they'd kill a thousand tortoises or dolphins if it meant keeping their kids safe. That's just the natural way of things,"

"Turtles," Rodney says.

"Excuse me?"

"Turtles live in the ocean. Tortoises live on land."

The mayor stands dumbfounded, his hands planted firmly in his rain coat.

"I'm going to take another lap."

Rodney turns on the headlights and pulls out into the street. He slows to a stop at the crosswalk. A group of kids and their parents hustle across the street headed for the park. The older man raises an open hand and Rodney returns by lifting his fingers off of the steering wheel. Once they're clear, he's on the gas pedal and has no intention of returning to the park tonight.

THIRTEEN

A police SUV stops at the crosswalk. Cheyenne walks in front of her grandparents as the man driving waves them through. She can only see his hand above the glare of the headlights. After they're safely on the sidewalk the SUV speeds off down the road behind them. The wet tires creating a satisfying hum as water pelts off of the wheel well and pavement.

The park is full of people. Cheyenne looks around for anyone she might know. She makes her way to one of the tables and sees Jason, Rachel and her dad Glenn, and a few others hanging around a decorated table. They look to be adding some final touches. The two girls hug, though she's not sure who initiated it.

Gram admires the lights and candles all around the park. "You guys did such a wonderful job, Glenn."

"All thanks to this lot, how many ribbons did you two tie?" He asks Jason.

"Um, like 500, I think. Not that bad." Jason stands outside of the group as if he is purposefully putting some distance between himself and Rachel now that his grandparents have arrived.

"Chey, Jason told me you are on the cheerleading squad. That's so cool!" Rachel says.

She can't think of anything she'd rather talk about less but forces a polite response. "I guess. It's okay, I mean."

"Are you cheering at the game on Friday?"

"If you can call it cheering!" Jason sneers.

"Don't be rude," Rachel says before Cheyenne can eviscerate her brother with a humiliating rebuttal.

"She knows I'm just kidding! We're coming to watch you, aren't we Gram?"

"Of course, we are," Gram says with a hand on Cheyenne's back.

"Great," says Cheyenne with no intention of hiding the sarcasm.

Donovan and Manny burst into the group, bouncing around like billiards on break.

"What's going on losers?" Manny says. They're both sweaty and a bit dirty. He shoves Jason and puts an arm around Rachel who shrugs him off.

"Hi, Cheyenne."

"Hi, Donovan. What were you guys doing?" She tries not to embarrass him by noticing the state of his current appearance. Or the smell of the boys' sweat.

Manny loses interest in bothering Rachel and walks around the decorated table. He picks up the candles, then the ribbons, and then the origami shapes that rest on the black fabric tablecloth. Glenn reacts with every inspection as if the entire table will crumble to pieces under Manny's less than tender touch. Donovan brushes himself off before responding to Cheyenne.

"Nothing. Just hanging out at Manny's today. Do you all want to go run around with us?"

Cheyenne looks to her grandparents as Rachel looks to her dad. The adults nod in agreement.

"That'll be fine. Just meet us back here by 8:30, okay?"

"Yes. And you all stay out of trouble. Remember this is a memorial so no rough housing. Show some respect for everyone here," adds Glenn.

"Yes, sir," says Donovan.

Manny, Jason, and Rachel take off ahead but Donovan hangs back with Cheyenne as they walk slower.

"I'm glad you were able to make it," Donovan blurts out.

"Yeah, me too."

"It's pretty sad, huh?"

Cheyenne watches her feet imprint the damp blades of grass that show signs of browning. "Yeah. I still hope they find her but a year's a long time. She could be anywhere by now. Do you ever wonder about what might have happened?"

"Sure. We moved from the city. Nobody I knew, but sometimes there were kids who were either hurt or went missing for one reason or another. It always seemed to be a parent or someone close. Not to suggest Melody's family…" He looks around while lowering his voice.

"I know what you mean. Is that why you all moved here? Living in the city must have been cool, though. All those places open past six. More than one grocery store to choose from."

His laugh makes her feel warm and produces a flutter in her stomach.

"No, we lived in a pretty good area so nothing like that. My dad got transferred for his work. I don't mind the change, though. Plus, it has its perks."

Cheyenne hopes he's flirting but she doesn't have the courage to ask what perks he's referring to. They walk past a table where people are signing a book of some sort. She can't quite see what it says but suspects it's a memory book. They had one at her parents' funeral. She hated that thing and demanded her grandparents hide it afterwards. It's probably in the attic but she has no intention of looking at it anytime soon.

"Do you think the commotion will ever stop?" asks Cheyenne.

"Commotion?"

"Sorry. That was inconsiderate."

"Oh, you mean like all this? I understand," Donovan says as he points to the park decorations set up all around them.

"Yeah, and the news. Seems like it's all they talk about on TV or online."

"My dad doesn't really let us watch TV, especially not the news. We stream some shows together but that's about it. And he's pretty strict with my phone too."

"Consider yourself lucky, you're not missing anything." She feels weird saying that out loud because even though she detests the avalanche of stimulation, she would also fight to keep that chunky brick of plastic and glass in her possession. She imagines her hypocrisy is as noticeable as the boys' sweat.

Cheyenne slows as they walk by the group who speaks with Melody's family. The mayor stands hovering behind Jack and Molly with one hand on each shoulder. She watches Simone who is in front of her parents with bloodshot eyes and puffy cheeks, but at the moment isn't crying.

"It just feels so heavy. I don't know how they do it," says Cheyenne.

"The Andersons?" asks Donovan.

"Yeah. Constant attention and talking and talking with nothing changing. Speculations and that stupid picture of that horrible man. It never ends." Cheyenne feels bad for complaining and tries to come up with something more interesting to talk about.

Donovan's silence doesn't help. She didn't expect to be happy to see her brother but Jason, Manny, and Rachel circle back to them just in time to fill the gap in conversation.

"You guys wanna go do the lanterns? They're setting them on fire soon!" Jason is excited but tries to pull back to a serious tone.

"Sure." Donovan smiles at Cheyenne.

She's taken completely off guard when he reaches out and grabs her hand in his, their fingers inter-locking. A million thoughts run through her mind. She's simultaneously embarrassed and thrilled at the same time. Cheyenne wills the sweat away from her hand and prays she isn't squeezing too hard or too light.

When Jason looks back, brewing a comment, Cheyenne musters a stare that could melt a statue. Jason quickly turns back to Rachel and reaches for her hand but as she notices he fakes wiping it on his pantleg.

Manny bursts out laughing.

"What?" Jason exclaims.

"Nothing, big Papi!" Manny says with a forced accent.

All of the kids, except Jason, share a laugh. They quiet themselves when the attention of the nearby adults turn their way. Cheyenne hasn't felt this great in, well, ever. She feels guilty for the happiness that sweeps over her on such a somber night.

The week went by way too fast and she finds herself feeling better about almost everything. No fighting with her brother in several days, homework has been manageable, if not easy, and she hasn't really felt the need to be on her phone all the time unless she's talking to Donovan. But when Friday arrives it's as if clouds have rolled in over her sun-kissed day. Cheyenne was able to go through the motions at cheerleading practice during the week but now that it's Friday, game day, everything changes.

The last thing she wants to think about is cheering in front of everyone. Especially Donovan. Maybe she can give herself food poisoning at lunch. Unlike the rest of her squad, Cheyenne is wearing her regular clothes while the other girls walk the halls proudly in their uniforms. The football players that are scattered among the regular students between periods wear their jerseys. A gameday tradition she still doesn't understand, especially the cheerleaders.

"Let me get those." Donovan reaches for her books and she obliges. At first, she didn't quite get why he wanted to do it, but he insisted. It seems to make him happy so she saw no reason to protest.

"Thanks." It's only been a few days but she's living in a dream. He's sweet, and kind, and not immature like Manny or Jason.

The pair walks down the hall and pass a group of girls Cheyenne's age that are as boisterous as they are fake. They're all in their cheer uniforms.

"Aw, how sweet," Simone calls out from the center, appearing to materialize among her own cheerleaders. "Ya know, just because she's a girl doesn't mean she can't carry her own books."

Donovan stops and addresses her with a direct, but calm, response. "Well, my dad taught me that it's not about her being a girl. But about me being a man. What do you care, anyway?"

"Oh, I don't. Just thought the extra exercise might be good for her."

Cheyenne's face turns red. She feels hot. Claustrophobic. Donovan steps in front of her, maybe sensing the coming outrage. "You know, if you weren't so evil maybe a guy would carry your books too," he says.

"Please." Simone rolls her eyes and then looks Cheyenne up and down. "So, where's your uniform? Is your grandma spending the day letting it out so it will fit for the game tonight?"

"Whatever, Simone. I hate being there as much as you hate having me there. Trust me," Cheyenne says.

Where's the stupid bell? If she storms away, they'll mock her. If she stays and plays Simone's game, she can't be certain she won't make it worse. She's barely holding her composure as it is. Cheyenne doesn't believe in mind power but she tries to make the bell ring anyway. It doesn't.

"You know something?" Simone steps past Donovan, changing her tone to something resembling genuine kindness. She walks a half circle around Cheyenne. "I bet if you taped down that chest of yours, cut off what's left of your hair, and changed your name to say, Chad, people might actually like you. You've already got the voice for it."

The girls in the group audibly gasp and groan. Some mock Cheyenne. Once again, the tears backfill but she holds them off. She can see Donovan's fist clenching. She knows he would never hit a girl but doesn't want him to say anything that would get him in trouble, either. Not on her account, she couldn't bare it.

Cheyenne steps up to Simone. "I don't get it. Melody was so nice. What the hell happened to you?"

A range of emotions flood Simone's face until finally she bursts into tears and storms off. The girls give dirty looks as they chase after her down the hall.

"I wasn't trying to be mean…"

"I know, Cheyenne. She needs help. Not your fault."

Manny bumps into Donovan. "Hey guys, what'd I miss?"

"Hey, nothing man."

"You think I could catch a ride with you to the game tonight?" asks Manny.

"Sure, my dad's picking me up today though. I think he wants to mess with the car," says Donovan.

"Shit, I didn't bring a note." Manny puts a finger to his chin.

Cheyenne takes her books from Donovan before walking into class. "Has that ever stopped you before?" She asks.

"Good point," the boys say in unison.

FOURTEEN

A football flies off of the tee and sails through the night sky under the lights of the Hawksboro High School football field. The school's outdoor sports practice and play at Pine Island Park where the Sappony River splits to the south of it and rejoins to the north. It's one of the few rivers flowing the opposite direction and such a fact is ingrained in each student during elementary geography. The name of the park comes from the towering longleaf pine trees that fill the center of the park, some towering over one hundred feet tall.

The main set of bleachers for the home team sprawl the middle third of the field and were recently renovated from wood to aluminum, the expenditure a hot button item of debate and its controversy delayed the upgrade for several years. A three-windowed announcers and coaches booth sits atop the new structure, audio booming from the also new sound system. Across the field a modest by comparison single section of wooden bleachers holds a packed crowd of the away team's fan base. The long walk for opposing spectators to the concession stand that sits off of the south endzone near the home side was no mistake in planning, it would appear.

Donovan rips a bite of a soft pretzel as his eyes follow the ball through the air and into the visiting team's grasp. The crowd cheers as the home team makes a tackle. Those that opposed the upgraded seats seem to be enjoying them just fine now. He chases the ketchup on the corner of his mouth with his tongue and applies a dab more only on the piece he plans on biting. If he had a dollar for every time he heard "Ketchup? On a pretzel?" he'd be rich enough not to care what others thought and would dip away as if mustard was the unusual option.

He scoots over as Manny plops down beside him, panting. He doesn't ask what he's been up to as he's sure it's some sort of nonsense that will come with a long drawn out story that he doesn't feel like pretending to listen to. Especially not when Chey is about to go on the field. He's quick to bite the end with the ketchup so there'll be no questions asked.

"Yo, give me a bite."

"Come on, man." Donovan extends the pretzel and Manny tears a chunk.

"What, no mustard?"

"Ew, no." He reaches his hand out indicating Manny is welcome to one bite only.

Rick and Cynthia make their way up the stairs, taking a good amount of time to navigate the metal steps which nobody could argue have more traction and space than the planks of rotted and moss-covered wood that looked to come off of an eighteenth-century pirate ship. They look up and down the rows for a moment before selecting the same bleacher as the boys. There's plenty of legroom in the new stands for other fans to stay seated as the couple moves to an empty section a couple dozen feet down from Donovan and Manny.

"Hey your future grandparents in-law are here." Manny points with an outturned thumb.

"Shut up. You're such an idiot sometimes."

"Where is she?"

Donovan gestures with the remnant of the pretzel toward the home sideline just off the stands. Manny cranes his neck to look over the people in front of him. A group of cheerleaders bounce pom-poms behind the players. Cheyenne struggles to keep up and looks uncomfortable and awkward among the other girls. Donovan feels guilty for thinking it and maybe it's guilt because he feels sorry for her. He's torn between support and wanting it to end for her own sake.

"Damn, she's not very good, is she?" says Manny.

"Bro, you're going to get hit."

"What? I'd never say it to her face."

"Still. She's trying her best. And her grandparents make her do it. If Simone wasn't such a bitch maybe the team would help her out instead of treating her like a leper." Donovan looks over his shoulder to make sure nobody overheard him slight the town's darling.

"A leper? How old are you?"

"Shut up, you know what I mean.

"Calm down. I'm joking. Besides, I'd do it. Male cheerleaders get the most action, anyway. Pretty smart if you think about it."

"Action? Like you know anything about action. You still have Ninja Turtles posters."

"Whatever. April O'Neil was my first kiss."

The home team offense runs out onto the field. The crowd yells in support. Rick looks down the bleacher and waves at Donovan just as he finishes off the pretzel, dry as a bone without the rest of the ketchup that he's hiding among his napkins.

"Heya, son!"

"Hi Rick. Gram," he tries to say without being rude as the wad of bland dough clings to the inside of his cheek.

"Gram" still sounds weird to him but he managed to call her Cynthia just once before he was told there would be no more of that talk. Never meeting his own grandmother, he didn't mind the condition. Jason and Cheyenne are her only blood grandchildren, but a true count of all of the kids she would put into that bracket would be a hard task.

They both smile in their puffy jackets, breath clouding from their open mouths and masking their wrinkles that have tightened in the air. It's just cold enough for them to wear gloves but almost everyone else, including the boys, wear only hoodies or light jackets. The football players and cheerleaders wear long-sleeved white shirts that extend the length of their arms from underneath their blue jerseys and uniforms.

The crowd erupts as the home team scores a touchdown, the majority on their feet cheering and clapping. The cheerleading squad runs out onto the field and turns to face the crowd. Cheyenne is in the front row. It seems she purposely doesn't look up into the stands. Donovan tries not to stare in case she does catch his eye, hoping to save her further embarrassment. Parents throughout the stands hold up phones, snapping photos and recording the routine that their friends at work and church will feign interest in watching when cornered.

Simone, from the back of the group, kicks off the cheer and the cheerleaders go through the routine. Donovan notices the girls begin looking at one another mid-cheer, which seems out of place. Simone shouts out another part of the cheer and it's as if she cues her teammates. One by one they back away from Cheyenne, who doesn't notice and is focused on remembering each move. The vocals continue but the girls stop cheering behind her as they huddle together. She's unaware that she's alone in the front, moving her arms and going through the motions.

"Oh no," Gram says loud enough for Donovan to hear.

He looks between Gram and the field. The girls keep shouting though they make obscene and mocking gestures with their arms and hands. Cheyenne is so focused on her routine she still hasn't noticed. Murmurs and laughter in the crowd cause Donovan to lose his cool. He means to stand up and wave at her but then, without warning, Simone holds up a hand and the girls stop the cheer, leaving Cheyenne to call out by herself. Her voice cracks as it carries across the stands. Laughter from the cheerleaders seems to spill over to the crowd and the football team.

A look of terror falls over Cheyenne's face as she goes silent and lowers her pom-poms to her side. She turns to the girls who are doubled over behind her, pointing, mimicking, and clinging to one another at the joy they're experiencing. Cynthia places a hand on Rick's shoulder to help her to her feet and she moves as fast as she can to the stairs and down the bleachers.

Cheyenne breaks into tears and storms off of the field.

"Honey, please. Wait!" Gram calls from above.

"Stay away from me, this is all your fault!" Cheyenne shouts as she runs past the stands, headed for the park between the field and the school, which sits just across the pedestrian bridge that spans the east branch of the river.

Rick places a hand on Cynthia's shoulder. "It's okay, dear. She'll be alright, just give her a minute."

Donovan seethes in his seat. If Simone wasn't a girl he'd run out onto the field and clock her between the eyes. High-fives between the squad and even the smug expression on the coach's face with no hint of condemnation, almost break him. The cheerleaders return to the sideline as the game continues. Donovan stands from his seat and moves across the aisle in front of those still seated who are again invested in the game as if they're all the type of people who would defend such behavior as "kids being kids." They can all fuck off, he thinks.

"Want me to come with you?" Manny asks.

"No."

Manny shrugs.

Donovan walks around the base of the bleachers. The light from the field casts a dim light out into the park and is absorbed into nothingness by the towering pines. He squints into the darkness, scanning the area to see any signs of where Cheyenne has gone. Maybe a hundred yards out, he can see the outline of her uniform. She's hunched over on a park bench, with her head in her hands. The white sleeves of her uniform are a contrast to the black of night behind her. He hesitates, thinking it better to give her space.

He walks to the front of the bleachers, pretending to watch the game but all he can think about is running to Cheyenne. Donovan watches the clock on the scoreboard, willing it to go faster. He'll give her a couple more minutes and then check on her, understanding that two minutes of game time is more like five minutes in real time.

As the whistle blows an end to the first quarter Donovan spins around and jogs to the back of the stands. He jerks his head left and right trying to locate the bench in the park. It was harder to find this time as it didn't stick out from the trees. He realizes it's because it's now empty, the wooden bench just a shade lighter than the woods that try to swallow it. An uncomfortable feeling tightens his stomach.

Donovan runs to one side of the bleachers and then the other, sure that Cheyenne must have returned to the field. No sign of her. He sprints out into the park and makes his way to the bench where she was last sitting. It takes only a few seconds for him to make it out there and he worries for a moment how stupid he must look to Cheyenne if she's watching him.

Once he's at the bench he's uncertain which one she was sitting at. A single bench is really three that are spread out along the edge of the park. They all look the same and he can't recall from memory where she sat. Donovan circles the area and then stops in his tracks. At his feet in front of the center bench, all of the pine needles have been disturbed. It looks to him like shoes have been dragged through the dirt, forming channels in the debris that was on the ground. The lines cut around the bench and fade in the thick of the trees behind it. Donovan can't make out anything in the darkness. He begins to panic.

"Cheyenne! Cheyenne!" Fuck!" Donovan sprints back to the field as fast as he can.

FIFTEEN

The line for the concession stand is taking way too long and Jason's battling his desire for a slice of pizza and wanting to go find Rachel. His grandparents gave him five dollars before making their way to the bleachers and he rolls the wrinkled bill between his fingers, fidgeting with it impatiently as the people in front of him stand idle under the yellow lamppost. Grampa joked about what that used to be able to buy and the fact that he can now get no more than a single slice of cheese and a can of Cheerwine did not go unchastised.

A loud cheer from the field causes the entire line to turn to see what they've missed. The scoreboard at their side of the field, just off of the endzone, gives six points to the home team. A few of the adults in line clap before turning their attention back to the glow of the rectangular window. Jason can hear the beginning of the home cheer but a commotion draws his attention to the dirt road that runs in front of the booth and around the park.

Feet pound the dirt as a boy, a little older than Jason, runs through the crowd and bumps into people in line. He stumbles and staggers away as another boy, someone Jason does recognize, slides to a stop. It's Greg Pullman, a junior, and a real asshole.

Donovan used to have a problem with him but it's been awhile since he's come up, Jason guesses because he's found a new mouse to toy with.

Frustrated that he lost the pursuit, Greg runs a hand through his shoulder length hair and stomps off behind the concession stand and into the trees of the park. Some of the adults in line murmur among themselves but again their curiosity is pulled to the events on the field. A rumble of laughter carries over the fans and it's surprising to hear. Jason wonders if there's some sort of mascot routine, that stupid Hawk costume that looks more like something out of a horror movie than a representation of team spirt. Jason can see neither the bird nor the source of the laughter and he turns back just in time to shuffle a few steps forward in line.

Looking back at the field, still intrigued by what caused the outburst, he bumps into the person directly in front of him. He hadn't paid them any attention before, but the sudden recognition as the man turns and look down at him, is unsettling.

It's Mr. Alexander, the old science teacher, and Jason is shocked to see him at the game. He never had his class as the man only taught the older kids, but he remembers him enough to realize Mr. Alexander's appearance has drastically changed. He looks to have aged by ten to fifteen years and his eyes look tired. Nothing like what you'd expect a teacher to look like, he thinks.

Jason tries to stammer out an "Excuse me" but he fumbles the words and ends up looking to his feet as he backs up several steps. Mr. Alexander stares at the boy, not in anger or with any emotion at all, more like a robot processing information and waiting for further instruction. Finally, he looks around and abruptly steps out of line.

The former teacher digs into his pocket as he walks along the dirt road toward the parking lot, looking over his shoulder at Jason several times as if he's waiting to see what the boy will do. It all comes across very weird but Jason doesn't feel threatened, guilty if anything, as he believes his stuttering and sudden retreat probably made Mr. Alexander uncomfortable or embarrassed and prompted his exit from the line. He's surprised the man still lives here, let alone would show up to a game after everything that has happened.

"Next!"

Jason ignores the voice of the cashier until the woman behind the counter yells it again, twice as loud. He turns to the open window and his eyes adjust to the searing brightness of the booth, a stark contrast from watching Mr. Alexander scurry to his car in the dark.

"Huh, oh sorry," he says as he walks the several vacant steps to the counter. "Can I get a slice of cheese and a Cheerwine, please?" He slides the five-dollar bill across the stainless-steel counter and the woman just looks at it before pointing at a sign with a tightly gripped blue pen.

It's less of a sign and more of a paper plate with thick marker writing taped to the window.

"Son of a bitch," Jason says under his breath as he reads the SORRY, NO PIZZA sign.

"Fine, just the soda."

The woman reaches somewhere under the counter and places the crimson can next to his money. Jason grabs the can but quickly lets go, sliding it back in her direction.

"It's warm!"

"Sorry, son. Just dropped them in the cooler. Got water, Powerade, and Rockstar cold at the moment."

"No thanks." He lands his flat palm on top of the five and slides it back off of the steel and balls it into a fist as he walks away.

"Next!"

The woman's voice makes him jump. Then his frustration turns to elation as he sees Rachel standing next to one of the towering light poles that illuminate the football field. He hurries over to her but his smile quickly fades with the look of worry that she wears.

"What's wrong?"

"You didn't see?" she asks.

He shakes his head no, suddenly worried. Is it Cheyenne or one of his grandparents? Jason looks all around expecting to see an ambulance or something to help him understand what she's talking about. Then his eyes find his grandparents who are standing on the bleachers and making their way down the stairs. He looks back to Rachel and her sympathetic expression makes him feel sick to his stomach.

"Rachel, what happened to my sister?"

SIXTEEN

The outburst from the crowd pulls Rodney from his crime scene vision, just as the sheet was about to slide off of the face underneath. His position at the corner of the endzone, leaning against one of the scoreboard's support posts, gives him a clear vantage point of both sidelines, the field, and the concession stands area where the restrooms are located. Any mischief would be well within his field of view, though these games rarely produce much more than a rowdy visiting parent who's channeling the disappointment in their child's performance.

As the laughter dies down, a flash of blue and white pulls him fully back to reality. A cheerleader runs off of the field, past the bleachers, and off into the park. He's not sure what the issue is but doesn't appear to be something he should concern himself with. When some people stand up, their unsteady movement suggesting they share a worry he doesn't, Rodney decides to go check things out. Plus, his back hurts from leaning against that cold concrete beam so he uses the event as an excuse to get the blood flowing.

First, he looks for Darren who's supposed to be over by the opposing team in case some fans or coaches get out of hand. It's not uncommon for the deputies to walk around, chat it up with the locals, or grab a hot dog, but Rodney's more annoyed that he might have to address an issue himself should any parents get into it. Feeling the pressure to be proactive, despite a lingering buzz from his pre-game thermos, he calls Darren over his radio.

"Zero one to zero seven, over." Rodney releases the button and listens for a response among the cheering fans.

"Dammit, Darren." He waits another beat before jamming the button again.

"Zero one to zero seven, over."

"Go for Darren. Uh, zero seven, over." The voice crackles on the other end.

"What's your twenty? You better not be at the concessions stand, might need you to check on something. Over." He's aware of the colloquial pluralization as he speaks, thanks to Darren's OCD of pointing out anything technically inaccurate. If he brings it up now—

"Zero-seven. I'm uh, 10-100 at the moment. Over."

"Jesus Christ," Rodney says off radio before depressing the button again. "10-4. Over."

"You need me to 10-19? Over."

"I got it. Just try not to catch it in your zipper. Over and out."

"Copy that. Two minutes. Zero-seven, out."

The radio crackles and goes silent. Rodney first looks to the brick building connected to the concession stand with the men and women signs on each opening. He could wait but sees more of a gathering at the stands and decides to investigate. He walks his way around the edge of the football field and greets Rick and Cynthia who are standing on the stairs. He knows the elderly couple, albeit not well, but remembers their situation and the loss of their daughter and son-in-law.

Rodney, just a deputy back then, was the new guy on the force. The big city cop assigned to the night shift. He was one of the first responders to arrive at the scene of the accident just a few miles out on route 17. It wasn't pretty and even a strong drink won't erase the images that return to his memory all these years later, though that doesn't stop him from trying on an almost nightly basis.

He seems to recall the young kids, maybe two or three, were home with their grandparents at the time and thankfully not in the car. The poor mother, who was in the passenger seat, got it the worst. Not much left to identify after the fire was extinguished. The dad somehow survived the car's initial impact after dropping off of the highway overpass and bursting into flames on the county road below. An out-of-town truck driver made it down the embankment and was able to pull him out, but the fire engulfed the rest of the car before he could extricate the mother. She was still screaming when Rodney arrived, but not for long.

With severe burns over most of his body, the father and son-in-law never regained consciousness and died a short time after making it to the hospital via a Life Flight helicopter. There were rumors going around town within hours that drunkenness and substance abuse were the cause of the accident, but the toxicology report following the autopsy indicated only trace amounts of marijuana, and accident scene analysis backed up the truck driver's account. According to the distraught man with severe burns of his own, the car swerved to miss a deer and lost control, hit the concrete barrier, rolled over, and then landed on its wheels sixty feet below.

Rodney bats his eyes, attempting to erase the horrific images behind them. Rick and Cynthia stand before him, grasping the railing as if on a ship in a storm. He allows them to explain what happened, taking much longer than needed he realizes once they got to the point of it, and takes a long, considerate breath to demonstrate how serious he was taking the situation.

"She going to be okay?" he asks.

"I think she'll be fine, Sheriff. Cheyenne's a tough girl," Rick says while rubbing the arm of Cynthia's jacket. She looks fraught with guilt, more culpable than worried.

"Kids can be cruel. Don't take it to heart."

Rodney scans the seats and the field before turning back to the couple. He didn't notice before but they not only look but feel frail. Like the lightest breeze would turn them to dust. His eyes do another round, not wanting to stare. With the exception of a few children, nobody seems to be invested in the current incident. It's all about the football game still going on with the boisterous excitement of small-town sports.

"Maybe it'd be best if you get her home for the night. Let her sleep it off. I'm sure the last thing–Cheyenne is it? The last thing Cheyenne wants is to have to face her friends after that. I can give Jack a word if you think it'd help."

Rodney prays they don't ask him to follow through on the offer. Jack was always intimidating, but after a year of distress and unending attention, not all being well-intentioned, he's become a monster. Maybe it's that he feels it can't get worse, giving him a confidence to say and do whatever his temper demands. Or it could be, as Rodney suspects of most people, that Jack places the blame of Melody's unsolved case on the sheriff's office, and any chance to speak out to someone in power is delivered with fervent repudiation. It's gotten to the point where Rodney avoids going into the office if the front desk has let him know Jack is waiting to see him.

"No, no, that won't be necessary. I don't even blame the poor girl. They've been through so much." Rick guides Cynthia as they descend the bleacher stairs.

A boy runs from around the corner of the stands. He's panting and trying to catch his breath. His face is distraught, a clear indication that it's more than the usual rough-housing. Rodney steps around the couple, careful not to knock them over on the way down and hurries to meet the frightened child.

"Donovan, what's going on?" Cynthia calls out.

"Help! Help! She's gone!" Donovan fights to get the words out between gasps.

"Who's gone? Cheyenne? What do you mean, son?" Rick steps in front of Cynthia.

Rodney grabs Donovan by the arm with a gentle squeeze, his intention to help him focus.

"Take a breath."

The boy puffs in and out with arms overhead, trying to control his breathing.

"Okay, good. Now tell us exactly what happened. What did you see?"

"I. Am. Trying!"

The sheriff takes a knee to reach eye level with him though it makes the boy a head taller. "In your own time, son." He looks around hoping the boy's father is nearby to help. Rodney's not one for dealing with kids.

"She's gone. One second she was sitting on the bench, crying or something, and the next she disappeared. Something's not right!" Donovan's frustration bleeds through, like a tantrum from someone half his age.

Cynthia covers her mouth with her gloved hand.

"It's alright. Let's not get worked up any more than we already are, okay? Donovan, right?" The boy nods. "Donovan, can you show me where you saw her last?"

Rodney stands, wiping the dirt from his knee. His hand finds the shoulder radio but he hesitates as he looks around, not knowing what his eyes are even searching for. Dizziness sweeps over him. He pep-talks himself back into the moment. Two more children run over to meet them.

"Gram, what happened?"

"Nothing, Jason. Everything is just fine, come here." Rick pulls him into a hug. "Rachel, why don't you go and get your dad for me?"

The girl agrees and runs off.

Rick rubs Jason's hair and extends the boy to arm's length. "Can you stay here with Gram for me? I'm going to go with the sheriff and give him a hand. I'm sure your sister just went for a walk to cool off."

Jason nods and hugs Cynthia who is holding it together, though it seems by a thread.

Rodney depresses the radio. "Zero one to zero seven."

"Go for zero seven," Darren's voice comes in with no delay.

"What's your twenty? Over."

"Just got back over to the visitor's side. An unruly parent I might need to put in his place if he doesn't calm down. Acting like it's the dang pros or something."

Rodney's eyes roll back waiting for Darren to shut up and clear the channel.

"Just stand by for me, don't go anywhere. Over."

"Copy that."

Donovan leads the sheriff as they jog across the park. Rick does his best to keep up. Donovan shows them a bench that sits in front of a large wooded area that is adjacent to the river, and beyond that and over the pedestrian bridge is Hawksboro

High School.

"I was over by the bleachers and looked over. She was right here sitting, and I looked away for just a second, I swear. When I looked back, she was gone!"

"Did you see anyone else around?" Rodney asks as he shines his flashlight on the bench and surrounding area.

"No. I mean, I don't think so. It was just her. Look around, besides the trees it's all open. I would've seen her and anyone else, but it was empty."

Rodney shines his light into the wooded area, the tall, slender pines look like bars of a cell that go on, far out of the reach of the luminance of his beam.

"No way she'd go in there!" Donovan says as if the sheriff is wasting time.

Thunderous footsteps announce Kenneth's arrival. Rodney had met him when Kenneth and his family first moved into town. His service record was as impressive as the shape he keeps himself in. Maybe he should be the sheriff, Rodney thought at the time, still thinks it now. They've been cordial since, not friends, but it seems Kenneth has taken a liking to him, though he couldn't pinpoint why to save his life. Something about his arrival brings comfort, as if for once Rodney isn't alone.

"What do you need, Rod?" Kenneth asks.

"I don't see anything out of the ordinary. You sure you didn't just miss her getting up?"

Rodney takes a few steps into the growth beyond the bench. He thinks to radio Darren to check the restrooms and under the bleachers with the field equipment where some of the kids like to play, even though it's supposed to be locked. Rick joins the group and Rodney lets the radio fall back to his shoulder. A girl walking away from a bench and her boyfriend frantic over her whereabouts is hardly eventful, let alone criminal, however the distinct feeling he had in the first days of Melody's disappearance has returned.

Donovan points to the scattered pine needles at their feet.

"I'm positive. It was a split second. Look at all the scuff marks around the bench."

"That doesn't seem unusual, son. Just looks like someone was sitting here swinging their feet back and forth." Rodney moves back to the front of the bench dismissing the ground cover.

"No! Look!"

The boy storms over to the bench and sits all the way back. The tips of his shoes just barely touch the surface of the ground

"See, and I'm taller than her!"

"I appreciate the point you're making. And all I'm saying is nothing here looks suspicious, that doesn't mean anything other than that."

"You're wrong! Why don't you believe me?"

"Hey, Don. Look who you're talking to. Take it easy. We believe you," Kenneth says while putting his hand on the back of Donovan's neck.

"I'm not saying you weren't right to come get help. You were," says Rodney.

Donovan's eyes drift to his feet.

"The most likely thing that happened is she was too embarrassed to return to the game and decided to walk home. It's not far right, Rick?" Rodney asks, turning to the man who has been staring at the bench with a hand under his chin since he arrived.

"You're probably right," Rick says.

"That's not what happened!" Donovan bursts out.

"Hey! What did I say? I know she's your friend, but you need to cool it," Kenneth says.

"I won't cool it. Something is wrong and none of you are helping!" Donovan storms off toward the football field.

"It's okay. I'll get him a ride back and then we can look around a bit more."

Rodney nods and scans the area with his light. Kenneth jogs to catch up with his son. Rick moves to the bench and takes a seat. He rubs his hand on the worn wooden planks.

"Why don't you get Cynthia home as well in case she did decide to walk?" Rodney suggests.

He doesn't mind the help but the older man doesn't need to be out in the cool night air if there's no good reason.

"I suppose you're right." Rick sighs as he stands and pats Rodney on the shoulder as he walks toward the bleachers. "You call us if you see anything, Sheriff."

Rodney continues to walk around the benches and the wooded area. There are scuff marks and trenches dug into the needles, but that's far from troublesome. It just appears highly-trafficked and it's a park. He can't shake the feeling that something is off though, but resists the urge to apply Melody's disappearance to that of a bullied cheerleader who didn't wave goodbye. Guilt strikes him like a slap across the face as he recognizes his dismissal is more avoiding what it would mean for him if she was taken, rather than concern for a young girl in possible danger.

He engages the button on his radio once again. "Zero one, zero seven. Over."

"Zero-seven," Darren replies.

"I'm over in the park looking into something. Can you canvas town, let me know if you see anyone out walking by them selves? Over."

"10-4. I'm already in the parking lot. Had to break up some

kids throwing bottles. Got a description? Over."

"Just relay if you come across anyone and I'll advise. Meet you back at the station in an hour. Over and out."

"Copy."

As Rodney releases the radio, Kenneth and Glenn make their way to him.

"Thank God for the emergency road kit," Glenn proudly holds up a bulky flashlight.

Kenneth has a small tactical flashlight out and shining at their feet while they talk. Rodney suspects it came from a concealed holster under his hoodie, and if he was a betting man in a constitutional carry state, there's probably a handgun under there too. This thought, in addition to the formidable man's presence, also provides some comfort. Kenneth being here reduces the chances of Rodney missing something if he were alone. Less of a chance to fuck things up.

The three men walk along the wooded area circling almost the entire way to the high school. They pass the pedestrian bridge but don't cross it and see no signs of anyone. The trees continue in a thick patch with high brush covering the gap between them and the river. Ahead, past the tall grass, a concrete bridge spans the river. The road going across it goes from the park and travels up the forested hillside and out of town.

"If she didn't cut through the school, she probably made her way to the road and then followed it back into town." Rodney points to the bridge and overgrown bank with his flashlight. The bright moon makes it easy enough to see what's in front of them.

They high-step through the brush and thicket where the trees meet the rocky edge of the water. All three shine their lights on the ground all around them as they place each step with caution. They're near the end of the overgrowth and a few feet from the shoulder of the road when Rodney's light catches a glint.

"What's that?" Kenneth is the first to call it out.

"Not sure."

Rodney moves to the object, keeping his beam centered on the sparkle.

Glenn beats the side of his fat flashlight trying to enhance the output. They gather around the shiny object tangled in the grass that lines the shoulder of the road. Rodney pulls it out of the natural snare and examines it in his palm. All three lights shine bright on his hand.

"Looks to be tinsel of some sort, wrapped with blue thread."

The Sheriff twirls it between his fingers.

"Probably came off her uniform, looks right doesn't it?" Glenn suggests.

"I think you're right." Kenneth kneels to get a closer look. "Hey, it's a good sign. Show's we're headed in the right direction."

Rodney stands from his crouching position and illuminates the road and then back to the grass and again to the road.

"Most likely got tangled in those briars when she cut through the woods. Could have been hanging off her to begin with, not exactly new uniforms. My guess is she walked along Davenport Drive back to Main Street." Rodney drops the beam to the muddy shoulder of gravel at his feet.

"Why wouldn't she take the walking bridge to the high school and then go through town?" asks Kenneth. "Seems about the same distance and less of this junk to go through."

"I don't have an answer for that yet. Not exactly the wilderness, we're chasing kids outta here all the time, but sure the other way would have been easier," says Rodney.

"Regardless, her house is only about a half-mile that way. She's probably home already," Glenn adds.

"I'll have Darren give us a ride back to the field, we don't need to walk through all that shit again."

Rodney moves the focus of the light along the ground, still rubbing the tinsel in his other hand. Thick tread marks look fresh in the shoulder of the road, just before the bridge. He's seen people fish off of it before but usually not this time of year. There's something about them that triggers his instinct, but he can't quite put a finger on it.

"See something else?" Kenneth asks.

"Huh? Oh, no. Just thinking." Rodney tilts his head to his radio. "Zero one to zero seven. Over."

SEVENTEEN

Plates of cookies, muffins, and brownies cover the entire Formica counter. All of the baking dishes and utensils that were used in the creation of this bounty are now spotless and drying in the rack next to the sink. Cynthia sits at the kitchen table awake, but resting in her chair, eyes drifting open and closed. A newspaper crossword is sprawled out and completed in front of her. The soft blue light from early dawn seeps into the room from behind matching laced curtains that cover the single window next to the table as well as the entryway.

Cynthia is startled by the porch screen door rattling shut and stands to her feet as fast as she can manage, with the assistance of the table, as Rick enters through the front door and stops on the mat in the kitchen. He removes his gloves one at a time and kicks off a pair of muddy boots. She stares at him, the anxiety welling in her eyes, looking for any sign of news from the overnight search.

Rodney had stopped by late the night before to ask about a bit of her uniform. When he pulled into the driveway it was about as much as she could handle. The lack of lights or a siren were somehow less comforting. Cynthia could tell that the sheriff was counting on Cheyenne already being home, though he made no remarks. They looked at each other with disappointment from across the lawn, realizing that neither carried the good news that the other was hoping for. That she was desperate for. Rick wasted no time gathering his things to go back out and aid the search.

Now, as he stands just a few feet away, his eyes finally meet hers. In their 57 years of marriage she can count the number of times she's seen him cry on one hand and it looks like he's doing everything within his power to hold it back.

"We didn't find her. Searched the whole town. Knocked on doors. Retraced the entire wooded area behind the school and back over to the park. Nothing."

"Oh, Rick." Cynthia moves to him and stumbles into his arms.

"She'll turn up. Sheriff thinks she probably just stayed at a friend's house. They're getting someone to open her locker this morning to retrieve her phone. That's why we probably haven't heard from her, he said."

"Rick, I know you don't believe that. Cheyenne doesn't have any friends except those kids who were all worked up at the game."

"I...Sheriff said—"

"No, there's more happening here and you know it."

Cynthia buries her head into his chest and they sink to their knees on the kitchen floor. Rick pulls her close and she sobs into him. He places his hand on the back of her head. Her permed hair grasps his swollen knuckles in a soft, twirling embrace.

"Do you remember back when Wendy musta been about eight years old and I lost her down at Kaufmann's department store?" Rick asks.

Cynthia looks to him with tears in her eyes. She nods.

"I drove around town for hours looking for her. When I got home, I wasn't just worried about her being gone, I was worried about how much I let the both of you down. My mind obsessed over how you would never forgive me. I honestly imagined you would leave."

"How could you even think something like that?"

"And do you remember where she turned up later that day?"

She laughs between the tears that run down her face. "Of course. When she saw how angry you were in the department store for wandering off, she hid in the bed of your truck. There you were driving all around town looking for her and she was with you the whole time."

Rick's smile wraps her like a warm blanket. "And she's still with us, dear. Michael too. Their spirits are still with us, we get to see them every day in those kids." He gestures to a photo of Cheyenne and Jason on the wall. "They entrusted us to take care of them and I'm promising you we're going to do whatever it takes to get her home."

Cynthia rests an ear on his chest while looking out of the kitchen window.

"Your faith has been my anchor through all these years, especially after the accident. And I need you to be my foundation now, too."

"Always," she whispers.

Cynthia can feel his head rise from atop of hers and move back and forth.

"When did you do all of this?" he asks.

She looks around the counter, only now noticing the quantity of sweets she's put together.

"I wanted to have something special ready for her when she got home."

Rick lets out a deep sigh. A groan from the stairs as Jason walks down and enters the kitchen, wiping his groggy eyes.

"Where's Chey?" asks Jason.

"She, uh—" Rick starts.

"It's okay, honey. Come here," Cynthia says, quick to interrupt.

Jason, not picking up his feet, slides on his socks across the linoleum and takes a seat on her knee.

"Why are you two on the floor? And why isn't she home yet?"

"Grampa was out all night looking for her but don't you worry about your sister. She'll be home very soon. You know that, don't you?" Cynthia tries hard to believe her own words.

With a tired nod he rests his head on her shoulder. "I didn't mean it."

"Mean what, dear?" she asks.

"All the mean things I said to her. I didn't mean any of them."

"We know that, Jason. And she does too. You had nothing to do with this, understand?" Cynthia says.

"I guess so. What are you going to do, Grampa?" he asks, looking up to Rick.

"We're going to keep looking. Last night at the game was a pretty mean thing they did, but your sister is strong. She'll show up. You gotta be strong for when she gets back though, okay?"

"I will."

"I know you will." Rick kisses his forehead and tussles the boy's bed hair.

They sit together in the center of the kitchen floor in a tight huddle as the first full rays of sunshine dance through the blinds behind the curtains. Falling leaves cast their shadows on the translucent fabric as they drop from the safety of the tree in the front yard and land on the curled blades of grass that have yet to be kissed by the sun.

EIGHTEEN

"Knock, knock." Marcus sticks his head into the open door of Erin's office.

She doesn't look up from the laptop in front of her. The screen reflects off of her blue light filter glasses. Marcus enters and sits on the corner of her desk. Erin types vigorously and then leans in to read.

"Two seconds?" he asks.

Erin removes the glasses and leans back in her chair. It's been weeks since they've had any physical contact, be it a flirtatious swipe of a hand when no one is looking, or a full-on desk-clearer. Strictly business. Something about his wife catching on, but Erin doesn't buy it. In fact, she's seen this before, almost verbatim. He's lost interest. Something shinier, tighter, more submissive, has his attention.

"You see this?" Marcus shoves his phone into her face.

She pulls her head back to adjust focus on the small screen before squinting and grabbing it out of his hand. He's reluctant to give up control of the device but she's too quick and she's already scrolling the story with her index finger. Erin can feel his pent-up anxiety, she should close out the browser and open another app just to fuck with him.

"Hawksboro? Why does that sound familiar?" She reads more and hands it back to him. She can feel his relief when it's back and safe in his hands.

"That girl, Melody Anderson. A year ago. Same town." Marcus raises his eyebrows, his way of insinuating there's opportunity to be had.

"No shit. What's the story on this one?"

"Well, source on the ground says this other girl hasn't been seen since Friday. Up and vanished at a football game."

"Who's the source?"

"Local beat writer. Some acne punk kid with a decent following on social, why?"

"A kid?"

"I don't know how old he is. Yes, he's an adult but he looks like a kid. Does it matter?"

She puts a pen in her mouth and watches his eyes follow it to her lips.

"We have an angle? Four days is a little early to be making connections. Especially if no arrests have been made."

"That's the hang-up. Sheriff's office is holding a press conference tomorrow but my money is on runaway. Or at least that's what they're suggesting without saying as much."

"Hmm. What's the girl look like? She have a good story?"

Marcus gestures to her laptop and she spins it to face him. He begins typing and clicking. After a moment he spins it back to face her. Erin slides her glasses back on, intentionally drawing out the movement while playing with the pen. She looks at the page in front of her.

What appears to be a yearbook photo with a name typed below, shows Cheyenne among a column of text.

"Hawksboro Gazette. Riveting," Erin says as she reads. "She's not exactly a looker, is she?" Erin scrolls back up to the photo at the top of the page.

"You could say that. We could run it? Light segment tonight," Marcus offers.

"You're kidding." Erin removes the pen and glasses and delivers an icy stare.

"What, so there's no connection but people can make the jump themselves."

"And what if the news conference tomorrow makes us all look like fools when we find out she ran away because, well did you read this? Of course she ran away. Or someone did her a favor."

"That's a little cold, even for you."

"Seriously, my point is Melody was the story. It told itself. You put her picture up and the whole country is dying to know what happens next. You show this poor girl's mug, let alone try to explain her backstory, people will lose their jobs."

Marcus stands, slapping his phone on his pant leg with one hand and biting a finger of the other. "What about the POC angle? Hate crime?"

"Jesus, Marcus. Show me one picture of a slur written on her locker and we'll talk. Besides, you know that doesn't work for indigenous. Polls are atrocious. You want to be the one to connect the dots on her dad's heritage and alcoholism?" She violently points at the article in front of her.

"It says that?"

"No you ass, it doesn't, but it also doesn't take a genius to put two and two together just by us describing the setting. A single car accident. Passenger dies, driver survives but dies later, and happens to be a full blood Native American."

Marcus seems to be taken aback by the suggestion. She

continues, unfazed.

"Look, I'm not saying it's true but my job is to understand the public. The consumer. I have to anticipate what they're going to think based on every word that comes out of my mouth, even better than they do. If you're mad at someone, be mad at them."

"What if there was another way we could pitch it?"

"And what's that? She have a dark-skinned boyfriend with a record, or better yet, immigrant status that we can scare the suburban moms with?"

"Fuck you. I'm talking about Finely."

"For Christ's sake. I think we've milked that cow to death." Erin makes a show of pulling her laptop closer and putting her glasses back on. "I've got to get ready for the show. Mind closing the door on the way out?"

"Just listen to my pitch and I'll let it go?"

Her silence is enough permission for Marcus to continue.

"We dropped the Finely storyline, what, three-four months ago? Hasn't been seen since going AWOL. But what if I told you his lawyer randomly dropped dead over the summer?" Marcus beams a smile.

Erin smashes keys on her keyboard and turns the laptop to face him. His smile fades.

"You mean this fat fuck? Nothing random or suspicious about eating twice as many calories as your heart can handle."

The obituary on the screen shows a headshot of an overweight man in a suit.

"Have it your way. But if anything of note comes out of the press conference tomorrow, you're running it."

"Sure. If anything of note we'll grab a soundbite from the locals, give it thirty seconds before mid-break. Can we please be done talking about this?"

Another knock at the door surprises them both.

"Excuse me, Marcus?" A very young and very beautiful brunette hangs on the door frame.

"Hey, Julie," he says.

Erin looks her up and down. What she wouldn't give for the twenty-year-old's body. She can't blame Marcus. She would probably fuck her too. To be desired by someone who looks that good, wouldn't be the worst way to spend an evening. And she knows from experience she could show the young plaything a better time than Marcus ever could.

"Sorry to interrupt, but this just came in." Julie holds a paper in her hand.

"You're not interrupting. Let's go back to my office and look it over."

He doesn't even look back. Erin watches them leave her office. The sleight of hand on the small of Julie's lower back. Her tight ass moving perfectly underneath that even tighter skirt. The prick even has the audacity to adjust his chub as he walks behind her.

Once they're gone, she clicks back over to a tab featuring Cheyenne's photo. She punches a key to zoom in on the image. Erin pictures it blown up on TV's in homes all across her viewing base. Her having to keep a straight face while describing the horrors this girl may be facing at the hands of Finely. She doesn't buy it. This girl's entire life is a horror. She wouldn't be surprised if the press conference revealed they found a body with self-sustained injuries. Erin shudders as she clicks the X button, closing the open tab.

NINETEEN

odney walks through the halls of the police station. Officers and detectives work at their desks, each acknowledging with a wave or a greeting as he passes by their desks. He grabs a mug and fills it with lukewarm coffee and sips it as he makes his way to his office. Throwing himself down into his chair, which screams under the sudden occupation, he places the mug on a stack of papers in front of him and lets out a long, slow exhale. It's been hell the past few days and to have a moment of peace and quiet off of his feet is almost euphoric.

"How ya holding up?" Darren calls from the door.

Rodney groans as the moment to himself is spoiled and hopes the "dammit" he sputtered wasn't loud enough to carry past his desk. He gathers some papers and draws his attention to Darren, who still waits in the doorway.

"Morning, Darren. Any luck from the hotline? Credible tips? Witnesses? Anybody call in or heard anything at all?" Rodney asks, hoping to get something in return.

"Not a one, sir. I'll keep on it, though. You about ready for the press conference?"

"Shit. Balls. Shit." Rodney looks at his watch and to his

wrinkled uniform. He instinctively touches the rough patches on his face. "I can't go in there like this."

"No, sir. You can't." Darren motions with his head toward the desk. "Top drawer."

Rodney looks down and pulls open the top drawer. Inside is a small shave kit and aftershave.

"Point taken. Tell them I'll be out in five."

They share a smirk and Darren pats the door frame as he leaves the office.

After washing up in the rest room, a quick shave, and a spritz of cologne, Rodney flattens his uniform with his hands and walks down the long hallway toward the small conference room attached to the police station. Before he can make it through the side door an arm hooks his, pulling him to an abrupt stop.

"Mr. Mayor," he says, trying to sound cordial as he can muster.

The mayor's grip on the inside of the bend in his arm is firm but not aggressive. Not yet, anyway. Rodney tries not to stare at the man's unmoving swath of gray hair that has been glued into a perfect combed-back form. Beads of sweat collect on spray-tanned temples as he looks into Rodney's eyes, indicating his presence is of a serious nature.

"Sheriff. Just wanted to sidebar with you real quick so we're all on the same page."

"What page is that, sir?"

His hand slides off of Rodney's arm and the mayor relaxes his body language.

"Oh, you know, Rod. I just want to make sure we're not blowing this whole thing up until we have more facts to support that kind of narrative."

Rodney shudders at his unapproved nickname as it slides across the mayor's lips. It reeks of a snide, "all-good buddy" tone.

Not immediately granting the request is an apparent invitation for the man to further plead his case.

"You remember what is was like this past year." The mayor swats Rodney's shoulder for effect. "Whole town turned upside down. Sure, the extra business was good but having a microphone shoved in our faces every day and those bugger internet trolls thinking they can come down here and do our jobs, your job, well I just don't think the citizens here have the stomach for it again."

The mayor must feel like he properly sold his point because he steps back, folding his arms, and shows a smile that Rodney wants to flatten with the hard side of his flash light.

"We'll go where the truth leads us." Before the mayor can turn a full shade of red, Rodney places a hand firmly on the breast of his suit. "But in the meantime, I can assure you we have no new information to indicate that there would be any benefit to telling the media it's anything more than what we know."

He doesn't wait for a response and pulls open the door in front of him. As he enters the room, he's surprised to see an almost entirely empty space. Of the twenty-some chairs, two are occupied in the front center. A single cameraman stands in the back behind his tripod.

Rodney approaches the podium with some apprehensions. An American and North Carolina State flag stand upright behind him. He liked it better when other people were up here with him, but this time he's alone. He clears his throat before leaning into the single, unmarked microphone mounted on the podium.

"Thank you all for coming." He pauses, thinking how stupid that must have sounded, but manages to continue. "On Friday, September 20th at roughly 7:30 p.m., Cheyenne Holt went missing while in attendance of the Hawksboro High School football game. She was last seen sitting alone on a park bench just off of the field that is about a half mile from the school.

"For the past several days, myself, and all of the Lincoln County Sheriff's Department, have been diligently searching and checking every lead. At this time, we have no reason to suspect foul play as it appears more than likely a runaway case resulting from a bullying incident that took place shortly before she was reported missing.

"We will continue our search and ask that if you have any information regarding Cheyenne's whereabouts to please contact the station directly. I…We are working hard to bring Cheyenne home and I know her family appreciates your cooperation and respecting their privacy. Thank you."

Rodney steps away from the microphone, with no real media presence he doesn't expect any questions. Of course, the lone reporter speaks up. The young woman is from a local affiliate that he's seen on the evening news. She's not terribly charming to watch, he thinks.

"Sheriff, one question."

"Yes, go ahead." Rodney hopes he sold the desperation of needing to get back to work.

"How is it you're so certain it's a runaway case? Don't you feel it's at least plausible that her fate could be related to that of Melody Anderson's unsolved disappearance in this very town just over a year ago?"

He clears his throat again and leans back to the podium, unwilling to commit to fully standing before it again.

"It's obvious the coincidences are chilling, but we have no significant evidence to suspect that scenario. While no possibility has been taken off of the table, my experience and first-hand knowledge of the case leads me to believe it's an unrelated runaway and nothing more. We're going to do our due diligence of course and follow any lead, wherever it takes us."

"Significant evidence?" The young man next to the reporter asks with a hand thrust into the air. Rodney thinks it's the local reporter from the Hawksboro Gazette but can't be certain. The kid looks like he can't be more than in his early twenties. One thing he does know is that it was his Pulitzer-worthy, back-of-the-issue column that generated the need to even hold a press conference. It's nice to put a face to the blame for his current discomfort.

"Yeah, I just meant the two cases are very different. With Melody we knew almost immediately that something nefarious had taken place, but in this instance, there just isn't anything that reaches out to us to suggest foul play."

"What about—"

"Andrew, is it?" He hopes he got it right to avoid the embarrassment of correction. The kid nods. "Andrew, I promise if we receive any additional information you all will be the first to know. In a case like this, the public's participation is crucial to law enforcement."

The TV reporter is already packing up with her cameraman. Andrew, looking to want to continue his questions follows her lead and puts away his phone and handheld audio recorder.

"Will that be all?" Rodney says, not so much a question but a farewell.

"Yes, thank you, Sheriff."

"Where uh, where's everyone else? Some breaking news I don't know about?" Rodney has his hand on his hip and an elbow on the podium.

"They're piggy-backing our coverage. Until there's more development there's just not much interest in the story. Less so now, I suspect."

"What do you mean?"

"You know the saying, if it bleeds…may be just a one-liner on the evening news. We've got the fall festival over in Sherill's Ford and that new Amazon Warehouse breaking ground down in Prembly. Busy news day."

The reporter slings her bag and the cameraman shoulders his tripod.

Rodney steps aside as they exit the conference room. Andrew stops with that look in his eye and he gives him a hearty slap on the shoulder.

"Thanks for coming out, Andrew. I'll be sure to let you know personally if anything develops."

Deflated, the beat reporter drags himself through the door. Darren gives him a thumbs up from the back of the room which draws an eye roll from the sheriff.

"Don't you have somewhere to be?"

The remainder of the shift crawled to the end with no new information. He spent most of the time reshuffling the blank job applications stacked on his desk. When it came time to call it a day, Rodney couldn't leave the suffocating environment of the police station quick enough. With two missing girls in the small town of which he is responsible, the station and what should be a symbol of safety for the community, had turned into a prison for his mind. Small crimes keep the department busy enough, especially with the influx of opioids that have altered the entire protocol of how they patrol and respond to calls, but the face of Melody and now Cheyenne in every cubicle and on every computer screen serve as a constant reminder that feels as cold as the trail leading to their whereabouts.

Now in the comfort of his living room, a dinner which

consisted of a case of beer, is nearly finished. Empty bottles compete for floor space with the remnants from the night before. Rodney has nailed down a routine to go to a different store every day as not to draw any questions on his consumption. Between the gas stations, Ingles, and the local liquor store known as "the beer distributor," he could cover a week or more without visiting the same location twice. If the same worker happened to be on shift as his last stop, he would buy a pack of gum and go on to the next. A year of this would probably look daunting from the outside, but for him it has become muscle memory. A necessary inconvenience to keep the fog present.

Loud music and bright graphics pull Rodney from his alcohol-induced slumber. Erin Heart appears on the screen that sits atop a cabinet, even though the mount for it hangs empty on the wall behind it. He dials his vision to focus on the woman who looks to be as likely a digital creation as a real live person. Her hair, perfect. Her makeup, perfect. Even her outfit is color coordinated in such a pleasing way that it complements the busy, monitor-filled background of the so-called newsroom. God, he hates the news, yet here he is, another night, another rotation. Another chance to chase an answer that won't come.

"Good evening. I'm Erin Heart with tonight's top story, how a toxic spill twenty years ago could still be contaminating the drinking water and harming local children. But first we report on another missing persons case." Erin reads the teleprompter with dramatic highs and lows in her voice.

Rodney eases forward in his recliner.

"Cheyenne Holt of Hawksboro, the same town that suffered the disappearance of Melody Anderson last year, has also gone missing. Officials from the Lincoln County Sherriff's Department have called this mystery a runaway."

An edited video clip of Rodney at the earlier press conference plays. He looks away from the TV, once again wincing at the sound of his voice.

"At this time, we have no reason to suspect foul play as it appears more than likely a runaway case. We will continue our search and ask that if you have any information regarding Cheyenne's whereabouts to please contact the station directly."

Erin again fills the screen. The number of the police hotline displays on the lower third.

"Our thoughts and prayers are with her family tonight. Now on to the shocking story of a company's neglect that may have residents under a boil water notice sooner than you think. After the break."

The image goes to black and a prescription drug commercial takes over. Rodney kicks down the recliner's foot rest and knocks over the clutter of bottles in the process. He points an angry finger, the only one not holding the bottle in hand, at the TV.

"What the hell was that?" His equilibrium tumbles with the change of position. "Not even a God-damned photo?"

Rodney fumbles for his phone on the side table. It's buried under wrappers and receipts. He brings the screen close to his face and punches each button with careful focus before placing it to his ear. He checks it twice to make sure it says it's ringing.

"Yeah?" a muffled voice answers on the other end.

"Did you see that load of shit?" Rodney asks.

"Sheriff, that you? See what? Everything okay?" Darren asks, his voice now perked up.

"I can't believe it."

"Rodney, do you need me to come in? Where's Hugh?"

"Huh? No. I don't know. He's probably sleeping in his patrol car outside of the Taco Bell." Rodney shakes his head for clarity.

"I'm talking about the TV."

"Sir, it's late and you've lost me."

"The news. They didn't even show her picture! How is anyone going to recognize her if they don't know what she looks like?"

"The news? Look, I'm sure it was just an oversight, whatever you saw. We can call the local station in the morning and make sure they have our current APB."

A pause on the other end.

"Did you need something, sir?" asks Darren.

Rodney looks at his phone and then his watch. It's 1:30 a.m. which doesn't make sense at first. "Ah Christ, I must have paused the live broadcast. Sorry to call so late." Rodney's eyes feel like bricks and they struggle to stay open. The streets of Baltimore pull at his lids.

"You can release another statement tomorrow. Maybe not lean so heavily on the runaway angle," Darren says.

"So, it's my fault? I'm responsible for the news now, too?" "I didn't say that, Sheriff. It's late—"

A whimper and a muffled, angry voice. Rodney bats his eyes, analyzing the phone's screen before putting it back to his ear.

"I didn't mean to wake you," says Rodney.

"Shit. The baby's up. I gotta go. You need me to come in or not?"

"No, Darren. Sorry. Sorry." While hazy, he still recognizes a tone in Darren he hasn't heard before. He hopes he can remember to ease up on the kid tomorrow. He also hopes that he doesn't remember any of this come tomorrow.

"Goodnight, Rodney."

"Goodnight Dar—" the line is already dead.

As Erin's face returns to the screen, Rodney fumbles for the remote and turns it to a sports channel. A recap of the day's games plays as he drifts into unconsciousness. The half-empty bottle of beer tilts from his hand and pours into his lap. He doesn't even stir as the beer soaks into his pants while the colors of the TV flash on his face and the wall behind him.

TWENTY

Sunlight. That means it's now Monday. She's not sure what time, but it feels early. Her head is covered with something porous enough to let the light through and if positioned just right she can see, although a hazy view, from the threaded weaves that push close to her eyes.

Cheyenne goes through her new daily routine. Before he comes, she replays the first night hoping to recall something that will help her. Any detail to learn who he is, or how she might escape. A hint to her location. With each night that passes, it becomes harder to recall it in as clear of detail as the first, so she runs it again, grasping for every sense and memory she can summon to return.

It's been three days since she was grabbed in the park, violently pulled into those tall pines that looked like soldiers standing guard. Except they didn't protect her like soldiers are supposed to, they didn't so much as move a branch on that windless night. She can still feel the gloved hand over her mouth, the inability to catch her balance as her white tennis shoes dragged through the soft dirt and needles, the motionless trees that seemed endless above as she was pulled backward.

Maybe she was imagining it, but the sounds of the football game seemed so loud despite being so far away. The crowd cheering, happy screams and whooping. A coordinated gasp. No, think of the man, she reminds herself. Strong hands, bony grip. A lean but strong arm across her body holding up her weight, the pressure of his squeeze painful on her chest. His arm. Dark fabric and a glove, the same as the one covering her mouth as she tries to scream against it.

What else? His breathing. He's struggling to get her through the wooded area as she can feel his exhales against the back of her head, his heart pounding. He doesn't speak, but grunts with forceful turns and pivots over the uneven ground. She never stops fighting and squirming, trying to make it harder for him, but she's tired and knows the fight has worn out of her as much as the resistance to that fighting has worn out of him. A moment of relief when the darkness of the trees gives way to the open air. Something stings her bare legs below her skirt and pulls at the cotton of her long sleeve. Briars in the tall grass.

The man swears under his breath but somehow continues to pull her. Cheyenne pushes her eyes as far back as they'll go to try to catch a glimpse of his face. Even though her face is presently covered, she squeezes her eyes shut to try to picture the moment. Almost. The memory is but a silhouette, the terrifying shape only looking from the direction he's pulling briefly down at her before again looking away and out of her sight.

She couldn't see his face, but there was something. A hat. What kind of hat? A ballcap maybe. The man coughs a disgusting, wet discharge and spits it as they make their way through the grass. Cheyenne tries to grab something, anything but if she lets go of his arm it feels as if she's going to suffocate. He doesn't react to the fingernails that dig into the sleeve. The material is heavy duty so she doubts she's breaking the skin but she applies all of her strength to the tips of her freshly painted nails. Daggers of school spirit.

The sounds of the game have long faded but she hears something else now. The low rumble of an engine, idling. The very distant sound of wheels on wet pavement. This strikes a new fear into her because she knows that if she's put into a vehicle her chances of survival almost vanish. She could be taken anywhere, at least here she's still close to people, to her grandparents, to Donovan.

Cheyenne thrashes her elbows into the man who grumbles at the reinvigorated fight of his prey. Letting go of his arms causes her to sink again and she can't get the air she needs. Flailing makes it worse as all of the oxygen is driven from her lungs and can't be replaced. Her vision begins to fade as the sound of the engine grows. She settles, hoping to save one last effort should the moment present itself. It's unclear what he'll do but she thinks when the man tries to get her into the trunk there will be a moment and she'll give it everything she has to get away.

As the grass thins near the road, she thrusts a hand down to her uniform and grabs a handful of the tinsel that adorns her skirt. She yanks as hard as she can but only a single strand breaks free between her fingers. Cheyenne casts it out and tries to watch where it lands. She wills it not to get lost in the dirt or caught on her shoes. There, it grabs onto a tall spur of grass and dwindles there, high above the rest. A brief moment of hope that is quickly extinguished.

The gravel from the shoulder of the road pulls at her shoes. Before she can get a look at the car, she's whipped over on her stomach onto the edge of the pavement, the two-inch rise in the asphalt dividing her from feet to chin. The sharp stones dig into her skin and the scratch from the fall burns across her cheek. Before she can push herself off the ground, both arms are pulled behind her back and bound, a ratcheting sound with the tightness constricting her wrists.

Cheyenne pushes her head forward to be clear of the gravel and takes a deep breath to scream as loud as she can. As the sounds drive from her stomach a gag stops any noise from escaping. The application cracks her upper lip and jostles her teeth. She screams against the object anyway but can't hear it herself over the engine.

In the room where she's captive, she exhales the air that she was holding in, feeling the hot air hit her face under the bag. This is the last moment she had true sight so she thinks hard about everything she can remember. Seconds before the bag was placed over her head she was pulled upward by her bound hands. A flash of car lights far off in the distance. The town naïve to her struggle. Cheyenne turns in an attempt to get a view of the vehicle but before she can, the cover slams over her eyes.

A loud bang of metal and she's again being dragged backward, this time both of his hands are under her armpits. She tries to go limp, to make her weight harder to pull, but he doesn't go far. She's flipped over again and this time something hits her stomach high off the ground. It knocks the wind out of her. A sense of vertigo as both of her feet leave the ground. It happens so fast but she's on her side and rolled into the bed of a truck, she thinks.

Cheyenne tries to roll back the way she came, bracing for a fall back to the road, but the man grabs her feet and ties them to something. She can only move her shoulders a little from one direction to the other. Then, the bed of the truck is slammed closed and she's plunged into darkness.

Her heart beats fast as her memory is interrupted. Her heavy breathing has caused sweat to cover her face and is getting in her eyes inside the bag. She shakes her head from left to right to try to get a better hole to look through. A sickness rises in her stomach as fear has returns to steal away her thoughts. The rattle of his truck on rough terrain and the low rumble of the engine, the sound that takes her right back to that first night, grows louder and then settles. He's back and she has nowhere to hide.

TWENTY-ONE

The teacher drones at the front of the class as Manny scribbles on the inside cover of his math book. The crude shape of a rabbit with giant fangs and missing chunks of fur jumps out from the book's title which has been scratched out in lead and replaced with the word CHUPACABRA. His non-drawing hand supports his face, smashing his cheek as Manny's head is tilted to the side.

"Manny. Eyes forward," the teacher says.

Mrs. Edwards is old. Not old, old, but gray hair starting to show up, old. Her glasses are thick and it magnifies her eyes, which Manny finds hilarious. He hates math. Putting down his pencil and closing the cover of the book to hide his handiwork, Manny sits back in his chair demonstrating his undivided attention. Another incident and he'll be stuck cleaning the diner's bathrooms again, something he hates more than math. Why is it so hard for people to keep their piss and shit in the bowl?

"For all of you who didn't turn in your papers today, remember they are due no later than Friday. You will lose ten points off of your total score for every day it is late. If you turn it in by end of day on Thursday, that's tomorrow, you will receive ten extra bonus points. Any questions?"

Mrs. Edwards looks at the clock above the door and moves back to the whiteboard which is decorated with complicated math equations in various colors of marker. There are more letters and symbols than numbers, which is also Manny's go-to response when his dad presses him on his homework. He finds himself thumbing the cover of his notebook but resists diving back into the illustration.

"Before you go, keep in mind for those of you who are waiting until the last minute, permission slips and the $20 fee must be handed in on Friday by first period or you will not be able to go on the field trip on Tuesday to the Georgia Aquarium. I can promise you that you don't want to be the only one left out. The bus leaves promptly at 6:00 a.m. so be sure your parents have you here no later than 5:45. I know that's early but it's about a three-hour bus ride and you can sleep on the way. In fact, I prefer it."

A few of the kids laugh.

"The slip your parents sign has all of the details regarding meals, contact information, and times. We should be back to Hawksboro by 8 p.m. Anyone who isn't picked up by 8:30 will be forced to stay with Principal Wheeler in the auditorium."

The same kids laugh.

"Seriously though, please ask your parents to be prompt. I don't want to be waiting around all night."

Different kids let out an audible sigh.

"That's right, I'm one of the chaperones. But I promise it's going to be fun, and if you've got a camera or phone, you'll be able to take some great pictures. Please get permission first if you're going to bring anything of value with you."

The bell chime signals the end of the period and the kids waste no time heading for the hallway. Manny is one of the first out of the door. Donovan and Rachel exit from the classroom across the hall and merge with Manny who gives them both a playful fist bump.

"Hey look, Jason's back!" Rachel calls out, pointing ahead.

Donovan and Manny look up to see Jason not far down the hallway at his locker.

"Hey buddy, good to see you back," Manny says.

Jason looks at them briefly and then back to his locker.

"Yeah man, how are you doing?" Donovan asks.

"I'm okay." Jason closes the door with a soft latch and spins the combination lock then turns to his friends. "Hi, Rachel."

"Hey," she says softly.

Jason walks past them with his lunch in hand, headed for the cafeteria.

"Are you going on the field trip next week?" Manny asks, catching up to Jason's side.

"To the aquarium?"

"Yeah, should be pretty cool."

"I don't think so. I'd like to stay home and be with my grandparents. They're not doing so good."

"Oh." Manny tries not to sound disappointed.

"That's okay, and awful sweet of you to think of them," Rachel adds, flanking his other side.

Donovan steps between Jason and Manny. "Hey, I brought you some of my dad's homemade chili. Do you want to try to get Big Mike to snort it again?"

Jason chuckles and nods. "Thanks, guys."

"For what?" asks Manny.

"For trying to cheer me up."

Manny reaches across Donovan and puts a hand on Jason's shoulder. "No sweat man. Cheyenne will be home before you know it."

Jason drops his head and Rachel gives Manny an icy glare. Donovan elbows him in the ribs. It genuinely hurts but so does the thought that he said something wrong.

"Ow. What did I say?" Manny complains.

"Just be quiet, Manny," says Rachel.

"What, I just—"

"No, it's okay. He's right. I just don't get why she ran away and why for this long. I know we've all wanted to do it at one point or another but to really go through with it and be gone for so long? I'm really worried about her." Jason doesn't look up from his feet as they walk.

Donovan looks to Manny and Rachel, perhaps contemplating if he should speak. Manny mouths the word "DON'T."

"She didn't run away, Jason," Donovan says.

Manny can feel the tension of the group change. It's as uncomfortable as he can imagine and he searches for any comedic remedy to deliver them from the moment. No jokes come to mind and then it's too late.

"I know what you told my grandparents and the police, Donovan. But they all think she just ran away."

"Come on, Don. Please leave it alone," Rachel adds.

"But they're making a mistake. Someone took her. I know it! She DID NOT run away!" Donovan's hands flare to his sides.

"I already tried saying that but my grandparent—"

"Your grandparents are wrong! The sheriff is wrong! We need to find out who did this!" Donovan is nearly shouting now. Manny tries to put a hand on his shoulder but it's shrugged off with a powerful swing of his arm.

Jason looks up from the floor and stops walking.

"You better be quiet, Donovan. My grandpa hasn't slept in

five days. If there was something that could be done, he would be doing it."

"Well, he's not doing enough. Nobody is! Jason, she's your sister. You have to believe me!" Donovan grabs his arm.

"Stop it," Rachel says.

Manny doesn't like the look in Jason's eyes and he notices Donovan's free hand is clenched and beads of sweat are forming at his temple.

"No, I won't. Unlike everyone else in this stupid town, I actually care about Cheyenne and I know she's in danger!"

Jason throws off Donovan's loose grasp and shoves him with both hands.

"Shut up, you asshole!" Jason screams.

Donovan shoves him back and Jason charges, tackling him to the hallway floor. They wrestle, exchanging superiority. Manny circles the scuffle with his hands on his head.

"Stop it, you guys. You're being jerks!" Rachel pleads.

Kids gather and Jason bursts into tears while throwing punches down on Donovan, who is successful at deflecting most of them. Manny waves on teachers as they arrive and pull the two boys apart.

Once separated, Jason begins crying even harder, sobbing into the teacher who grabbed him. The PE teacher holds Donovan by one arm, who doesn't resist the restraint. The realization of what took place seems to wash over him.

"I'm sorry. It's my fault. I'm sorry," Donovan says to the teachers.

"You're going to have to tell that to Principal Wheeler. After we call your father," the PE teacher says as he pulls Donovan in the direction of the office.

Jason is already being led down the hallway by the other

teacher. Manny and Rachel grab the boys' belongings off of the floor and stagger to catch up, unsure if they should follow or hang back. Manny slows, realizing he left his own stuff at the scene of the scuffle.

"I'll meet you there," he says to Rachel and she jogs to catch up to the boys and the discipline procession.

Manny is glad to see his books still lying propped against the wall. Papers are scattered, he's not sure whose, and a large puddle soaks some of the edges. An open water thermos is the culprit and the last of its contents trickle out of the open mouth. He scoops up his books and kneels over the papers where he looks for a name to see who they belong to. If not his friends then he's leaving them.

A shadow covers the floor where he's picking up the paper and he imagines that the PE teacher has returned to scold him for the mess.

"Look, it's not my stuff," says Manny as he looks over his shoulder and up to the figure standing over him.

It's not the PE teacher or any teacher. It's the custodian, Mr. Belsky. The only reason he knows the man's name is he's heard it called out a dozen times in the cafeteria by the lunch ladies. This is the closest he's ever been to him and Belsky, as the kids call him, is much broader than he realized. The man's shoulders are wide, with long, thin arms. But he's not lanky, he's got old man muscle as Donovan would say.

Manny shuffles what he can and jumps to his feet.

"Sorry, uh, sorry about the water. I don't know who that belongs to."

Belsky blinks just once but otherwise doesn't break his concentration on Manny. Dark circles surround inset eyes of some dim color. He doesn't want to look long enough to figure it out. The smallest gap separates the man's upper and lower lips. No teeth are evident, but he has to have teeth, right? Manny finds himself pressed against the lockers behind him, not realizing he was backing up while lost in the man's stare.

Finally, Belsky groans and goes to one knee. He retrieves a more-gray-than-white towel from his back pocket and wipes at the floor. Manny steps over the water, careful not to make the scene any worse. He contemplates going for the sideways bottle but decides to leave it. He'd rather buy a new one than stick his hand past Belsky. The custodian places a hand on the purplish thermos and gently sets it upright. Manny doesn't believe his eyes but he swears the man sniffs the rim before returning to his towel. It takes all of Manny's willpower to turn his back on the man and bolt down the hall toward Principal Wheeler's office.

TWENTY-TWO

onovan holds a cloth to his cracked lip while staring at the ceiling tiles in the waiting area of the principal's office. A few chairs away, Jason holds an ice pack against his right-hand fist. Neither speak for several minutes. Donovan is less worried about the conversation with the principal than he is about the one that will take place with his dad when he gets home from school. Pulling the cloth off of his mouth, he examines it. Only a speck of red on the white fabric.

"You okay?" Donovan asks, to no one in particular.

"Yeah. You?" comes a reply.

"Yeah."

"I'm sorry I hit you," Jason says with a wince.

"It was my fault. I shouldn't have said anything. I mean, I know it's hard for me so I can't even imagine how difficult it's been for you."

"Well, you were right."

"What do you mean?" asks Donovan.

"I agree with you. And so does my Grandpa. We both know she didn't run away but nobody will listen. There isn't any proof."

"Then why'd you get so upset?"

"I don't know. It's just frustrating, I feel so horrible all the time. Seeing my grandparents, knowing how helpless they feel. It's eating away at me." Jason chokes on his words.

"Can't he talk to the police again?"

"He tries talking to the sheriff every day, but it hasn't done any good. It's to the point where we think he's avoiding my Grandpa and not returning his calls."

Donovan runs his tongue across the crack in his lip, tasting the familiar iron flavor that comes with the injury.

"How's your Gram doing?" he asks.

"Not good. She won't talk about it. I feel like I'm the only one capable of doing anything and I have no idea what to do."

"Well, if it helps, you're not alone."

"Thanks, Don. Hey, your lip isn't looking too bad. Good thing I was going easy on you."

Donovan laughs and nods to Jason's hand. "Yeah, yeah. Good thing. Sorry my jaw is so solid, can't help being hard-headed."

Jason laughs as the principal's assistant opens the glass door and looks around the room.

"Malcolm?"

To Donovan and Jason's surprise, a small boy pulls himself out of a chair in the corner and shuffles toward the assistant before stopping in front of them.

"You guys are weird," the boy says.

He then enters the office and the door closes behind him and the assistant. Donovan and Jason look at each other and laugh at the fact that they weren't alone.

"Man, your dad is going to be so pissed. What are you going to tell him?" Jason asks.

"Yeah, he is and I don't know. Still working on it."

"I hope he doesn't ground you from the field trip," says Jason.

Donovan perks up. "That's it! Jason, you're a genius!"

"I am?"

"Yeah! Listen, I've got a plan."

Donovan jumps over to the seat next to him and whispers in Jason's ear.

The rest of the day was a flood of ideas racing through Donovan's mind. Something was growing inside of him, confidence, if he had to put a name to it. But that didn't quite describe the feeling because he didn't fully believe his plan would work or that he would even have the guts to go through with it when the time comes. It's not lost on him that he got lucky with the principal, who was understanding of Jason's outburst given his sister, and since Donovan was the worse for wear and took responsibility, neither boy was suspended, which is the mandatory punishment for fighting in school. A call home and two strikes were a relief, considering if either of them had been banned from next week's field trip his whole plan would have been ruined.

As the kids emptied the school and he met the fresh air, a feeling of happiness washed over him. Elation that someone, even if it is himself, was finally going to do something to find Cheyenne.

"Don!"

Kenneth's voice drives the feeling of joy out like a priest with holy water. Donovan can feel it leave his body. If his dad is here it's because the school spoke to him and not his mom and he knows about the fight. Donovan could try to play dumb but that's always gone worse than owning it. He'll face the music, even if it means crushing his speck of hope before it could materialize.

"Hey Dad," he says as Jason and Rachel meet them on the sidewalk outside of the school.

He can't tell from the blank expression if his dad is angry, disappointed, or perhaps still doesn't know. Yeah right, he already clocked both of the boys' injuries and didn't say a word, which means he's not surprised. Damn, this is going to hurt worse than the punch.

Donovan walks to his dad's side who places a hand on his shoulder. He braces for a squeeze but it's just a guide to show him where the car is parked. It's in an adjacent lot to the bus loop and just a short walk along the sidewalk in front of the school.

"Kenneth," a voice calls out with the patter of feet.

"Dad?" Rachel says with the shock undue of seeing only her father and not an axe-wielding murderer.

"Heya, hun!" Glenn says as he meets the group.

Kenneth extends his hand and Donovan shrugs his shoulder where the grip was pressed, trying to get the blood and feeling back into the muscle.

Glenn accepts the shake and looks over the kids.

"Rough day, I hear."

"Yeah, we were just headed home to talk about that." Kenneth looks to Jason and then to Donovan. Both boys turn their attention down deep beyond the concrete at their feet.

"They called you, too? I didn't do anything!" Rachel says.

"It's true, sh—"

The thin man with wood grain rims and clear lenses holds up a hand, beaming a perfect white smile. His hair always looks like it was just cut, Donovan thinks.

"No, no, heard it through the grapevine. Gosh, does anyone still say that? I must sound like an old goat."

"Oh my God." Rachel looks as if her dad is reading her diary, cheeks flushed red and focusing anywhere but on the boys.

"It was nice to see you Glenn, if you don't mind—" Kenneth places his hand back on Donovan's shoulder but this time the boy is ready for it.

"Sure enough, hey just one more thing." Glenn leans in way too close to Kenneth who doesn't retreat but turns his brow to suggest he doesn't understand what's happening. Then Glenn whispers, but not nearly quiet enough, "I just wanted to let you know, you've got an ally in me."

"Make it stop," Rachel cries.

Jason looks between her and Glenn who takes a step back and slaps Kenneth on the arm. His thick bicep ripples but otherwise doesn't budge.

"Wowzer," Glenn says while shaking out his hand.

Kenneth lights up and makes a rare animated gesture.

"Oh man, you're serious? You served? Who did you deploy with? Canadians, Brits? You weren't with the Australians, were you? Those guys were insane. I guess that's what you get when you live where everything is trying to kill you."

The three kids stare at Glenn, who quivers as he tries to speak.

"Well no, not like that." He leans in again and raises a clenched fist close to his chest. "An ally, ally."

"I have to move," Rachel says to the universe.

Manny stifles a laugh that surprises everyone since nobody saw him arrive.

Looking embarrassed, Glenn walks backward with a hand outstretched, maybe to suggest to Rachel that it's time to go. If so, she doesn't get the hint. Kenneth appears to do his best to move on, pulling Donovan in the opposite direction as well.

"Got it. Thanks, Glenn," he says.

Still walking in reverse, Glenn reaches Rachel and gives her a gentle pull by her backpack. "I just mean, Ethan and I. We're not like most of the town, ya know. We're very open-minded."

"Dad, stop talking." Now Rachel has taken the lead and is

pulling her dad away.

"Understood, have yourself a good evening." Kenneth gives a polite wave.

"I don't know if you saw the sign in our yard or not—" Glenn is far enough away that he adjusts his volume to make up for the distance.

"Bye, everyone!" Rachel shouts over her dad.

Kenneth's phone rings and he holds up a finger and steps to the side.

Glenn complains about Rachel's interruption as they finally detach and go their own way. She sneaks a peek back and mouths, "Sorry."

All three boys acknowledge with a wave, unsure of who she's apologizing to.

Donovan can sense Manny and Jason trying to think of something to say.

"Don't sweat it guys, yeah it happens and it's always weird but I'm sure her dad is coming from a good place."

"Your dad was like a statue. Mine swears at kitchen appliances," says Manny.

"Not much bothers him now, I guess. He once carried a body for thirteen miles while getting shot at."

Jason and Manny's eyes show disbelief.

"Hey!" Kenneth's voice is raised, still calm but elevated for his demeanor. The fear in Donovan's look is unmistakable.

"Boys, stay out of trouble. Donovan is grounded for two weeks, with the exception of the field trip and that's only because we already paid the twenty bucks, but I may still change my mind. We'll see how the rest of the week goes."

"Goodnight, sir," says Manny.

"G-Goodnight," adds Jason.

Kenneth leads Donovan away along the sidewalk, his grip now tighter than before. Donovan winces, not because it hurts but because he knows he's in trouble.

Neither speak until they're inside Kenneth's Jeep. After clicking his seatbelt, Kenneth rests an arm on the wheel and turns his body toward Donovan.

"Son, I didn't tell you that story so you could go on sharing it like it's outta some comic book or video game."

Donovan tries to look anywhere but at his dad.

"Eyes up."

He does.

"You want to have an adult conversation then I'm going to tell you some adult information. It wasn't a body, as you dressed it for your friends. His name was Craig and I made a promise. Now, I told you that story because you asked, and because I thought you were old enough to hear that the real world is ugly. Understand?"

"Yes, sir."

"And I think what your friend, Chey, might be going through is ugly. This world is spoiled with it."

"Why did you do it, though? You said before it almost got you kicked out of the Army."

"That's right, I went against orders and put my team in a spot. But I made a promise and I did what I thought was right. I was ready for whatever consequences that were coming my way."

"So sometimes it's okay to break the rules if it's for the right reasons?"

"All I'm saying son, is that you have to own your decisions. As long as you do what you believe in your heart is right..." The jab with the pointer finger hurts a little, but Donovan wouldn't trade it. "...I'll always have your back. Roger?"

"Roger," Donovan says.

"Now, you know what you're going to be doing whenever you're not doing homework the next two weeks?" asks Kenneth as he turns on the Jeep and shifts into reverse.

Donovan shakes his head no, afraid of what he might be signed up for and now questioning if he really did get off easy.

"Betty needs some TLC."

Not Betty, Donovan thinks to himself, unwilling to vocalize his displeasure for fear of what that might bring down on him. He hates tinkering with that stupid old beater in the garage. The rusted-out car is older than his dad and whenever he's asked to help work on it, not that there's an actual choice involved, it seems like they're always messing with the same problems. If it's not the belts, it's the battery. If not the battery, the tires. Donovan tells himself it's worth it if it keeps him out of more trouble and so he doesn't say a word, just gives a thumbs up as he looks out the window of the Jeep.

TWENTY-THREE

"**N**o way! I can't," says Rachel. "We're going to get caught, for sure."

Jason looks from Rachel to Manny who sits on the opposite side of the tent that has been semi-permanently pitched in Manny's backyard, awaiting a witty rebuttal. The impromptu Saturday night get-together was something Donovan insisted had to take place and couldn't wait. Only fitting that he's late to his own secret meeting. Not to mention what he's risking if he's caught while on house arrest. Jason's grandparents are fairly easy-going and Manny's dad has a way of ensuring obedience that Manny seems careful to adhere to, but Jason would never test Donovan's dad, not in a million years.

"It's the only way. Nobody else is going to do anything, so I have to. You don't have to go but I'm not going to change my mind." Jason folds his arms in defiance.

Manny speaks up but it's Rachel's response he's waiting for. "I'm in! You know it."

Neither one so much as gives him a glance of acknowledgment.

"I can't let you go alone. Are you sure about this, Jason?" Rachel asks.

"Definitely. Donovan and I have worked out all the details. Don't worry."

"Hey, I said I would go too," Manny says.

"Do you guys even have any idea where to start looking?" she asks.

Jason retrieves a phone and stares at it for a moment. It's Cheyenne's, the one they retrieved from her locker after she went missing. He opens the screen and shows Rachel the satellite map of the area that Donovan pointed out to him earlier. Manny cranes his neck to see the image from his vantage point from across the tent.

"I think so. I mean we know where Cheyenne was last seen. We know where the sheriff found that piece of her uniform. Grampa has also told us all of the places they've searched. I say we start here, just past the bridge." Jason zooms into the map and points at a pin marker.

"I agree. What about—" says Manny.

"Hey guys, I made it!" Donovan pulls himself into the tent.

"How'd you manage to sneak out? Aren't you grounded?" Jason asks.

"Dad's watching cage fighting. It's the girls' card so I've got twenty minutes before he'll notice I'm gone," Donovan says.

"If you're grounded how can we go through with all of this?" Rachel asks.

"He agreed to still let me go on the field trip in exchange for helping him work on the car all day tomorrow."

"Awesome!" Manny says louder than the small tent requires.

"And! Even better, he said I could stay here with Manny the night before so he doesn't have to bring me all the way in so early. Everything is falling into place!" Donovan says.

"Great. Donovan go over the plan once more now that we're

all together." Jason nudges Rachel to pay attention, appearing proud of what they've put together.

"Manny and Jason will say they're staying at my place and that my dad will take us in the morning. Myself and Rachel will say we're staying over here. You think you can sell your dad on that, Rachel?"

"I don't know, one maybe, probably not both. Dad-E is out of town at least but Dad-G didn't like me staying tonight, let alone on a school night. Plus, I haven't even agreed to take part in whatever this is yet."

Donovan takes the first hurdle in stride and continues laying out the plan.

"So, Monday after school we'll all go home and pack some extra clothes and snacks, be careful as it needs to look like enough just for a sleepover. At 6 p.m. we can all meet at the playground by the field and head out from there."

"That gives us a night's head start but they'll notice something is up when none of us are present for the roll call on the bus Tuesday morning," Rachel says.

"Ah, true!" says Manny.

"I've got it covered. Nedry and his sister, you know the twins? They're going to cover for us on the bus by saying 'Here!' when our names are called."

Jason puts a fist out and Donovan gives it a bump. "Nice."

"We have until 9 o'clock on Tuesday night to be back at the school to meet the bus, and our parents," Donovan says.

"Maybe one of us could go unnoticed, but you think the chaperones won't figure out that four of us on the roster aren't seen at all during the day?" asks Rachel.

"It's a fair point. But being the entire grade, maybe 200 kids, we could get lucky, or at least by the time they figure it out hopefully we'll already be on our way back."

"And if we find her?" Manny asks.

"We will find her," Jason says.

"Well, then we'll be heroes and it won't matter what we did. Just that she's home," says Donovan.

"I'm still not sure about all of this," Rachel says.

"I'll understand if you don't go. It could be dangerous and we have no idea what to expect," says Jason.

She seems to consider it for a moment. "I'll go. She's my friend too. But we can't come back until we know what happened."

"Seconded," adds Manny. "Even if it's days."

"We'll need to leave notes then so everyone doesn't think we've been taken, I mean, missing too," says Jason.

"Hide them so you don't get us caught before we leave the schoolyard," says Manny.

"Then we're agreed. I gotta get back before my dad knows I'm gone or this whole thing is bust. Just remember, if we don't do this, nobody else will. Cheyenne is depending on us."

"Thank you, guys," says Jason, rubbing the phone in his hand.

"We're gonna find her," says Donovan.

Jason nods.

"Alright. See you Monday." Donovan crawls out of the tent.

Manny calls after him. "Hey, couldn't we just have done this over a video call?"

"Shut up, Manny." Donovan's voice is faint as he runs out of the yard.

Rachel laughs but Jason continues to rub the phone with his thumb. The stupid device that's the source of so much pain, maybe even somewhat to blame for his sister's disappearance, may also be what helps them find her. None of them know how to navigate a map, but looking at a satellite image, zooming in and dropping pins, feels like progress. Like he's doing something to help instead of just being a bystander or victim. The kid with dead parents and a probably dead sister.

Manny's annoying voice is for once a welcome contribution as it snaps Jason out of his funk. "Hey, you downloaded that map image, right?"

"Yeah, I don't know what service will be like up there so as long as I have battery, I can still reference it."

"Good thinking, send it to me. I want to look around." He waves his phone at Jason as he lies on his stomach, blocking the entrance to the tent.

"Reference it? You sound like you're auditioning for the CIA," Rachel asks Jason, sounding surprised by his initiative.

"What?" Jason asks, playing dumb.

TWENTY-FOUR

She bats her eyes, the lashes brushing against the coarse fabric in front of her face. Its roughness feels like burlap, she's come to recognize, and if it wasn't for the weaves having just big enough gaps to allow pinhole light to pass through, she would have lost her mind by now. Like every other time that she's awakened in this position, Cheyenne first moves her head to try to see out of one of these holes.

Vertical wood planks are not far from her face. A wall. It feels like she's in the same room where she's been kept for several days. Cheyenne maneuvers her hands but they're still bound behind her. Feeling the back of her thighs and down to her bare feet, her fingers scrape the wooden floor. She can feel the dirt or dust gather in her nails.

Cheyenne scoots as best she can to the corner of the room. She's still in her uniform and it's soiled and uncomfortable. Splinters and cuts everywhere, so many that she can't pinpoint the pain from any single one as her skin from the waist down burns non-stop. But she's further from the door. The blurry rectangle through the bag that she doesn't take her eyes off until she knows for certain that she's alone.

"He's gone. He's gone," she says to herself.

During the times when she's been left alone, Cheyenne has worked the board next to the door almost free. She first tried the sole window but it was boarded so heavily with thick and rusted nails that she gave up. Besides, the panes are too small and she'd have to break them all to squeeze out. Break them with what? And if she were to fail, the idea of being moved somewhere without a window, without sunlight, convinced her to try the door instead.

Cheyenne labors at the loose board, unable to see her bound hands while she faces the window. After several minutes, the bottom nail wiggles free and she can push it outward just enough to stick her hand through. Her fingers swat and scrape at the other side, searching for the knob or latch or whatever is keeping the damn thing shut.

When the tip of her middle finger swipes a piece of cold iron, she taps it again. It rattles. Cheyenne flicks at the arm, what feels like a latch, as hard as she can despite the cramp in her hand and the wood cutting into her wrists. The metallic clank signifies success and the door drifts open into her room. She's so shocked she freezes for a moment, making sure he's not inside.

Once she's confident that it's just her, Cheyenne sticks her head out into the hall and looks around, shaking the bag so the holes line up over her eyes. She glances at the table in the center of the structure. A plate of food sits to one side. Cheyenne considers it and then the main door. Back and forth. She crosses the threshold, more in her mind than a physical barrier, and scurries to the table setting, careful to stay below the windows.

"Where are you?" she asks, no higher than a whisper.

Next to the plate, a fork and knife lay as he left them. Cheyenne grabs the knife by turning her back to the table and begins working her way at the bind on her hands. It's smooth, whatever it is, not rope. She shuffles her wrists, paying attention to the texture against her skin. She turns her head over her shoulder to try to get a look but can't position the bag. Then she recalls the night of her capture and the clicking sound that accompanied the tightening.

"Zip-ties."

Adjusting the knife between the loops, she begins twisting it as the constraints get tighter and tighter. Cheyenne endures and twists way past what she thought she could handle. It's the first time that the dulling of pain arrives outside of when he's here and it scares her, worrying what that might mean, but she focuses on the ties. The plastic snaps at the buckle and one wrist is free. The remaining tie hangs from her other hand. She rips off the bag that covered her head.

The food looks old and she can't tell if it's meat or something else but she forces a handful into her mouth. It tastes as bad as it looks but she chokes it down. Overcome with thirst, she grabs the glass and takes several gulps before spitting it across the table. Cheyenne covers her mouth to stifle the gag. Not iced tea.

Looking around the space there isn't much to take in. She moves to the door, or what passes as a door, and peers through the large gap in the frame. Nothing outside the cabin that she can tell. Cheyenne slips the latch from the inside, careful not to make a sound, and uses the slowest movements to open it. When it's ajar just enough to slide through, she does and guides the door closed.

She stumbles across the leaf-covered ground. Trees tower overhead in all directions. A small dirt road, more like a logging trail with high grass in the middle, leads away from what she sees as a rundown cabin. Stones and twigs pierce her feet but she doesn't so much as limp. Cheyenne tries to control her breathing but she's panicking, thinking how nobody could ever find her here, wherever here is, and doubting if anyone is even looking for her.

Making her way to the tree line, and what seems like an endless forest beyond, she keeps looking over her shoulder. She prays he's not around. She would rather die, alone in the forest, than have him find her. Cheyenne snags a foot on a concealed root and faceplants into the leafy undergrowth. She looks around to see if anyone heard the fall. Still nothing but herself and the breeze carrying between the trees, begging her to run to safety.

She rubs her toe that she jammed into the ground. It's not broken but she can already feel the joint swelling. Something isn't right though. It wasn't a root at all. There was a give to whatever she tripped over. Her eyes scan the leaves at her feet, retracing her steps to the cabin.

Cheyenne covers her mouth as she discovers what caused her fall. There, a few feet from where she sits on the damp ground, the tip of a sneaker protrudes from the earth. It's not more than an inch above the bright orange and soft brown blanket of leaves. But the colorful splotches of forest that once thrived above are now as dead and rotting as the foot they're trying to hide.

Spinning over to her hands and knees, she crawls toward it. First, she hesitates, then begins brushing the leaves away from around the sneaker. Cheyenne hopes it's just a shoe. But something tells her otherwise. Maybe because it didn't rip out of the ground when it tripped her. Or maybe what she's endured whispers to her, warns her there's no way in hell it's just a shoe. She knows what she's going to find before her hands touch the ground.

As the leaves spread away from the toe cap, the walls and laces appear. Working further into the dirt, she finds that the rest of the shoe is covered by a thick sheet of plastic. Cheyenne carefully works her way up the thick, opaque material, pushing leaves and wet dirt to the sides. She follows the tarp for several feet before coming to what appears to be a ragged sweatshirt draped over whatever is contained by the plastic.

Cheyenne looks back to the cabin and to the woods. Everything inside screams to run. Any direction, just run. She can't ignore the draw of the tattered clothing before her. She grabs the corner and looks away before pulling it hard toward her and tossing it over her shoulder.

She holds her eyes tight as she turns her head back to the ground and then forces herself to look.

"Melody."

The semi-decomposed skull of Melody Anderson rests facing upward toward the canopy. Blonde hair swirls from the patchy skin drawn taught against the bone beneath. The tarp stops just below the neck. Cheyenne turns her upper body, looking for the sweatshirt that she cast aside. She shakes it free of leaves and gently places it back over Melody's face.

Cheyenne turns to her side and throws up what little food she just ate. She spits it from her lips and wipes her face with her forearm. She gives one last glimpse to the body at her feet wanting to memorize the look and location so she can lead someone to recover Melody. But first, she has to escape herself.

As she rises to a knee, a glint of light just above the plastic catches her eye. Something reflects the sunlight that falls between the trees. A necklace. It lies on the body, still clasped and hanging around the caved-in neck but just below the sweatshirt. Otherwise, she would have missed it. The chain sparkles like a beacon. A lighthouse among the waves and rocks of decay.

Pain shoots through the back of her head and she doesn't hear the impact as much as she feels it in her neck and back. Something falls to the ground beside her. She struggles to see between the stars in her vision. A wooden plank.

"There you are." The voice is low and distant, but she knows it's him.

Cheyenne struggles between wanting to fight and trying to maintain clarity as her brain is stuck in a fog from the strike.

"Please, let me go," she manages to say.

Cheyenne can see the light from the canopy above as she's being dragged through the leaves toward the cabin.

"Nobody really wants to know their future, do they?" The voice laughs and she tries to make sense of what it means.

She manages to mount a resistance and breaks free of the grasp on her hair. Cheyenne crawls, dizziness and nausea fighting every push forward. She lunges and reaches for the body as a hand yanks her by the ankle. She's dragged on her stomach back to the cabin, watching the tree line of the forest get smaller and smaller, the tip of the sneaker vanishing among the leaves.

The rickety door bounces shut as Cheyenne is pulled to her room and tossed inside. Her head impacts the wall and the stars return. A dark shadow stands over her body. The silhouette leans close. She cowers as the burlap is pulled over her face. She can still hear the muffled voice above despite the ringing in her ears.

"Let's not try that again. You may find yourself sharing her fate sooner than you need to. Understood?" A boot kicks her in the shin.

"Yes!" she screams.

Pressed as far into the corner as she can scurry, she hears him close the door to her room and then cross the floor of the cabin. The front door opens and closes and then what sounds like a lock being latched, metal on metal. Cheyenne hears the boots walking away from the cabin on the wooden porch and then the ground.

A moment later they return, but this time accompanied by something else. Paws claw at the dirt outside the door. A snout huffs and kicks up the dust around the wood. The dog begins growling and barking, its nails scratching to get inside.

A knuckle knocks on the door.

"She's got the scent now. I dare you to run."

The footsteps and paws retreat from the door. A leash drops to the ground and the dog settles on its belly, panting, whining.

"Stay."

Leaves swirl under the door and into the cabin as the man walks off. Wood creaks as he passes the window. In the distance an engine turns over and brakes squeal as a vehicle drives away, its rumble fading in the distance.

Cheyenne pulls off the bag and looks at her hands. She rubs the musical note pendant on the necklace between her dirty fingers before squeezing the charm between her fists. She puts the horrors of what's been done to her out of her mind. She focuses on the will to get home. She prays someone will find her. She prays for Donovan, and her grandparents, and Simone. She prays for the dog guarding her door. She prays for the man who has done unspeakable things to her, things that she'll never tell a soul. Finally, she says a prayer for herself, and for the courage to survive.

TWENTY-FIVE

As darkness falls over Hawksboro on Monday night, there isn't a cloud in the sky. Manny is being watched as he walks alone near the football field. He's carrying a backpack that sags low and sways as he moves toward the playground. The parking lot lights have just kicked on and cast a wide ambiance onto the area. The mixture of dusk and halogen almost makes for a green eerie tone, like the fabled sky when tornadoes are inbound. But the only storm looming is the parental meltdown when their plot is eventually discovered.

The watcher peers around an obstruction in the playground, one of those climbing towers with the plastic finger holds. Manny sits on the down side of a see-saw. He whips off his backpack and retrieves a candy bar. Tearing the wrapper with his teeth and spitting it into the rubber chips that cover the ground, he takes a bite and chews loudly while looking around. A car sits behind the school at the very end of the lot near the pedestrian bridge that leads to the park.

"Pssst."

Startled, Manny drops the candy bar at his feet. "Ah, dammit!"

"Over here!"

Donovan, Jason, and Rachel wait inside the playground dome. Donovan's head sticks out of a hole in the dark blue structure made of hard plastic. It's an upgrade from the old metal bars that were here prior, long before Donovan came to town, but he's heard plenty of stories of the good ole days on the playground with equipment that could probably decapitate or paralyze you without a second thought.

"Man! You made me drop my Snickers." Manny picks it up off of the ground, examines it, and then blows on the end before tucking it back into the wrapper and placing it in his bag.

"Let's go, hurry up!" Donovan calls out.

Manny scurries toward them. "How long have you been here?"

"Not long. Some teachers driving around so we hid in here," says Rachel.

"Any problems at home?" Donovan asks the group.

They all shake their head no.

"Rachel?" he asks.

"No, your dad didn't tell you?"

Donovan looks confused.

"My dad called yours this morning and I guess since yours said he was okay with it, mine felt compelled not to be the problematic one. Or that's my guess anyway because he told me the news over breakfast." Rachel shrugs.

"Great. Now it's in the hands of the twins," says Donovan.

"Hey, you all see Belsky's car?" Manny asks pointing to the decades-old Toyota.

"It's been here since we got here, but haven't seen him," says Donovan.

"He creeps me out," says Manny.

"Me too," adds Jason.

"I wonder what he's doing over here, well his car anyway,"

Manny says as the rest exit the dome and follow Donovan across the playground.

"Who knows, one mystery at a time, huh?" Donovan says with an abrupt ending, deciding for the group that there are more important things at hand than wondering about the custodian. He leads them out of the park and toward the wooded area where the sheriff found the bit of uniform. The only reason they even know about that is Jason overheard his grandpa telling his grandma.

"How did you get the twins to agree? They usually kinda suck," says Manny.

"I told my dad lunch and dinner weren't provided and needed another twenty. He complained but my mom made him cough it up. I gave both of the twins $10 and said they would each get another $10 after," says Donovan.

"Well played!" says Manny.

"I know, and the other twenty's on you."

Manny furrows his brow and puffs his arms out.

"We've got a long night ahead. I want to be well into the woods before we make camp," Donovan says.

"Where exactly are we going?" asks Rachel.

"Show her, Manny," Donovan says.

Manny slides his phone from his pocket and illuminates the screen so Rachel and Jason can see the display.

"My dad always has hunters coming into the diner. I've heard them talk about their camps and whatnot in the mountains outside of town. It's miles of open wilderness between Hawksboro and Sherill's Ford. Based on the map Jason sent me, it's our best bet."

"You think it was a hunter that took her?" Rachel asks.

"No, not necessarily. But I did some digging and there are a ton of old hunting cabins a few miles outside of town. I looked at more satellite images and was able to highlight the ones that looked abandoned, though we won't know until we get there."

"It's a long shot. But it gives us a place to start looking," says Donovan.

"Makes sense, right?" adds Rachel. "If she was taken by someone, the risk of getting caught on the road or in another town is pretty high. Sure, they could be far away by now but there's nothing we can do about that, so it's on us to check around here. Where could they take her that would be fast and less traveled?"

Jason stops and looks at Rachel with a contorted expression. "And I thought I overprepared."

She laughs. "What? My parents watch a lot of Dateline."

Donovan puts a hand up and makes a fist to signal to freeze. Manny points to him, mocking the seriousness, but Donovan pays him no mind. He's shushed by Rachel, anyway.

"Wait here. I'm going to cross first and then wave you over."

At the edge of the tall grass, Donovan darts through the remainder of the weeds and briars and then across Davenport Drive which is identified by a tilted sign on the other side of the small bridge. He takes up a hiding spot behind the edge of the concrete guard rail. He looks both up and down the road before gesturing for the rest to follow.

Once they're all on the other side of the road, he again looks both ways before hopping the concrete guard and back onto the road.

"Let's go!" Donovan runs the length of the bridge and then jumps into the bushes where the road takes a sharp turn up the wooded hill.

Jason and Rachel follow. Manny takes a long loop around the concrete barrier instead of jumping over. Donovan wakes up his phone showing the group the map from the safety of the thicket. The illumination glows on their faces and he pulls down the brightness to help conceal their position, though no cars can be seen or heard.

"We'll cut over and pick up the trail where Melody went missing last year. You guys ready? No going back after this," says Donovan.

Jason and Rachel agree.

Manny, out of breath, holds up a finger.

"Get it together, man. We've got a long way to go."

"Shut up, I'm good. And what do you mean there's no going back? We can just turn around."

"We're coming Chey!" says Donovan.

"We're coming Chey," Manny says in a distorted and poorly imitated voice.

Donovan pulls a headband from his bag and slips it over his forehead. He clicks a button and a headlamp shines bright. With a childlike energy, he bounds through the trees and leads the others up the hillside and deep into the night-engulfed forest, high above Hawksboro. The lights of the school, and the town beyond, mimic a reflection of the unobstructed stars overhead. Adrenaline makes him shiver but he suppresses any indication of fear or apprehension for the sake of the others. His only thought, aside from willing Cheyenne to hold on if she's still alive, is imagining that his dad is watching his every move with a look of pride that his boy is doing the right thing.

TWENTY-SIX

Rodney is engrossed in a stack of papers and folders on his desk. On the top is a photo of James Finely. Reading glasses hang on the end of the sheriff's nose as he licks a thumb and digs through the papers. With a red marker, he makes a large circle and compares it to another page. He taps his knuckle on the desk, staring into the mugshot and looking far beyond, lost in all of the possibilities and scenarios that led to the current situation.

A soft tap on the door pulls his attention from the research piled high in front of him. Darren leans in, as he always does, and gives Rodney a wave.

"Thought you went home for the day?" asks Rodney while checking the time. His eyebrows jump at the lateness of the hour. "Christ, it's past seven already?"

"Carla came by to pick me up, she's waiting in the car. She, uh, made these for you. Asked me to bring them." Darren holds a plate of cookies covered in plastic wrap.

Rodney looks surprised.

"Yeah, took me off guard too. I can't promise she didn't put a little something extra in them," says Darren.

"Not thrilled about the late-night call, I take it?"

"She got over it. Just told her that you called to let me know you gave me the day off tomorrow." Darren smiles and raises the yellow plate.

Rodney returns the smirk and waves him over. Darren places the plate on the desk. He picks up the photo of Finely and looks it over.

"That's our guy, huh? The hunter of Hawksboro." Darren wiggles his fingers with a spooky effect.

Biting into a cookie, Rodney brushes off the crumbs before answering.

"Yeah. That's him."

"You really think he has something to do with this new girl?" asks Darren.

"Cheyenne. I just can't tell. It makes sense when you look at his record and timing, but there's no evidence to put him in the area. And all that hype last year didn't help. If anything, it probably scared him off."

"Last thing I remember hearing was his lawyer turning up dead. Gotta be more than a coincidence, right?" Darren places the photo back on the desk.

Rodney types on the laptop that sits on the corner of the desk, pulling up the photo of the lawyer. He rests his chin on his hand, trying to see if there's any connection that he missed.

"Hard to say. He represented a lot of clients so there's no shortage of motivation out there from those that he couldn't get free, but if I recall, his wife was the one who called dispatch. If anyone suspected foul play it'd be her and she's not singing."

"You're probably right. Besides, what's a wife going to know about her husband's work, anyway? Carla couldn't tell you anything about what I do in a day. By design, frankly."

The sheriff thinks for a moment focused on the lawyer on the screen of his laptop. He wags a finger at Darren and begins typing. The loud clacks of the keys raise an eyebrow of his deputy.

"Sir?"

"You might be on to something."

Rodney grabs the marker and jots down an address on one of the papers.

"Want to fill me in?"

He closes the laptop and gathers the papers into their folders before tucking them under his arm. Rodney leads Darren toward the door. He turns back and juggles the plate of cookies before exiting the office and closing the door behind them.

"Most of these types of lawyers also work from home. I'm betting he's got a duplicate file sitting in a cabinet somewhere under lock and key. I'd never get so much as an appointment at his old firm and a records request would take weeks, assuming I even knew what to ask for. But maybe I'll have some luck at his home."

"What about the FBI?" Darren asks.

"I fumbled this thing from the start. As soon as I leaned into the runaway theory. Without some hard evidence tying his whereabouts to the area, if not to Melody or Cheyenne, they're not going to send someone all the way from Charlotte. Not until more people go missing and the public starts demanding answers. And once that happens, I won't be around to call anyone."

Rodney walks ahead of Darren as they move swiftly through the station.

"So, you don't think she ran away anymore?"

The sheriff stops and places a hand on Darren's shoulder.

"Look, you deserved better leadership from me and I'm sorry. You've been vocal about your support of all of my positions and I appreciate it. You're a good deputy."

"What can I do to help?" Darren asks.

Rodney opens the front door of the station and it's nearly dark out, just a hint of dusk remains. A car sits idling at the curb.

"Nothing, Darren. Enjoy the day off tomorrow. I'll call you if anything comes up but we should be able to handle it."

"What are you going to do?"

"I'm going to pay his wife a visit. Address shows it's a couple hour drive. I'll keep you posted. Tell Carla thanks for the cookies."

Darren nods and opens the passenger door of the car. Rodney leans down and waves with a cookie in hand. Carla glares at him and speeds off as soon as Darren's door is closed.

Rodney looks at the cookie, considering it for a moment before taking another bite.

"Sherriff?"

The gravelly voice comes from the shadows of the station sidewalk. He tucks the remnants of the cookie to the corner of his cheek and clears his throat as a shape steps into the light. It's Rick, walking with his hand up as if hailing a cab. Rodney looks to his SUV and back to the man, knowing he can't make a run for it but wishing he had acted like he hadn't heard.

"Hi, Rick. What are you doing out here so late? Everything okay at home?"

"Fine as can be, considering. Just thought I'd swing by to see if you had any news for us. Haven't heard from you in a few days figured there must be something we hadn't heard yet."

He guides the man away from the station and toward the crosswalk that leads to the visitor parking lot, assuming that's where he's parked. It's not likely he walked the distance from his house though it isn't far.

"I'm sorry, Rick. I can't imagine how frustrating this must be but I don't have any news to share just yet. I promise as soon as I do, I won't even call, I'll stop by myself."

Rick stops walking along and leans back, lingering and not getting the not-so-subtle hint.

"I was out there with you all night and we both know our poor girl didn't run away. Why did you even suggest that was a possibility? Look around, does this look anything like the events of a year ago? Nobody outside of this town even knows Cheyenne's name let alone what she looks like. How on earth can someone identify her if whoever has her is on the run?"

Rodney agrees with everything that Rick is saying and it's all he can do not to unclip his duty belt, tear off his badge, and chuck his keys into the bushes, never returning to this god-forsaken station and this cursed town. Then he notices a small yellow ribbon pinned to the man's jacket just over his heart.

Rick must have noticed Rodney checking it out and looks to his chest and raises the ribbon toward the sheriff.

"Yellow's her favorite color. If I have to put one of these on every lamp post, tree, and parking meter in this town, I will. Cheyenne deserves to be remembered."

"You have my word. I won't rest until I have some answers." Rodney tries to reassure him with his eyes but at this point, he can't blame anyone for thinking he's full of shit.

The nod he receives feels more like coming to terms than an understanding or one of being reassured. In fact, it's more painful than if the man had cussed him out, that sad, defeated look on the elderly man's face as he turns and walks away from the crosswalk and back toward the shadows. Rodney makes his way to his SUV and plugs in the address on his phone.

During the entire two-hour drive Rodney's thoughts were consumed by the events of the past year. Everything he'd done and didn't do. No music over the radio, just the sound of the tires on the two-lane, winding highway. He arrived just after 9:00 p.m. at the large brick home centered among towering magnolia trees. A light is still on in the window and he could go for a drink. There's a liquor store around the corner and its call to him is almost victorious, but he kills the motor before he can reconsider and the urge fades as if powered by the engine.

It hadn't rained back in Hawksboro but there's a dampness to the driveway here. The dead leaves on the yard sparkle with the water that has accumulated on their surface. Rodney steps out of the SUV with his laptop and folder under his right arm. A dog barks somewhere down the street as he closes the door. His boots smack on the new-looking asphalt driveway as he approaches the front stoop. A motion light next to the entrance kicks on as he gets closer.

He skips the doorbell and knocks with a roll of his knuckles. Years of police work have sharpened his senses to situations like this. Rodney hears a stir in the house and waits a moment. When nobody answers he rattles the door again. This time the curtain in the window next to the entryway shifts. He tries to present his chest so his badge is evident without looking at whoever is checking. He looks back to the driveway where his police SUV is parked. The bolt on the other side slides free. The thick wooden door cracks just enough for a woman with frazzled hair wearing night clothes under a bathrobe to peek out.

"Can I help you?" she says with a hand bracing her side as if she's ready to slam it in the sheriff's face.

Rodney has to check his folder to recall her name. "Uh, Mrs. Bartlow? I'm Sheriff McDougall with the Lincoln County Sheriff's Office. I know it's late and I'm sorry for that, but would you have a moment to speak?"

"This about Allen? I've recalled everything, many times over."

She begins closing the door but Rodney places a hand against the wood. Her eyes go wide.

"Sorry." He withdraws his hand from the door. "It's Janet, right?"

She nods.

"Janet. Like I said, I hate to bother you so late but I believe your husband might have some information that could be of use in a case I'm working on."

"My husband is dead—"

"I understand, I mean I believe there might be something within his files that could help me track down a very dangerous person. And time is of the essence."

"I'm sorry, I can't help you." Janet closes the door and it locks with no delay.

"Ma'am. We have another missing girl and I believe there is a link between her disappearance and what happened to your husband."

Nothing. He doesn't hear her walking away either and imagines that she's wishing him away from the other side of the door. At least she's listening.

"It's about James Finely."

A moment goes by and Rodney drops his head, tucking everything back under his arm except for a photo of Cheyenne and his card. He places them through the mail slot in the door.

"I'm just going to leave this here and be out of your hair. If you think of anything please give me a call." Rodney steps off of the landing and then the door unlatches and reopens.

"I'll put a pot of coffee on." Janet vanishes somewhere inside.

Rodney heel-turns and tries to hide the pep in his step as he hustles inside and closes the front door behind him.

The interior of the home is dated but nice. Boxes line the walls of each room. Blankets are draped over furniture. He cases the place as he walks toward the kitchen light at the back of the home. Janet clanks about, filling a pot with water and scooping grounds into a filter.

"You can put your things down." Janet points to the kitchen table which is already stacked with mail and clutter.

"You, uh, planning on moving?" asks Rodney as he sets down his laptop and folder on the only unclaimed spot on the table.

"No point in keeping up this house on my own. Kids are all off doing their own things. Just me here now." She presses the brew button and the water steams and trickles into the pot.

"I am very sorry about your loss. From what I've read Allen was a well-respected and accomplished attorney."

"Loss? I didn't lose Allen. He was taken from me. I don't care what the coroner says."

Rodney isn't sure what to say and she must see it on him.

"Could he have eaten better and gone for a walk once in a while? Sure. Who couldn't? But there wasn't a damn thing wrong with his heart. He had his yearly a month before and it was glowing. Doctor even joked he himself was going to start the Allen Bartlow diet."

"Why haven't you filed a report? You could have requested an autopsy, for peace of mind, if anything."

"I tried telling one of the officers who spoke with me, I guess he and Allen had a history, and he warned me of all the red tape if I turned it into a criminal investigation, especially with no evidence to support such a claim."

"Well, sure that's somewhat true but—"

"I just wanted to bury him and let him rest. What would it matter anyway? He's gone and it wouldn't bring him back."

"Do you remember the name of the officer or which

department he was with? I'd like to have a chat with him."

"I don't, and it's been months. I can't even tell you what he looked like. It could have been you. That whole time is a blur in my mind."

"Well, I have no reason not to believe you. But unfortunately, I'm not here to solve that case. Not today, at least. What I can tell you is if the same person is responsible, helping me answer my questions may bring some closure to yours."

Janet eyes him up and down a moment while the pot fills behind her.

"This way." She's out of the kitchen and into the hallway before he hears her finish.

Rodney follows to an office down the hall and around the corner. Janet opens a glass double door and flips on a light.

"All yours." Janet steps past him and heads back to the kitchen.

He steps into the office and looks from wall to wall. Boxes are stacked three to four high with little room to navigate between the columns. There must be fifty of them and not so much as a Sharpie mark in sight. Rodney lets out a long exhale. He peels open an ear of a box with his index finger and lets the flap close, not knowing where to start.

"Lucky you came when you did. This is all headed to the shredder tomorrow. His firm has everything they need. These are all working notes or duplicate documents, they said."

Janet hands Rodney a piping hot cup of coffee.

"You look like the kind of person who takes it black, but there's cream and sugar in the kitchen."

Rodney takes the mug and blows across the surface. "Thank you, Janet. This will do fine."

She turns to leave the office. "I'm headed up to bed. Bathroom's back off the kitchen. Take whatever you need and you can see yourself out when you're done."

"Thank you," he calls as she reaches the end of the hallway.

Janet raises a hand and turns the corner, out of sight.

Rodney sips the coffee allowing it to burn his tongue before setting the cup on the corner of a desk. He takes another long look at the room before opening the box nearest to him.

TWENTY-SEVEN

The single envelope, no larger than a postcard, seems to take up the entire Milpa Burl coffee table in Erin's posh downtown apartment as she stares at the contrasting rectangle from behind her second glass of viognier. The crisp, white liquid magnifies her expression through the bulbous glass. Scribbled handwriting, like that of a child still learning the basics, displays her name and the network's address in a slanted block just off-center on the dirty white envelope.

A return address, that she recognizes as the same fictitious location as the previous letters, is written on the upper left with matching penmanship. This is the eighteenth letter that she's received from the sender. Sometimes they arrive every couple of days and other times several weeks in between. Up until now. She hasn't gotten another letter in three months and hasn't read this one yet. The last one.

Erin places her glass down in the damp ring next to the envelope, ignoring the custom-stamped leather coaster altogether. She ponders the contents of the letter. The others made no mention of Melody, other than very broad denials of being associated with such "utter bullshit," as he claimed. Nobody else knows about the correspondence, not even Marcus. She keeps the bound stack in a shoe box in the back of her closet, the New Balance box not the Valentinos, in the off chance someone breaks into her twenty-four-hour security-staffed high-rise.

Thankfully, the mailroom clerk in the network building is a typical gross old man who doesn't speak English well and all it took was batting her eyes and telling a story about a nephew that didn't exist. A boy writing her fan mail was enough to kill his broken questions on the frequent deliveries. He bought the story so well that he even drops the letters off with shared excitement, unaware hers is as fake as the nephew. It would take siblings to have nieces and nephews and her dysfunctional parents decided they would rather tell each other to get bent than provide her a lifelong companion.

She reaches out for the letter but bypasses it once again, this time reaching beyond the glass and picking up the remote. It takes her only a moment to get to her station in time to catch the late replay of her show. A good one by her assessment, except for that deplorable guest who kept speaking over her. Erin watches segment after segment, from the drug scare to the political shit Marcus makes her run that is so boring she could claw her eyes out live on the air. Sure, people like it. What's not to like about getting viewers perpetually pissed off, and he's shown her more than once the metrics with and without those hollow, hot-button stories.

Paying her dues, Erin justifies those stories the same way she accounted for sleeping with Marcus. Yes, she could be a bull and cause a stir to get what she wanted, but sometimes the easier route is the best one. The whole bees and honey, flies and shit, thing. For a creature of performance, she really hates catchphrases. Maybe because none are of her own creation.

After slipping an Ambien and finishing off the bottle–a gift from someone who she couldn't recall if she was deposed–Erin slides back into the sky-blue Boucle wool Diane sofa as the final segment of her show comes back from commercial break. It's the part with the dick-in-a-suit who wouldn't shut up. She prides herself in her composure but is disappointed that she allowed herself to show a rare glimpse of frustration and embarrassment. The man danced around every point she made, leaving her tongue-tied and reddened. Marcus swearing in her ear did little to help her regain control of the discussion.

She watches the exchange, allowing the salt of the interaction to pack into the wound in her ego. The worst part is Erin knows that the clip is likely being circulated online by the scrotum's posse of trolls as an epic dunk on the *bimbo* queen. The same keyboard cucks who threaten to assault her in every creative way known to women. It doesn't faze her, in fact, sometimes she finds herself laughing and in awe of these incel's imaginations.

The show fades to black and as she moves her index finger to turn off the TV a commercial fills the oversized screen. For a reason that she can't explain, she watches the ad. Maybe it's the imagery of the family, walking in a field with wild text swirling around their heads, or the look on the boy's face as he adores his miscast mom. Erin suddenly feels sick. It's not the overpriced wine, her body takes it like water by now. She knows what she's seeing is fake, especially being in the business, there's no connecting with those that live behind the glass. But this family. These four actors who probably didn't know one another the morning it was filmed, make her feel something she doesn't like.

Her throat tightens and her eyes suddenly fill with water. *What the fuck.* As the commercial ends in a warm embrace with a dog running through the yard in front of the family, because of-fucking-course, the tears finally let loose and stream down her face. This makes her angry more than anything. Erin feels weak, disgusted by her momentary outburst of emotion.

Erin slams down the remote on the coffee table and hits the off button, plunging the TV to black. Her empty glass rattles and tips. She reaches to save it but fumbles to grasp the wet sides and knocks it hard into the surface of the table. It shatters, sending shards and the envelope onto the floor.

Sleep wills her to the bedroom as the medication and wine merge in her system. Despite her neat personality fighting the idea of leaving a mess for the morning, she pulls herself off of the couch, careful to avoid the chunks of glass on the floor. Her foot kicks the envelope and it slides out of sight. Morning. She'll pick up in the morning. With her phone in hand, Erin makes it to her king-size bed in the adjacent room and plunges onto the comforter among a pyramid of decorative pillows.

TWENTY-EIGHT

A small campfire among sprawling roots casts shadows onto the surrounding trees. Smoke rises with sparks toward a cloudless, star-filled sky. Donovan, Rachel, and Jason sit on logs and stones around the teepee-style flame. Manny breaks through the trees with a flashlight carrying a bundle of dead branches. His cumbersome stomp echoes into the otherwise quiet night.

"Wow, could you be any louder?" Donovan asks.

"Huh? Hey, how'd you get it started already? Man, you're like a survivalist or something!" Manny says, admiring the fire as he throws the sticks at their feet.

"My dad taught me," Donovan replies, staring into the flames while poking the coals with a pointed stick.

"No way! You gotta show me how you did it." Manny plops down beside Donovan on the log. Jason and Rachel sit on a boulder across the fire from them.

"Maybe some other time. It's getting late," says Donovan.

Jason wakes up the phone to check the time and is quick to turn it back off to help save battery. Rachel leans over, the contact of her shoulder surprising Jason but he doesn't move.

"You have service?" Rachel asks, checking her own.

"No, haven't for a couple of miles," says Jason.

"I wouldn't rely on us getting any either. Maybe at the top of the mountain if there's a clearing but I'd be surprised. Not much out here," says Donovan.

Jason rubs his thumb over Cheyenne's phone but doesn't wake it up this time.

Manny grabs the stir stick and pokes at the fire. "Come on, this took you like five minutes, just show me. What else are we going to do? I'm not even tired yet."

Donovan takes the stick back. "It's complicated. Takes a lot of practice. When we get back, I'll show you. Promise."

Jason elbows Rachel and nods to Donovan. "Come on, Don. Just show him." He adds a wink but can't tell if Donovan caught it or not since he doesn't react.

Manny stares at his shoes as he digs them into the dirt.

"Alright. Grab that straight branch over there," Donovan says.

Jumping up and finding the stick on the ground, Manny eyes it for straightness.

"Good. Now it's crucial that the stick be as straight as possible. No bends or knots. Oh, and keep it around fifteen inches or so. You can break it, if you have to."

Manny examines the stick and holds it down to his crotch before making a stupid-looking smile. "Hey looks about fifteen inches to me."

Rachel rolls her eyes before burying her face in her hands.

"You're such an idiot," says Jason.

"Give it here."

Donovan takes the stick and looks it over before handing it back to Manny.

"Now what?" Manny asks.

"I'm getting there. Now this is the most important part. You've got to hold the stick long ways against your lips like you're playing a harmonic or flute."

Manny scrunches his eyebrows.

"I'm serious. You want me to show you or not?" asks Donovan. He raises the stick to his lips.

"Alright, now you've got to take a deep breath and blow air all across the top of it. This will make sure the wood is dry enough to take a spark."

"I've never heard of this before and I've seen everything online," says Manny.

"Well, duh. If you had you wouldn't be asking how to do it. Besides, it's just Ranger stuff my dad taught me. Classified ya know, can't put that shit on the internet."

"You better not be messing with me."

"Fine, toss it into the fire. You were the one who asked."

Manny looks from Donovan to Jason and Rachel, perhaps looking for any signs of a tell that this is all a setup. He takes a deep breath and exhales across the stick.

"Good! Now don't stop, blow on it as long as you can!" Donovan says.

Several seconds go by as Manny's face turns dark red, his eyes watering from the effort.

Jason and Rachel are the first to burst out laughing but Donovan joins and can't control his as he doubles over on the log.

"Man, not cool!" Manny shouts.

"Oh, because you've never pranked anyone," retorts Jason.

Manny snaps the stick over his knee and throws it into the fire. He storms off to the nearby tent.

"Sorry, man. I couldn't resist!" Donovan calls over his shoulder. "You think I would come all the way out here, unprepared?" He holds up a lighter and flicks the flame on for good measure.

They continue laughing. Donovan uncaps his canteen and takes a mouthful of water. A shoe hits him in the back of the head, sending water all down the front of him. The splash sizzles on the rocks around the fire.

The laughter continues.

"Feel better now?" Rachel asks the tent.

"Shut up!" Manny calls from behind the fabric.

Donovan wipes himself dry and caps the canteen. "Alright guys, seriously though we should get to bed so we can get up early and head out."

"Should we have a lookout or something? Maybe take shifts?" asks Jason.

"Look out for what?" Rachel asks.

"I don't know. Animals. Bears. What if someone else is in the woods?" asks Jason.

The kids look to the ground, perhaps all of them considering that they might run into the person responsible. That real danger could be out there. At least that's where Jason's thoughts lie.

"It's not a bad idea," says Donovan.

"Well, I'll take first watch then. I'm not tired yet," says Jason.

"You sure?" asks Donovan.

"I'll stay up with you. I'm not too tired either," says Rachel.

"I'm sure."

"Okay, well goodnight guys. Wake me up in a few hours so you can get some sleep, too."

Donovan stands and brushes his pants free of dirt and bark. He walks to the tent and unzips the flap, climbs inside, and pulls it closed behind him.

Inside, the skirmish continues.

"Move over!" Manny yells.

"You're such a baby," adds Donovan.

Jason makes small talk to pass the time. The commotion in the tent, bickering if he had to put a word to it, subsides after almost an hour and Manny's snoring is unmistakable. He'd be lying if he said he didn't feel less safe with Donovan asleep and not on watch. It's not that he feels weaker, but that it seems Don just doesn't get scared. He always knows what to do.

Holding hands happened out of nowhere as he and Rachel stared into the fire. He doesn't think he initiated it, maybe their fingers intertwined on accident, but neither pulled away. The small pile of branches, many the thickness of his arm and intended to keep the fire going, have dwindled as he's tended to the only source of light and heat. It should last until it's Donovan's turn to watch so Jason is glad that he doesn't have to decide what to do about keeping it going or letting it go out.

Rachel's responses have gotten softer and fewer questions come back. At first, he's self-conscious that he's boring her, but when he finally has the courage to steal a glance, he sees that her eyes are closed. As if she can feel his attention, her eyes jolt open and he's quick to look away, pretending not to notice.

"Sorry, what were you saying? I got lost in the fire."

"Nothing, I was rambling anyway."

He pokes the fire with the designated stick, the end now charred black and sharpened to a point thanks to the rock closest to where he sits. Straight lines of soot mark the gray surface where he repetitiously moved the point back and forth to form a spike.

"Ya know, this would be kinda nice, if the reason for us being out here wasn't so…" Rachel hesitates, maybe uncertain of how to describe what they're trying to accomplish.

Jason hates this part of the whole thing. The way people have treated him differently over the past week. He just wishes they would be honest and speak their mind. Even though Donovan pissed him off at school, at least he wasn't afraid to say what he was thinking.

"I know what you mean."

His thumbs find the phone but he leaves it dark. There's no point, he's scoured through it for anything that might help. Guilt led to anger as he saw the things Cheyenne was exposed to prior to the game. When they get back, he was going to make it his mission to take these people down, starting with Simone. He doesn't care if her whole family was taken from her. It gives her no right—the thought is interrupted by the realization that he's in that exact position. Jason loves his grandparents, but if Cheyenne is really gone and doesn't come back, his whole family will have been taken from him. The tightness that comes, signaling he's about to lose his composure, makes him snap out of it instead of risk the embarrassment in front of Rachel.

"You okay?" She squeezes his hand.

"I'm fine."

They exchange a quick look and just like with their hands, he doesn't know who leans in first. It'll be his first kiss and in any other situation he would find an excuse to bail out, but maybe the setting, a fire in the woods, nobody around to ridicule, exhaustion from a week of emotional torture, causes him to embrace the moment. A rare spout of courage, and he likes the feeling. Just as their lips are about to press together in a trembling collision, a sound strikes fear into both of them.

A crashing thud. The echo that follows. It continues and he pictures a bear the size of a van barreling through the woods, knocking down trees and plowing over the tent with the boys still inside.

Rachel's hands grasp his shoulders as it gets closer and louder. His courage vanishes and is replaced with helplessness. Jason lifts the pitiful stir stick with the end pointing toward the forest. The sound stops and an eerie silence returns. He peers into the darkness over the fire, somewhere between himself and the tent. Neither of the boys so much as stir.

The air leaving Rachel's lungs makes his hair stand on end. Not a gasp so much as a reverse breath. And then he sees what she must have seen. A shape moves in the black. Sparkles reflect in what must be the eyes. It stands tall, as tall as a man. The glints of light are wider than a man's eyes, he thinks, but the way it gazes at them feels human. And then it grows taller. He pulls her down off of the boulder and braces them between it and the fire. Whatever it is will have to dig them out and risk getting burned.

Judging by the size, he thinks their fire probably looks to it like Donovan's lighter looked to them. Inconsequential. Then the shape, definitely a man's shape now, lets out a gruff, low call. The darkness adds to the confusion.

"We…we should run…I think…" Rachel whispers.

Jason is thinking the same thing but his instincts tell him to stay put. He eyes a rock from the fire circle with the intent to throw it at the watcher. Sensing the movement, the eyes move closer, its body still clad in darkness just out of reach of the firelight. Its steps sound human too. Heel toe, heel toe.

With the advance, his fight reaction is triggered. Jason grabs the stone, pain searing into his hand, and launches it at the two white dots among the black. The sounds of a stomp and the man lunges forward out of the dark. Except it's not a man at all. A massive deer, with antlers twice as wide as its shoulders, lands just off of the fire and stands alert between the tent and the two cowering kids.

Rachel slides her hand down to the stir stick that Jason still has propped up in defense. He lowers it to the ground, the pain intensifying in his right hand as it moves.

"I swear I saw a man," he says.

"Shhh. It's okay," Rachel says, though he doesn't know if directed at him or the deer.

It snorts and huffs at the leaves and dirt. The sharp hooves scrape and the dirt is blown away by its snout. The deer raises its head back up and looks off somewhere into the darkness from where it came from. Then it trots out of the fire light and jumps into the forest and out of sight. The steps, four hooves hitting the earth, sound unmistakably like a person's two points of contact for each foot.

They share a brief laugh of relief but Jason winces. He grabs at his hand as the burn has come on full strength now that his adrenaline is wearing off.

"Let me look!"

Rachel pulls his hand over without waiting for permission and examines the palm in the light of the fire. He yanks it back as the heat intensifies the burn.

"This doesn't look good."

"I'm okay."

"I think we should wake Donovan."

"No, let them sleep. I'm not going to be able to fall asleep anyway, not after that and not with this."

Jason raises his reddened hand.

"At least let me wrap it."

It doesn't sound like a question. He nods. Rachel retrieves a bright white sock from her pack followed by a tube of something.

"What is that?"

"Healing ointment. It's embarrassing okay but I have dry skin on my elbows and I apply this at night before bed."

"That's not embarrassing, you should see my feet."

They allow themselves to laugh louder this time and a voice calls out from the tent.

"Can you two lovebirds keep it down!" calls Manny. A thwack and then, "Ow!"

Jason watches Rachel as she carefully applies the ointment to the sock and then wraps it with a gentleness, not unlike his Gram. She gives it a soft tug and he holds up his wrapped paw for them both to examine.

"Already feels better."

She smiles and he leans back into the rock. Rachel returns the ointment to her pack before nestling in beside him. They watch the flames dance as Jason puts the rest of the branches on the fire. He dares not take his eyes away from the bright orange tongues lapping at the night sky, afraid of what he might see if he again looks to the forest.

TWENTY-NINE

oxes that filled one side of the room now take up the entire wall on the other side, blocking the doorway and entombing Rodney as he flips through, page after page. The coffee ran out hours ago but he was fortunate to be able to escape to the bathroom before the boxes barred the door. The urge has returned but with the end in sight, as just a handful of unchecked containers remain, there's no chance that he's going to take a break.

The lid of the current stack sits upright to the side. Thick black letters in permanent marker read MONROE JUVENILE DETENTION CENTER. Rodney looks over the faded documents, placing those he has already visually scanned face down on the floor. His eyes are heavy and the lines on the page blur. He rubs and squints but that only causes them to burn as he tries to make sense of the cursive writing of dull, gray pen.

A tri-folded stack of papers stapled together is stuck to the bottom of the cardboard box. It cracks and groans as he carefully peels it up, leaving behind the reverse ghost of ink that transferred from the paper over the decades. The document resists his attempt to unfold it as if it were trying to hide whatever secrets lie within.

Rodney runs his thumb over what appears to be a land deed.

"What is this doing in his juvie box?" he whispers to the room. The towers of boxes don't answer, instead, absorb all sound as if he were in a padded cell.

A soft square can be seen through the translucent paper and he's eager to flip over the deed as the shape looks like a picture. Just as he thought, a rust-brown photocopy fills the width of the next page. Rodney stares at the image, trying to clear his mind of the fog that has set in over the past several hours.

In the photo, a modest wood cabin, more of a shack really, sits below a forest canopy. In front, several older men pose with hunting rifles. A 50's era truck sits just inside the frame. A young boy and a hound dog are front and center of the group posing with a string of dead birds. The only writing is on the bottom right border and reads FORESTVIEW LODGE – 1962 in pencil.

Rodney flips back to the deed on the first page. He reads the filled-in sections as best he can as the years have taken their toll on an already illegible script. He finds the line that denotes the sale, the actual transfer of the deed.

"No shit."

The line in question is a release of the property from a JIM FINELY (DECEASED) to a JAMES FINELY, JR.

Rodney is back on the photo. "The boy," he says while dragging his finger to the middle.

The address on the deed is too faded to make out the numbers or letters. Pulling out his phone he does a quick search for FORESTVIEW LODGE but the results are not what's he looking for, unless this property was converted into a VFW in Pennsylvania or a high-end ski resort in Utah. Something about the shack looks familiar but he can't place it. There are dozens in the area of Hawksboro, probably more that he doesn't even know about, and who's to say if it's even a local cabin, without a readable address.

This photo could be from anywhere there are tall trees and an abundance of wild game. He thinks he may have to go back to one of the earlier boxes, wherever it's located in the stacks, to cross-check the year with some documents to pinpoint Finely's whereabouts in 1962.

Then, a piece of the image screams at him. A spike of clarity more intense than any of the cups of coffee he had consumed during the night. On the porch of the cabin, a large sack is propped against the façade just off the door. The name on the burlap is smudged but still clear enough to read, the dark printed ink contrasting the soft haze of the rest of the photo.

"Miller's Feed," he reads.

Back to his phone, he pulls up a satellite image of Hawksboro and the surrounding mountains and zooms in using a reverse pinch of his thumb and index finger until the image of an abandoned mill just outside of town fills the screen. It had been closed long before he got to Hawksboro, probably not long after the cabin photo was taken, but the old logo, the one matching the bag, still hints in rust on the siding of the main tower where the old letters used to hang. Rodney zooms out some and sees that the factory sits at the base of the mountain to the west of Main Street and north of the high school. The quality of the satellite scan becomes less detailed as he scrolls over what seems like endless trees.

The paved road becomes a dirt road as it leads up the mountain. It has only a few branches off of it, all old logging roads from days gone by, and he chases each of these down as he comes to them. Most just take a long circle back to the dirt road or end without warning. One stops right at the edge of a wide and deep ravine. He's familiar with the canyon as he's had to answer more than one call at its base for injured hikers that have lost their footing on the shale-covered section of the trail.

As he swipes back along the logging road to find the dirt road, he sees something he missed when he first chased this lead. About a quarter mile up from the edge of the ravine and clear as he could hope, is a small brown rectangle sitting under wiry branches. Rodney realizes he's lucky the satellite passed over during the winter. With a full canopy, he never would have seen the shack. He compares the photo from the deed to the image on his phone. His detective instinct, the same voice he's been drinking away out of distrust for its fallible record, tells him to look at every detail in the deed. Rodney flips to the property line document, not a technical drawing as no survey was ever conducted, but someone years ago drew up the boundaries, including a rough sketch of the rectangular structure's dimensions. He traces the shape with his finger including the porch that juts out. Now that it's roughly scaled to the same size and sitting side by side with the document, it matches what the satellite displays on his phone.

Satisfied that this is his best shot, he puts a pin on the satellite map. He does his best to tidy up in haste, only to realize he has to move a couple of dozen boxes to clear a path out of the room. Rodney fights the urge to topple them over and make a swift exit. He still has some doubt and it battles with his eagerness to get on the road. He also doesn't have the heart to leave Janet with a mess of her husband's legacy for her to clean.

After hitting the bathroom one last time, Rodney is out the front door as the soft blue light of dawn illuminates the driveway. Dew covers the windshield of his SUV. He turns on the ignition and runs the wipers to clear the glass. He notices a curtain move on the second-story window as he backs out of the driveway.

As he accelerates on the damp asphalt, Rodney navigates with his phone and calls Darren. It rings over the sound system. For a moment he expects it to go to voicemail but the line connects with a throat-clearing grumble.

"Morning, boss." Darren sounds tired but alert.

"Darren, listen, I know what I said about today but I need you to meet me at the station. I found something and I think I know where Finely is."

"You're joking. Here in town?"

"No, an old hunting lodge up on the mountain."

A momentary pause. Shit, is it as crazy as it sounds? The lack of sleep makes him question his sudden burst of focus.

"You think he's up on Green? It's a lot of wilderness up there, not much more than old logging trails."

"Yeah, I know. That's why it's not a bad place to hole up."

"Nobody has seen him come around. You really think he's been up there this whole time without coming down for supplies?"

"I don't have an answer for most of my own questions, Darren, let alone everyone else's. Which is why I just want to take a look first."

"I'm grabbing my stuff. I can be up there in about an hour."

"Negative, I need you to go to the station and I'll meet you there. Don't want to risk spooking him if he's there. We might only get one shot at him."

"Roger."

"I'm a few hours out. Tell Carla, I'm sorry."

"Don't sweat it. I'll be ready."

"Thanks, Darren. I'm sending you a pin, have station records pull up documents on the property, if they have any."

"You want me to call in some support like State or Wildlife?"

"Not until we can get up there and get eyes ourselves. If I facilitate an operation with outside agencies off of what I've got and it's a dud, we won't get another opportunity. I'll be out of a job and both girls will be destined for the cold case boxes. I won't let that happen. I can't."

"Copy that."

Rodney hangs up the phone and sends the coordinates to Darren's. He plugs them into his maps app which displays 3 HOURS 18 MINUTES, not including his planned detour to the station first. He docks the phone and pats on the steering wheel as he flies down the two-lane road in radio silence.

"Come on. Be there you son-of-a-bitch."

THIRTY

Light trickles through the canopy in the early morning hours. A light fog hangs low in the forest. A few embers smolder in the firepit underneath a clump of white ash already cooled by the air temperature. Smoke swirls from the sole remaining log, its skin blackened on top and a white underbelly below, like a counter-shaded coat of dragon scale.

Donovan steps out of the tent, yawning and stretching his arms. He takes in the cool morning air and rubs his arms over his long sleeve shirt. He blows out a puff of breath and watches the moisture cloud carry upward before disappearing.

Jason is asleep on the ground next to the burnt-out fire. Rachel is also asleep at his side, her head resting on his arm. A thick blanket covers them both, their jackets stuffed behind them as pillows against the boulder.

"So much for keeping watch," says Donovan.

First, Jason stirs, confused and looking around trying to get his bearings. He then notices Rachel and nudges her awake with a gentle shrug of the arm she's lying against. She bats her eyes and takes stock of her surroundings and moves over, putting room between herself and Jason, a flush of red coming to her cheeks.

"I, uh, sorry, Do—" says Jason.

"Oooooo, how romantic!" Manny shouts as he stumbles out of the tent.

"Knock it off, Manny. You want me to tell them what you were mumbling in your sleep all night?"

Manny shakes his head no.

Donovan sits next to Jason and Rachel who kick off the blanket and stretch their arms and turn their necks to get the stiffness out.

"Anything out of the ordinary happen last night?" he asks while pushing around the dead coals with the pointed stir stick.

Jason and Rachel exchange glances and say "No" in unison.

"Alright, then. We need to get a move on it. Manny, put some water on these coals. Jason, why don't you get the stuff together and help Manny with the tent while Rachel organizes some snacks for breakfast from our supply?"

"That's sexist. Why can't I do breakfast?" asks Manny.

Rachel rolls her eyes and unzips a backpack.

"Maybe because some of us don't want candy bars for breakfast. And I don't mind. Good try, though."

"Well, what are you doing then captain while we slave away—" Manny stumbles mid-sentence as Donovan shoots him a glare.

Jason cracks a smile but tries to hide it with his hand.

"Oh, come on. You know what I mean. You're putting us all to work, what about you?" Manny asks.

"I'm going to go up ahead and try to find a good crossing point. Is that okay with you?" Donovan asks.

Manny fidgets, rubbing his knuckles on the side of his head. "Crossing point? What are we crossing?"

The ravine looks much larger than what the satellite image portrayed as there was no way to render depth on a flat picture. Far below, a stream trickles over polished stones. The distance from one side to another seems far, a hundred feet maybe. Donovan walks one way for a good distance before turning around and walking back the other way.

He's relieved when the canyon narrows to a point high on a ridge ten minutes from camp. A large tree has fallen and spans the gap. The trickle of a springtime waterfall runs from above it and ends far below. They could have crossed the shallow stream above but both sides of the waterfall are sheer rock face. He examines the uprooted trunk side of the natural tree bridge.

"This is the best option. Gets wider and deeper from here."

"That's what sh—"

Their looks are enough to stop Manny mid-sentence.

"As I was saying, you can see it just gets worse that way, and we don't have the time to backtrack and try to go up and over," Donovan says as he points to the top of the sheer above.

"You're joking," Manny says, his look lost in the ravine.

"Yeah, Don. I'm kind of with Manny this time. I don't think I can make it," says Rachel.

She puts her backpack down at her feet. Manny follows, dropping his. Jason slides his off and then Donovan does the same. They don't have time for this but if they turn back now it's a done deal. He searches for the right words to try to reassure them.

"It's safe. I promise. Look, this tree isn't going anywhere. Probably came down during the summer storms so it's not even rotting yet."

He gives it a good kick and shove. It's almost as thick as a car at the base and doesn't move an inch with Donovan's attacks.

"I don't know, man. I think they're right. There's got to be another way, maybe down the ravine a little further?" Jason suggests.

Donovan clenches his jaw and fists. "I already checked that way while you guys were playing summer camp. It only gets wider and deeper that way." He glares at Manny, daring him to make a remark.

"But—" Rachel tries to interject.

"But nothing! We have to go here. We don't have time to find another way. Cheyenne doesn't have time for us to find another way! Are you guys going to trust me, or not?" Donovan is hovering between anger and sadness, his voice quivering to match.

The others avoid eye contact. None say anything to either accept or question his outburst. Donovan grabs his bag off of the ground and shoulders it.

"Fine. Find your own way across, or head back. I'm crossing."

He stomps toward the uprooted trunk and climbs over the dirt-covered fingers that once kept the tree upright. Jason shakes his head and grabs his bag and follows.

"Jason, are you sure?" asks Rachel.

"He's right. Chey is counting on us. We can't waste any more time. We either cross or go home and I'm not ready to give up."

Rachel picks up her backpack and gets in line behind Jason.

"Come on, seriously?" Manny protests.

He waits in place as they begin crossing, sliding one foot in front of the other. Donovan carefully tightrope walks the tree until he can get to the first branch and find a hold. The rest of the branches are spaced not far from one another and allow him to slide between each until he's to the other side. He swings around the last branch and jumps down to the safety of the far bank. The tree bounces with a slight settling as his weight leaves the trunk.

Jason and Rachel steady themselves before continuing, following Donovan's path exactly.

"Let's go, Manny! You don't want to be left behind. The bears are trying to get fat for winter!" Donovan shouts over the ravine.

"Bears?" Manny asks. "This is so stupid. Should have just rode our bikes!"

"Bikes, genius? And how long do you think it would take to be found out if our parents thought we took our bikes on the field trip or some old farmer passed us on the road up here?" Jason says, gaining confidence as he approaches the far side. Rachel slows in front of him.

Manny shakes his head and finally shoulders his backpack. He makes his way to the first rock and begins crossing. He steps to the gnarled root ball that holds up the tree but hesitates before climbing onto the trunk.

"What's wrong?" asks Jason.
"Nothing," says Rachel but her voice isn't convincing and she's stopped moving.

"You okay?" Donovan asks as Manny has crawled onto the tree and is on all fours heading for the first branch.

"Not really. I think I'm stuck," Rachel says.
"Stuck? Where?" Jason catches up to her and examines her footing.

"My bag, I can't move."
He looks to her back and sees the side webbing has tangled into the dead spikes of the branch behind her.

"Let me try to get it free," Jason says, his voice trembling.

"Come on, you can do it. Just ten more feet!" Donovan calls from the bank.

Manny makes it to the first branch and pulls himself to his feet. He loses his balance and hugs the branch for safety. The entire tree rolls a small degree. Rachel screams.

"Hold on!" Donovan commands as he steps back onto the tree from the other side. It shifts under his weight.

Rachel's feet slip and she falls off the side of the trunk. She's saved by her tangled backpack as she hangs over the ravine, secured only by her shoulder straps. Jason grabs one of them with one arm and wraps his other around the same branch that holds her.

"I've got you!" he yells.

Rachel screams again, clawing at her bag, trying with no success to pull herself up, her shoes flailing in the open air.

"I'm coming!" Donovan is navigating the tree back to them.

Manny is rushing from his side as well. "Hang on!"

They arrive at the same time and the tree rolls again almost a half turn. All four kids are thrown downward. Donovan manages to hang on with two hands over a branch. Jason and Rachel are both hanging by her bag. The tree is now overhead and there's nothing but a long fall to rocks below.

"Where's Manny?" Rachel asks.

All three grab at the tree above while looking in all directions. Manny is gone.

"He fell! Oh my God, he fell!" Jason cries.

Rachel begins sobbing.

"I don't see him, where is he? I don't see him!" Donovan calls out as he looks between his dangling feet at the canyon below.

The tree turns again and Donovan's grip begins failing.

"I can't hold on," he whispers.

"No, Donovan. Shut up, do not let go of this tree!" Rachel says, both hands still gripping the shoulder straps like an ejected pilot stuck in her parachute.

"I'm sorry, I can't. They're slipping."

His fingers pull away from each other, just the tips digging into the bark. His fingernails ache like they're being pulled out with tweezers.

"Hey, bitch!" a voice calls out.

The three look around, panic still guiding their movements.

"What would your dad say if he knew you were giving up?" Manny asks, lumbering through the steep briars on the far side of the bank. He's cut up, clothes torn, but otherwise alright. He makes his way to where Donovan's bag lies next to the fallen tree.

"Manny!" Donovan yells, regripping the branch but his fingers immediately start sliding.

"Hold your horses, I'm coming. Sheesh."

Manny pulls himself up onto the tree and it moves under his weight. It seems to not affect him as he crawls first to Donovan.

"Alright, get up, buttercup."

Lying on his stomach, Manny reaches around the trunk with both arms and grabs Donovan's forearms. "One at a time. Left hand first."

Donovan nods and closes his eyes tight. He lets go with his left hand and expects to fall. Instead it's guided upward to the trunk by Manny's grip. He gains a strong hold and opens his eyes.

"Now right, let's go."

This time he doesn't blink or hesitate. His right hand finds the spot next to his left and he's able to pull his feet up. With Manny's help, he's up and onto his stomach just in front of Manny. The tree continues to move. Donovan thrusts a hand down to Jason.

"Her first!"

"We're both going to need to pull her up, grab on!" Donovan commands.

Jason releases his grip on the backpack and grabs Donovan's forearm with one hand and then the other. With Manny pulling at his back, Donovan is able to get Jason up and onto the trunk above Rachel.

"Now what?" Rachel screams.

"You're going to have to unhook your straps!"

"What! I can't! I'm sorry, I just can't!"

"Rachel, look at me," Jason says in as cool of a voice as he can muster.

She does, but not without darting her eyes back and forth to the ground below.

"We've got you, but have to get you out of the bag. Trust me."

The tree moves once more.

"It's now or never. You let go or we all fall!" Donovan says.

She looks down one last time and then agrees. Jason and Donovan already have her by the coat she wears inside the straps. Rachel closes her eyes as tight as she can and clicks both latches at the same time. She falls just as far as it takes for the boys to lock their arms.

"Pull!"

Jason and Donovan bring her up, slow with their knuckles turning white around her jacket. Manny reaches forward but realizes he can't be of any help from behind Donovan so he continues to hold Donovan's shirt in a balled fist.

"You're up!" Jason yells.

Rachel clings to the trunk.

"We have to get off this tree. Manny run!"

As if the tree heard the plan, it begins to roll. Manny whips around a branch and jumps to the bank. Donovan takes two large steps and lands right behind him. As the tree spins it slides down the bank. Jason guides Rachel to her feet and they dodge branches as the tree moves. He pushes her and they both jump as the massive trunk, branches and all, rolls and falls into the ravine, scooping Donovan's bag off the bank.

They land just shy of Manny, but safely on the other side of the canyon. The kids watch, panting, as the massive tree turns into a spear as it descends to the rocks below. The bright colors of their backpacks spin and fly in various directions before the wood impacts the dry creek bed and splinters like a bomb was detonated from the inside out.

"Manny, you saved us!" Rachel says while hugging his leg as they all lay sprawled out on the edge.

"Yeah, bro. We thought you fell." Donovan slaps his arm.

"I did! I tripped over your fat ass when the log turned. I happened to push off with one foot and it was enough to grab onto those briars." Manny holds up his bloodied hands.

"Damn. I'm sorry guys. This was all my fault, I almost got us killed."

"We're okay. No more risks though?" Rachel pleads.

"You got it."

In unison, they all take stock of what was lost. Their backpacks are all gone. One phone survived, Cheyenne's that Jason was carrying in his pocket, but the screen is cracked and is unusable, not that it had service anyway. Donovan has just his pocket knife.

"What are we going to do now?" asks Manny.

"We keep going. We don't have a choice," says Donovan gesturing to the now bridge-free obstacle at their feet.

"Where do we go from here?" asks Rachel.

"I left a note. When my dad realizes I didn't go on the trip, he'll find it and they'll come looking for us. But we have to get to one of the cabins or they won't know where to find us out here. These woods go on for miles in every direction."

"Okay, then. We press on. Agreed?" asks Jason.

The group agrees. They brush themselves off and take a

moment to reset. Jason removes the sock that was tending his burn and gives it to Manny who uses it to clean his cut fingers and palms. Jason flexes his hand and insists that he's fine. Manny does the same, testing the restriction of the new wrap.

"You're going to milk that for all it's worth, aren't you?" Donovan says.

"Oh, I'm sorry, would you prefer to be a pile of soup at the bottom of the canyon, Mr. Ranger's boy?"

"Touché."

Donovan smirks and gives a proud backhand to Manny's shoulder as he walks past. The others fall in line, again trusting their friend to lead them to Cheyenne, safety, or whatever lies ahead.

THIRTY-ONE

The soft rumble of an engine approaches the cabin. It's the same vehicle she's heard come and go countless times. The sound of the tires, creaking of the metal, even the thud of the door as he arrives, all sounds that churn her stomach and make her skin crawl. Her fingernails dig into the wood planks. The bag is crumpled at her feet and she's still bound in the corner of her small room. At least she's not stuck in the other room. Cheyenne hates that room.

She doesn't know what time it is, but judging by her hunger she would guess it's around breakfast. The light that cuts through the decaying walls and boarded window is the only indication that the sun is up. Cheyenne struggles at her wrists. He returned sometime during the night along with a fresh set of zip-ties. She had already managed to saw through one of the ties with a sharp sliver of wood but the shard broke, penetrating her forearm and pooling a small bubble of dark blood at the source.

The truck stops in its usual spot, judging by the sound and the door closing. The bass frequency carries through the thin walls. Footsteps on the dried grass and leaves get louder and at this point is all as routine as her getting ready for school, though she has a hard time recalling what that felt like. It seems like a fairy tale, or someone else's life. Incompatible with the current experience she's living, if she can call this living. She thinks it's not possible to ever return to that life, that having to explain this, him, what he does to her, could never happen.

So, what does that mean? Death is the only way out? Or could she escape and then run away, far away, where nobody would know her or what she's been through? Somewhere they couldn't see the tarnish on her, smell the spoil of her. The footsteps stop before getting to the porch. The mutt's paws scratch at the floorboards as it stands to greet him.

Cheyenne is shocked when he stops somewhere outside. His muffled voice sounds like the low frequency of the door being shut, the slight variations identifying it as speech and not something else. Who's he talking to, it's quiet so it can't be the dog. Is she so sure that it's him? Could it be someone else? If she tries to cry out and is wrong, he might kill her. But if she's right, it might be her one chance of escape. But why isn't the dog barking? If it were a stranger wouldn't the animal go nuts over the intruder?

She twists her hands at any angle that she can manage but the plastic cuts deeper into her skin. Giving up on her restraints, Cheyenne manages to push herself up to her feet. She knows the door is locked but she pushes against it anyway. Finding the rusted lever of the door, her swollen fingers push down. It doesn't move, as expected. The tail of the zip-tie bends against the door and pokes back against her arm. He tacked the board she had peeled away with twice as many nails but a small gap remains, though not large enough for a finger. She squats down and looks through the space at the door catch.

The idea strikes her and she places an ear to the door. His

voice is silent now and the dog doesn't move. Then, a loud curse causes her to jump and the boots stomp away from the porch. The truck door slams shut, she pictures it as a truck anyway, the same one that carried her out of town, hog-tied in the bed next to the tailgate. The engine starts up again and begins pulling away from the cabin. The dog whimpers outside.

Did she miss her chance? Why didn't they come inside or at least knock? She doubts it was anyone other than him, but can't trust her instincts anymore. Every sense seems to want to betray her in this hell hole. She decides to risk it.

"Hello!" she calls out in desperation, giving in to the consequences if she's wrong.

"Help! Can anyone hear me?"

The sound of the truck fades down the dirt road and her attention goes back to the door. She's relieved he didn't come in, but can't figure out why he left as fast as he did if it were him. He's been a man of routine, as much as she hates thinking of him as human. Every night around what she thinks is the same time, he shows up. But sometimes he shows up during the day at random times. The arrival and sudden departure do not sit well with her. If he's frantic then it's likely he'll take it out on her when he does return.

Cheyenne looks back to the door and guides the long tail of the zip-tie into the gap of the frame. She moves it down to the latch. The thick plastic sticks just above the door catch. Dust trickles into her eye and she bats it away. She turns her hands upward with the slightest of movement and then pushes down further into the catch. It moves a hair and butterflies fill her stomach. It's so close. Another push and the zip-tie is stuck firm between the latch and the frame. She pictures a thief using a credit card to sneak in, not quite the same as someone trying to break out. She grasps her left palm and fingers over the lever and in one swift motion, she turns both wrists while driving down on the handle.

The door pops open and drifts inward. Cheyenne can't believe it and it takes several moments for her to feel comfortable sticking her head out of the opening. She could always pretend it wasn't her if she could get back to her corner quick enough, feign sleep as if the old cabin had a mind of its own. When she's confident that she's alone inside, she takes a step out into the open room that serves as both the kitchen and living area.

Cheyenne moves toward the kitchen. Her eyes scan the wood counter and table for anything sharp. In one of the draws an old can opener sits stuck to the paper liner. She peels it up and places the square buckle of the tie in its jaw. Using the weight of her right side, she drives down onto the opener and the zip-tie pops. She rubs her wrists and examines the deep irritation. Her hands return to a normal, yet dirty appearance. The grime under her nails is as black as night.

She wonders what he'll do once he finds her out of her restraint again. He may just grow tired of her disobedience and bury her next to Melody. This is the first time she fully considers her death. Her body being eaten by bugs and worms, decaying in the ground and left unfound until after winter, if ever. It doesn't matter. It was always the way this would end, so she commits to taking control of the when.

Moving fast across the space, she's careful to be quiet to avoid giving herself away to the dog that is likely chained on the other side of the door. She looks for anything she can use to distract or kill the animal. Cheyenne feels sick at the idea, a certain empathy she shares that the dog is in a position not much different than her own. She pushes the apprehension aside and checks every cupboard for a weapon. Her eyes dart to the room at the back of the cabin. The door she said she wouldn't open if she got out.

She's only ever been inside with the bag over her head and she wants to keep the ignorance of what the room looks like intact as if she's holding on to one last refuge of denial that what took place in that room over the past week was all just a bad dream. A nightmare that she can tuck away in a deep vault in her mind the same way that room is tucked away. When Cheyenne realizes there's nothing useful to aid in her escape, she stops and stares at the looming door down the short hallway. Her fists clench as she musters the courage to look.

"It's just a room. It doesn't change anything."

The pep talk works and she moves with determined steps toward the back. She bypasses the space where she just broke out without hesitation and stops with a hand on the lever of the room in question. The chipped black paint over rusty iron is a feeling that will never leave the tips of her fingers. The unique, tactical depression under her thumb may as well be a new fingerprint permanently grafted to her skin. She exhales and pushes the handle down. Like her door, this one also drifts inward.

That awful but now familiar creak of rigid hinges prying open, serving both as an alarm of what's to come and a bell signifying that the act is over, alerts the dog outside. It moves in a circle and flops down at the front door. Deep inhales from its snout before the animal settles and she can hear it lie its head down. The chain rattles on the wooden porch. She turns and steps into the room forcing her eyes to take in every inch of the space.

The first thing Cheyenne notices is the smell. The sour notes of decay, mothballs, dirt, and alcohol that she associates with the worst times of her imprisonment. Another boarded window, but more light streams in than in her sleeping space. The room is smaller than she imagined. The small bed with tattered bedding sits alone in the center of the back wall. The door stops midway as she walks through. After stepping into the room, she closes the door to see what had stopped it.

She covers her mouth with her hand. In a small closet cutout, several shapes are stacked tightly wrapped. Some in sheets and blankets, some in tarps. Cheyenne backs up to take in the scope of what's before her as well as to put distance between her and the closet. She keeps moving backward until something grabs the back of her foot and she's falling toward the floor. She throws her hand out and manages to swat the bed, softening her fall.

An arm sticks out from underneath the bed. The skin is pale and dirty and she sighs in relief when she realizes it's void of life and poses no danger. The fingernails still have a hint of light blue polish. Cheyenne rolls to her knees and crawls along the edge of the bed. She has to look. She owes it to whoever was here before her.

Placing a hand on the hard mattress, she lowers her upper body and peers under the frame. Her eyes follow the arm that tripped her. It ends at a bloodied stump. Then, more body parts. Different shapes and sizes. Different people. Worst of all, staring back at her is a head. She closes her eyes so fast that all she can process is the sagging skin and lifeless eyes. It imprints on her mind the way the door lever did her thumb. Except she can't rub the image away.

At the sight of the discarded body parts, all of the trauma that took place in this room hits her at once. Her heart races, panic takes hold, her vision tunnels as she opens her eyes and it's all she can do to get to her feet. She blinks to find the door across the room and throws herself in that direction. Cheyenne stumbles into the doorway and drives it back into the stack in the closet. The pieces tumble and cascade onto the floor. A headless torso crashes at her feet, the covering unravels and spills before her. The way it moves seems impossible to have once been a living, breathing person.

Cheyenne plunges her grip into the edge of the door and yanks it toward her. It's stuck on the bodies at her feet and she puts all her weight between the frame and the edge. She's just able to slide through and slams both knees off of the floor. The skin burns and trickles of blood flow from the raw patches. Ignoring the pain, she climbs on all fours and hurls herself into her room. On the floor, she stares at the ceiling. Spiderwebs drape the beams above. Stars fill her vision as she fights to control her breathing by placing a hand on her chest.

She's unsure how long she laid in that spot but it felt like hours. She's pulled back by a distant humming. It's a sound she recognizes but takes a moment to realize what it is, clarity coming as her anxiety dissipates. A chainsaw, not close, some distance away but she's confident that it's the source. Grampa uses one every year to clear the trees in the backyard. She pictures it might be him out there now. It's a silly thought, but it could be someone, maybe the same someone who came by not long ago. Could it be a state forest worker? She has to find out, her foray into the back room accelerating her resolve to fight.

Cheyenne sits up as if coming out of a coma. She's leaving the cabin, even if it kills her. She looks to the room with the door propped open. She hates what she's thinking of doing. Her eyes ignore the tangle of limbs at the base of the door. Instead, they gaze beyond, to the base of the bed and the severed arm. She turns her head and looks to the gap under the front door where the dog lies, its shadow vibrating as it breathes.

"Give the dog a bone..." she whispers.

THIRTY-TWO

The first call came in over an hour ago with few details, only that some of the kids who were supposed to be on the field trip, weren't. They didn't know exactly who or how many so the school was asking if Jason was home. Of course, he wasn't as she had let him stay over at his little friend's house so they could go together. Even though it was a school night she didn't have the heart to tell him no after the week he'd been through.

Cynthia rolls her knuckles on the patterned tablecloth that drapes over the end table next to the brown corduroy couch. The receiver lies facedown next to her tapping fingernails. When it rings again there's a brief delay between the wall-mounted charging unit in the kitchen and the handset. As she flips it over and fumbles to answer, all of the buttons flash a neon yellow in unison with the ringer chime.

"Hello," she says in a soft voice, trying not to sound anxious.

Rick sticks his head in from the other room. She holds up a palm indicating she hasn't even heard who it is yet. He looks older. The past weeks seem to have aged him years and Cynthia wonders if it's done the same to her, though she hasn't noticed in the mirror. Just the tired, baggy eyes but she refuses to walk around like a zombie. She's done her hair and gotten ready for the day the same as she always has. Her bird sweater, a favorite, she chose today and she traces the embossed stitching of two blue jays with her free hand while the other holds the phone firm against her ear.

"What do you mean, he's not on the bus? Well, where is he?" she asks.

Cynthia can feel Rick's burning gaze from the doorway as she's trying to figure out what it means that Jason isn't on the bus headed for the field trip. The voice on the other end, Rachel's dad Glenn, says something she missed.

"I'm sorry, could you say that again?"

She nods and Rick's footsteps cause the floorboards to call out as he approaches the couch. Her hand has moved from her sweater to her necklace, now fondling the gold chain. His cold and still remarkably strong fingers wrap around her own as she struggles to concentrate on what Glenn is saying to her on the other end.

He's full of panic, and it's contagious as she can feel those same emotions that plagued her a week earlier, doubling down. They never went away, but have persisted with each day without news of Cheyenne. But now that Jason's whereabouts are unknown, Cynthia wants to drop the phone and give up. Crawl to the floor and let starvation or dehydration or whatever happens if she skips her medications, take her. First come, first serve.

"Okay. Yes, okay. Thank you, Glenn. We'll stay by the phone, please ring as soon as you hear anything more. Uh-huh, mmmbye."

Cynthia holds the receiver at a distance to make the buttons clear and presses the call button to disconnect the line. She places it face down in the same spot on the end table.

"What is it? What happened?" Rick asks, his voice cracking. An atypical break in the otherwise stoic persona.

"Nothing happened. That we know of, anyhow."

She knows he won't leave it at that and she thinks about what she can say that would even make sense.

"Well, where is he?" he asks.

"I don't know, Rick. That was Rachel's dad. Apparently, she and Manny haven't been accounted for either."

"What about that kid he pals around with, Donovan?"

"Glenn said he was calling Kenneth next. I'm not sure if he was on the bus or not. They're stopped at a rest stop a couple hours away waiting for the school to let them know the situation and what to do next."

"I don't know if I can bear it, Cynthia. I'm barely hanging on as it is."

"I know, Rick. Me too. But I have to believe he's alright. I know it's not like him to do something like this but since it's the lot of them, I'm sure there's some sort of explanation."

Rick draws his thumb and index in a hook shape to his mouth, his lips pursed tight and staring into the pattern of the brown sofa. She watches his eyes as they examine the drags in the corduroy that changes the color tone.

"What is it, what are you thinking?" she asks.

"Not thinking. A feeling."

"Goodness-gracious, Rick, what are you feeling, then?" Her voice is about as harsh and insistent as she's ever been with him.

"It's something Donovan said. The night Cheyenne went missing and we were with the sheriff. He was understandably shaken up, but I didn't sense that he felt he was overreacting. And you know Ken, there's not an ounce of BS in him."

"Well, spit it out."

"Ah." His lips smack and he waves at nothing in the air.

She grabs his hand, squeezing enough to make him pull back in surprise. Rick's eyes find hers and she is unwavering.

"I think they might have gone after her."

"Gone after her? Gone where? If they know where she is why haven't they told the police?" A thousand more questions come but she's desperate for him to answer those first.

"Hun, that's what I'm trying to tell you. I don't think they know, exactly. But Donovan, and probably the rest of them after hearing a convincing theory, believe she's been taken somewhere. It doesn't matter where she's gone right now. Only figuring out where they think she could be."

"Because that's where they're headed," says Cynthia.

"I hate to say it, but I believe so."

"We have to call the sheriff, and Kenneth, and—"

"Yes, dear. I'll do all that. Why don't you go check his room and see if he left anything behind?"

She agrees and makes her way up the stairs. Rick clears his throat as the person on the other end of the phone picks up.

"Yes, this is Rick Fuller for Sheriff McDougall. Well, I'll hold then."

Cynthia doesn't hear the rest of his conversation as she walks down the hallway to the two rooms that face one another. She taps lightly on the right-hand door hoping more than anything that Jason will cough or stumble his way out of bed and answer it. After several seconds she taps again as she turns the knob and steps inside.

There's little in the room that might offer a clue to what the boy and his friends are up to and she's quickly overwhelmed by all of the posters and electronics and visual noise that is so foreign to her. She tries hard to understand the kids' generation and can recall her own grandparents bickering about how hers was destined for hellfire because of marijuana and draft dodgers, but she still can't make sense of most of their interests, no matter how hard she tries.

The one thing she does find is a school notebook, it looks like his homework from the night before. It's already open with the cover pulled back so she doesn't feel intrusive leaning over it to have a look. One side is covered in complicated math equations, as confusing to her as his choice of wall art, but the other side, what was a blank page, has a block of writing. Cynthia scans the top line and realizes rather quickly that it's a note written from himself to Cheyenne.

She scans it to make sure there's nothing that would help her find him and once finished feels guilty that she encroached on his privacy. The note was a beautiful dedication to his sister and it's clear he believes she's still alive. Most of it is an apology for being a "crumby" brother as well as recalling fond memories they share.

Cynthia wipes away a tear and turns over the cover of the notebook, hoping to preserve the words in some small way. She exits the room and turns toward the stairs to see what Rick has heard but stops and takes a long look at Cheyenne's bedroom.

They've both been through it a dozen times in the past week, trying to turn up anything that could help them find her. The only thing they discovered was the extent to which she was being tortured at school. It was sickening, and to think these same awful kids will grow up one day to be the leaders of the country makes her glad she won't be around by then.

She walks to the bed and sits. The sun shines bright through the window and with the fallen leaves, she can see almost to the school from her vantage point. Cynthia stares out into the mid-morning sky, thinking of both of her grandchildren and how helpless she is in a world that seems like it left her behind long ago. If she can have one more thing before her time is up, it will be to see them both home safe and sound in their beds.

THIRTY-THREE

"**C**ome on, Don. We've been walking for hours." Manny kicks at the dirt of the animal trail that Donovan is using to navigate through the woods. "Trail" is a generous term, he thinks, some worn down weeds and brush more like it, he's not even sure how Donovan can see where it leads. His stomach does cartwheels as hunger is the only thing that he can think about. He feels guilty for complaining, given the circumstances, but it doesn't change the fact that his insides feel like they're eating themselves.

"It's not much further," says Donovan.

"How do you even know? We don't have any working phones," says Rachel.

Manny nods in support. His appetite is making him feel extra mutinous today.

Donovan stops and they nearly run into him. "Just trust me okay? The one logging road on the satellite image ran parallel to the gorge. If we keep walking this direction, we have to run into it. It was just a couple of miles if I remember right, so should be any minute now. We just need to keep going."

"Can we at least stop for a snack?" Manny begs.

"We lost all of our food too, genius. You know anything about what leaves or berries to eat out here?" asks Jason.

"Nobody is eating berries. Plus, the animals have probably picked what's left clean for the winter." Donovan turns and starts walking down the path.

"We didn't lose all of our food..." says Manny.

The three turn to look at him in unison, distrust that he's playing a most cruel prank very apparent on their faces. He retrieves a flattened candy bar from his back pocket and holds it up like a long-lost treasure.

"It's melted from my butt-heat and I smushed it when I fell, but we can still split it."

Donovan's sigh is loud enough to send a bird flying out of the bushes and that makes them all jump. "Fine, five minutes."

Manny tears the wrapper off the end, careful not to lose any of the soft morsels that have been ground together into an unrecognizable lump of chocolate and whatever nougat is made out of. He breaks off a piece, smaller than his fair share, and hands the rest to Rachel, who does the same. Jason is next and from his expression, he savors the lone bite like it's a gift from the gods. Donovan accepts the bar and looks the last piece over. He folds the wrapper and tucks it into his pocket.

"Cheyenne will probably be hungry."

The kids sit in silence. None say anything suggesting that maybe it's foolish to save the candy bar, or that they should have done the same with their share. Maybe they're all afraid to put their real thoughts into the air, that's Manny's assumption, anyway. He rubs his tongue over his teeth and the roof of his mouth to collect any pieces of sweet or salt that remain.

"I hope this cabin has some water," he says, breaking the moment of reflection they seemed to all be taking.

"Quiet," whispers Donovan.

"What, you can't tell me you all aren't thirsty," Manny says in defense.

"Shhh. You hear that?" Donovan tilts his head in the direction of the path up ahead.

"No, I don't hear anything—"

"Manny, shut it!" Jason says, throwing a stick in his direction.

Just then, the low rumble of a small engine fills the forest around them. It's not a vehicle but sounds more like a lawnmower. Then the unmistakable buzzing followed by the high-pitched scream of cutting wood.

"That a chainsaw?" Donovan asks.

"Oh, shit. We're in a horror movie," Manny whispers.

The noise grows but is still a good distance away. It ends in a matter of seconds and after a brief lull, the soft thud of a tree rattles the forest, though very faint.

"Come on!" Before they can respond, Donovan is moving in a soft-footed run down the trail. Jason is right behind him and Rachel is quick to catch up. Manny brings up the rear, still licking the flavor off of his lips.

They bob and weave through brush and trees, dried branches with brown leaves swat at their faces as they rush over the wooded rise in the direction of the sound. As they descend to the other side, another noise disrupts the natural ambiance.

Tires on the overgrown, dirt road kick up stones as the frame of the vehicle creaks and moans with the change in terrain. It starts fading and Donovan picks up the pace down the slope. Without warning, he slides to a halt and holds up a hand. The kids fall in behind him and he points through the briars and trees.

"It's coming from over there, anyone see it?"

Manny scans the woods, looking for any source of movement.

A motor travels from right to left but he can't find the source.

"Damn it," Donovan curses as the sound quiets to a low rumble before ceasing somewhere in the distance.

"Who do you think is all the way out here cutting down trees?" Rachel asks, her voice quivering.

"No telling, but they're headed in the direction of town. And the cabin is the only thing except miles of wilderness that way." Donovan gestures toward where the truck came from.

Jason bursts past Donovan and runs toward the road. The rest follow but struggle to keep up. It takes several minutes to get through the overgrowth and the vehicle is long gone by the time they emerge from the trees and onto the dirt logging road. The ruts of damp soil between a thick line of grass are all that can classify it as a road. Fresh wheel marks are depressed into the muddy areas at their feet.

"Come on, Jason. Slow down, we don't know what we're running toward," Rachel pleads as he turns away from them and runs along the path.

Donovan catches up, leaving Manny and Rachel behind by several paces. They move fast for several minutes and Manny begins to doubt the cabin is in the direction that they're headed. The two in front begin to slow and once again they're all grouped together but still hiking at a brisk pace.

"I thought you said it was just ahead. What if the vehicle was going and not leaving? We could be headed back toward town," Manny pleads while trying to catch his breath.

"Good!" adds Rachel.

"Look, I don't have it in front of me but I remember the rough distance on the satellite image it was like a thumb's width," Donovan retorts, still plodding ahead.

"A thumb's width?" Manny shouts. The echo of his voice

scares him in the quiet of the woods that surrounds them. "The entire state is a thumb's width if you zoom out far enough!"

"Manny if you don't knock it off, I'm going to smack you a thumb's width," Donovan calls over his shoulder.

"See, that! I don't even understand what that means."

Rachel hits him with the back of her hand and gestures with her eyes to quit egging him on. Manny rolls his own and throws out his hands feigning innocence.

"There!" Jason calls out.

Far up ahead just as the road begins sloping downward, a light brown shape sits along the edge of the trees.

"I told you," says Donovan.

"No shit." Manny's mouth hangs open.

Donovan leads them off of the road and into the trees on the other side, advancing toward the cabin with the light cover of the vegetation.

"We don't know who might still be here, so keep it quiet," he says.

They stalk through the growth, inching closer and closer until they are 50 yards or so away from the front of the porch. The face of the cabin sits back from the logging road, the grass in front worn down from being used as a roundabout for whatever vehicle has come and gone.

"Is that a truck?" Jason asks, pointing to a faded black hunk of metal sitting next to the cabin, its front facing away from the approaching kids.

"Damn, that's old," says Donovan as they take a wide sweep off the road and through the trees. "I don't think it's the one we heard but we need to play it safe."

Passing the truck from a good distance, Manny looks it over. It reminds him of the ancient delivery truck behind his dad's diner. The wheels sag, but otherwise, it looks somewhat intact.

"Looks like someone has been working on it," says Jason, pointing to an old leather tool bag spilled out in front of the rusted bumper.

"Not recently, there's leaves covering all the tools," says Donovan.

As they make their way through the woods where they can see the face of a cabin, Donovan grabs Manny's shirt and pulls him down. Jason and Rachel do the same.

"Shit. A dog!" Donovan exclaims in his highest whisper.

The mutt stirs on the porch. It paces in a circle–a chain wrapped tightly around its neck–and drops back down to the wooden floor. It lets out a soft whimper as it goes to its belly and chin. The pointy ears droop back from attention.

"Look we found the cabin. Let's just go call for help!" Manny demands.

"And what are we going to say? Hey, there's a cabin in the woods? Think, man."

Dogs have always brought a sense of fear to Manny and even though they've made it this far he doesn't have the stomach to go further. Fear sets in like he's out on the branch hanging over the ravine all over again, except this time he doesn't dare to climb back up.

"I'm going to go try to look in the windows," says Donovan.

"What about the dog?" Manny asks.

"You're going to have to distract it while I sneak around."

"I'm not going near that thing."

"You don't have to. Once I'm close, I just need you to throw something off to the other side, near the road. The chain doesn't look very long but it will give me time to get to the opposite side where it can't see me."

"I don't like this," adds Rachel.

"Me neither," says Jason.

"We didn't come all this way to turn back because of some dumb pet. You two need to be my eyes and ears. Any sign of someone coming or anything out of the ordinary make a bird call or something. Just give me a head's up. We'll split and meet back at the trail where we hit the logging road."

They nod. As Donovan steps onto the dirt to cross the roundabout, glass shatters on the porch of the cabin. He cowers back into the woods. A hand clears a pane of the window with an object. The shards fall to the porch. The dog jumps to its feet and extends its chain to the window. It barks and snarls at the hand, but can't reach it with its snapping jaws. It digs and pulls, standing up on its hind legs but held back by the thick chain.

The hand retracts, and to the kids' surprise, a face appears in the small black square that used to be milky glass.

"Chey!" Jason calls out but Donovan is quick to place a hand over his mouth.

"Oh my God," stutters Manny.

"Don, you did it!" gasps Rachel.

"Hold on, we still have to distract the dog and figure out how to get her out of there. She may not be alone."

Cheyenne's face disappears from the window and they all crane necks to see if they can pinpoint her within the cabin.

"I'm outta here, we need help!" Manny says as he stomps off into the forest.

"Manny, what are you doing! She's right there!"

The dog still barks at the broken window, not yet noticing the other children.

"Exactly. Now we need the police! You know, adults!"

He's undeterred and he's moving fast along the edge of the

road, away from the cabin.

"Let him go," he hears Rachel say as he leaves them behind.

Manny feels abandoned but he pushes the thought from his mind. He'll get help. It's the right thing to do. He looks back over his shoulder once more to see Donovan cross the road and move to the woods on the far side of the cabin. The dog's bark is incessant but begins to fade the further away he gets.

"Good luck," says Manny to himself, genuinely willing them success. He walks as fast as he can, following the narrow trough of the tire trail. He remembers from the satellite image the tangled web of roads with only one leading back to town. The fear of getting lost grows with every step away from his friends.

THIRTY-FOUR

Rodney slams a fist on the dash as he pulls into the parking lot of the police station. A small group has gathered outside on the steps. Cheyenne's grandparents, Rachel's dad, Manny's parents, a few teachers, and the usual tag-alongs of nosy locals, stand in a huddle, their hands and arms seeming to speak for them with wild gestures. This is the last thing he needs and considers for a moment blowing through the lot and avoiding them altogether.

"For Christ's sake, what now?"

The SUV squeals as the brakes engage and he stops on a dime, double parked at an angle. Rodney throws open the door and stands between it and the frame. Cheyenne's grandparents are the first to approach but they begin talking over each other. Rodney can't make sense of it so he holds up a hand.

Manny's dad steps forward with a piece of paper.

"Sheriff. It's the kids."

"What about 'em?"

Rodney accepts the note and scans it but looks to Manny's dad to elicit more detail.

"Kenneth found this this morning. I guess Donovan didn't

expect him to go into his room until after the field trip. They all went looking for Cheyenne."

"Looking where? And where's Kenneth?"

Rick steps up, a look of frantic despair that was worse than the night that Cheyenne went missing. *Please don't have a heart attack on me.*

"They went up the mountain. Don believes she might be in one of the old hunting cabins up there."

"Son of a bitch," he means to say it under his breath but they all hear. "And let me guess, Ken went after them?"

Manny's dad nods.

Rodney looks around. "Where the fuck is Darren?" he says to himself and he's surprised when Rick answers.

"You just missed him. He stopped in about an hour ago and when we told him what we found he sped out of here."

When he gets ahold of his deputy, he's going to ring his ass. He blames himself. Darren didn't call him because he knew what the response would be. "Stay put." The green deputy is braver than he gives him credit. Christ, all of them seem to have more courage than him. He shakes off the self-pity and pulls his shoulder radio close.

Rodney keys it up and calls into the black square. "Zero seven, this is zero one, you copy?"

A moment of static.

"Rodney for Darren, over."

"Sorry, go for Darren."

Trying to move out of earshot of the group, Rodney walks around to the back of the vehicle but they all step out to the parking lot to get closer. He has their undivided attention whether he likes it or not.

"Hey, I'm in town and just spoke with the parents. Apparently, some of the kids are up that way looking for her." He glances over the note once more. "Sounds like they've been out there all night, not sure how far they made it but I need you to head over to that cabin and have a look."

"Already on it. Just hit the logging road, should be there soon. But I'm guessing you knew that already."

"You guessed right. We'll talk about that later. Be careful, I'll be up there as fast as I can. Heading out now."

"Copy. And if it's empty?"

The parents perk up as Rodney tries to distance himself further around the back.

"Uh, just take a look, if the kids aren't there backtrack toward town with your windows down. Chirp the siren and listen for them."

"10-4, what about Finely?"

"Finely! That devil is here?" Manny's dad shouts.

Rodney holds up a hand. "I'm headed up that way, Darren. Just look for the kids. We'll regroup and deal with that situation later. Over."

"On my way. Over."

The people have surrounded Rodney's SUV as he makes his way back to the driver's door. "Please, go back to your homes so we can reach you as soon as we have any news."

"Aren't you going to get some help down here? Our kids are out there!" Rachel's dad exclaims, surprising everyone.

"Glenn, that's exactly what I'm doing. As soon as you all let me back out of here, I'm calling in search and rescue. We'll find the kids."

"And what about this Finely monster, he's really out there?" Cynthia asks. Rick wraps his arms around her shoulders.

"We don't know. But the priority is the kids. Please."

They back away from his SUV but as he shifts into reverse a tall, broad-shouldered man, who looks more like a skeleton in coveralls, steps past the parents and to his window. Rodney lowers the window while allowing the vehicle to roll backward, hoping it will expedite whatever the man has to say.

"Ey, uh, Sheriff, I'm Nikolas Blasky, I do the cleaning of the school here." The man's thick Eastern European accent is hard to decipher but Rodney tilts his head to tell him to get to the point. "I've been trying to inform someone since I heard about the kids. I believe I saw them last night. They were running off into the woods as I was locking up the school."

"Do you recall how many there were or which way they were headed?" Rodney asks, momentarily applying the brakes.

"Four I believe, maybe three boys and one girl but of that I'm not certain. They were headed out of the playground and up toward the concrete bridge. Thought they were just playing…" Blasky looks to his feet. The man genuinely looks sad, like he feels guilty for not saying something earlier.

"Thank you, Mr. uh, Blasky. No way to have known."

The man steps back, allowing Rodney to back out of the lot. Once onto the street, he flips on his emergency lights. In his rear-view mirror, the group of people disperse as he flies down Main Street.

On the way out of town, he passes the former teacher's house. He can't recall the man's name but a large for sale sign has been set up in the front yard. Rodney thinks it's for the best, hoping that he can start a new life somewhere that he can distance himself from the stain of accusations that unfairly fell on him. As he speeds past, the man leans out from behind the sign and the two make eye contact. Even from the distance of the road, the man's sadness is as clear as day as he secures the sign to the well-manicured lawn.

On his way up the mountain, Rodney makes the call to search and rescue. They're stationed about an hour outside of Hawksboro but he'll feel better if they can start before nightfall, in the event that he can't find the kids. Rodney allows himself to laugh for a moment, realizing that Donovan had figured out what took him so long to even look into. The kid has a future. He's motivated to do whatever it takes to track them down. They wouldn't be out there if he had been able to solve Melody's disappearance, or prevented Cheyenne's.

Rodney drives as fast as the small road will allow. It's about a 30-minute trip up to the cabin and he's hoping Darren will already have the kids safely in his truck. He grabs the radio to check in, then hesitates. *What if this asshole has a police scanner? Fuck.*

He pulls out his cell phone and instead dials Darren. It rings several times before going to voicemail. Rodney tries again but gets the same result. He should be up to the cabin by now. Once more he slides the radio off his shoulder.

"Zero seven, come in."

No response.

"Darren, this is Rodney, come in. Over."

There are a hundred reasons for his deputy not to respond so he doesn't push it. He calls the phone once more and this time leaves a voicemail, hoping the notification might get through, if there's spotty service.

"Hey, it's Rodney. I'm about twenty minutes out. Checking in. Couldn't get you on the radio. Ping me back, ASAP."

He floors the gas, pushing the RPMs as the SUV travels up the steep road. There are only a few miles left of pavement before he has to turn off onto the dirt logging road so he's trying to make up what time he can by traveling top speed while the terrain allows.

The radio on his shoulder chirps with static. No voice but the squelch of on then off, on then off. Rodney doesn't dare to call back over the radio.

It squelches once more, then silence.

Rodney takes the sharp turn, sending the entire contents of a massive puddle across the road as he pulls onto the logging road. The overgrowth and rutted tire marks are almost unnavigable. This is going to take a lot longer than he anticipated.

"Damn it!"

All he can do is drive slowly and aim his wheels for clear pathways. A breakdown out here would be disastrous. The pace is torture and he's about to lose it.

"Breathe. Breathe." Rodney wipes his brow. The anxiety attack clouds his vision but he's able to fight it off. His heart rate settles and he focuses on the road. He rolls down his windows both for some fresh air and to listen for any sounds. Someone calling for help, another vehicle, anything he might hear over the grind of his SUV.

A phone chime fills the vehicle's speakers and he answers it without looking, expecting it to be Darren returning his call. A woman's voice surprises him and he looks to the caller ID. It's not saved and he considers hanging up so he can focus on the task at hand.

"Sheriff McDougall, are you there?" she says.

"This is he, who's this?"

"Janet, you wer—"

"Yes, of course. I'm sorry I left in a rush, is everything okay? I'm sorry if I left a mess but it was truly helpful and I can't thank you enough."

The connection is spotty, her voice phases in and out.

"Everything is fine. I'm calling because I found the number of that officer I first spoke with. The one you were asking about."

For a moment he can't hear her and fears he lost the call. He looks down at his phone to ensure it's still connected.

"I'm sorry Janet, I'm in a bad service area. Can you text me a photo of his card when you have a moment? I've gotta run."

"He didn't leave a card, it's just a number that I jotted down on a scrap."

Unusual, he thinks. "Okay, can you text that number to me? I promise I'll get back to you as soon as I'm able."

He can't hear what she says in response. It's scrambled and then silent. The call disconnects. Rodney takes his eyes off of the uneven road just long enough to check the service bars. It flashes from one to zero, he's just on the edge of coverage and about to lose it for who knows how long.

A moment later his phone dings. He swivels it to glance at the screen just in time to see it display no service at the top. A message notification is on the home screen and he swipes it open. Janet must have heard him and the text just made it through.

Rodney glances at the bubble which is just a seven-digit number. A feeling of discomfort melds with confusion that rises from somewhere deep. He doesn't recognize the number, but the area code is local. He reads it over as many times as the road will allow his eyes to depart. One question begs to be answered and it eats at him as he drives painfully slow toward the unknown. Who exactly visited the lawyer's wife?

THIRTY-FIVE

Manny hears the distant sound of an approaching vehicle. He's on the edge of the rutted road and pinpoints the origin in the direction that he's heading, coming up the hill toward him. The squeak of the shocks as the wheels navigate the path. He's been walking for fifteen minutes and there's no way he can make it back to warn the others.

"Shit, shit, shit."

Manny jumps down into some brush and tucks himself beneath a growth of ferns.

The rattle of the vehicle overpowers the noise of the motor as every bump in the road is a stress on the axles, pushing the shocks to their limits. The roar becomes louder and a flash of color causes Manny to push himself even lower and further back into the woods.

A white truck spins and slides as it comes up over the road and moves to where he jumped down in hiding. It slows and Manny's heart pounds in his chest. Lying on his stomach, he looks over both shoulders at his feet, weighing if he should run away or stay still. Just as he's about to make his escape, the truck stops and the engine dies. He tries to sneak a peek but the sound of someone clearing their throat and hocking a wad of spit sends him back to the dirt.

There's a berm where the logging road was cleared however many decades ago and he can't see anything from his perspective, aside from the rocky soil that's covered with whatever is still green this time of year. Where his sight is blocked, he can still hear everything as silence has fallen on the trees. Boots on crunchy leaves and soggy earth. The loud thud of the door closing. He hears the sound of a tailgate dropping. A moment later that slams shut. More boots on the ground and a hand slapping on something. Sounds smooth—dry like bare skin—smacking something hard, immovable.

A sigh, followed by a groan, as whoever is above him struggles over something. And then as quick as the boots approached, they begin fading away down the road toward the cabin. After a few minutes have passed, he musters the courage to stick his head up out of the ferns. Manny first looks in the direction he came but sees no sign of anyone walking along the road. His eyes move back along the trail with slow precision until they get to the truck. It sits parked about thirty feet away on the road. A massive tree blocks its path, the trunk rising from his side and ending in a jagged, fresh cut. Leaves still hang from the sprawling branches.

Manny pushes himself to his knees and takes in the truck. Faint noises from within the engine still rattle as the parts settle. The longer he looks at the truck the angrier he gets with himself, every detail a screaming admission of his stupidity. A large antenna on the roof pieces it together and he feels like the biggest fool. It's unmarked, but he recognizes the truck as one belonging to a sheriff's deputy. Probably the tall, lanky one, if he had to guess. He's seen it around town many times, even at the diner. He scrambles out of the brush and up onto the road.

"I'm such an idiot." Manny wipes his knees and catches his breath from the brief moment of adrenaline. He considers running after the deputy, even screaming for him but a movement in the woods, in the direction from where they hiked in together, grabs his attention. A figure, far back in among the trees. His eyes shoot between the way the deputy went and the shape that stalks through the forest. It's in and out of sight, maybe a hundred yards into the trees. It's unclear who it is, all he can tell is that they're big. Not just tall, but thick. He conjures bigfoot lumbering toward him before shaking his imagination back to the very real danger that's lurking out there.

Manny rushes to the truck, maybe planning to reverse out of here, he isn't sure, but it's locked. Doubling back along the road, he pushes away from the cabin and into the woods where they first saw the road. He means to keep eyes on this figure. He won't let his friends be caught off guard. Stepping over branches and boulders, he's mindful to stay low and quiet. He's able to track the person for several minutes and they seem to be taking a longer way in the direction of the cabin. He still can't tell anything about the person, only that they're wearing neutral colors, almost camouflaged among the brown and muted surroundings. They're also carrying something. A spear? A stick? It's so far away he can't tell, but then he realizes it looks to be a rifle.

"It has to be him." He's terrified and feels helpless. Options race through his mind and none sound better than the last. He pushes on but is losing ground. The person in the woods is moving faster than him, like they know the area. The fact that they're armed doesn't exactly put a kick in his step.

At first, the figure would dip in and out of the trees with enough frequency that he could follow behind, but before long Manny has lost sight. Now, all of the directions look the same.

He's not even sure which way the road is, let alone the cabin. Panic sets in and the weight of feeling lost begins to grip him like a bear hug. He thinks he hears another engine, or maybe it's the same one, he doesn't even know how far he is from the truck. Manny can't even pinpoint the direction of the sound as every orientation his ears tell him that's the way.

He forces his breathing through his nose so he can better hear. It's difficult, and the numerous times he's been called a mouth-breather come to mind. Manny listens for any indication of the whereabouts of the new noise or of the person in the woods. Anything at all to help him figure out his location. He doesn't even want to follow them anymore. He would probably run the opposite direction if he could just catch a glimpse. Then, in a brief moment of fear that comes with the realization that he's not alone, brought on by the weight of a presence right behind him, a hand falls over his mouth and he's pulled backward in a violent jerk.

THIRTY-SIX

Avoiding detection by the dog wasn't easy, or quick. Donovan stepped carefully in a long arc through the woods toward the side of the cabin. He is now out of sight, but not earshot, of the chained animal and he inches his way along the side of the wall. A boarded-up window is just ahead but he hasn't seen anything since first seeing her hand in the front window several minutes ago. He pauses for a moment as the dog shifts positions on the porch, the rattle of the chain jarring his nervous system like the zap of an electric fence. The uncontrollable jerk of his neck and head as if an actual current were running up his spine.

Donovan looks out to the woods where Rachel and Jason have moved along his same path to maintain a line of sight with him. He can barely make them out among the leaves and brush. He takes another sliding step to get to the window. Using both hands, he cups his eyes and squints to see inside through the small gap between the boards.

It's dark and the glass is murky on the other side. He moves his head trying to make out anything within the room. He grabs a chunk of what looks like concrete from the crumbling foundation at his feet and doesn't hesitate to smash it where the boards leave the glass unprotected. The dog barks and growls, pulling harder on its chain. He crouches down, taking a knee to look in through the unobstructed part that is now open to the inside.

The room in the cabin is small, smells horrible, and is dark, but he can tell it's also empty. Donovan looks back to Rachel and Jason, shaking his head to indicate there is nothing in this room. Jason stands up and heaves something with a perfect baseball throw in the opposite direction of the cabin. It crashes off in the woods with a faint slap. The dog growls as it stands, the chain dragging across the wooden floor. It barks an ugly guttural yap at the intruding sound.

He turns back to the gap in the window and whispers as loud as he dares. "Cheyenne! Chey! Are you in there? It's Donovan! Say something if you can hear my voice!"

There's no response as the dog's barking quiets and it whines while circling in place, by the sound of its claws. Donovan looks to the others who are again hidden in the brush. He hopes his expression will show that he wants them to throw something else. He mimics it with his arm but there's no movement from Rachel or Jason. They're holding perfectly still.

A hand grasps the front of his shirt and pulls his face to the opening between the boards.

"Don?!"

After the initial panic, Donovan realizes he's staring Cheyenne in the face just a few inches away, separated only by the thin cabin wall.

"Chey! Chey! Oh my God, you're alive!"

Around the corner, the dog growls and pulls at its chain. He still can't see the others. He wants to wave and tell them she's okay.

"Don, who's out there? Tell me you brought help."

He snaps back to focus on her. "Are you okay? We need to get you out of here!"

"We, who's we? Where are the police?"

"Huh, no. They're not here. It's just me and Rachel and Jason."

"What?"

"Yeah, Manny too but he went back to get help when we saw you at the window."

"Don. We have to get out of here before he gets back. You can't be here when he gets back."

"I know, I know." Donovan pries at the boards. He looks to his feet for something else to use to rip them away.

"It won't work. The only way out is through the front."

"Shit. The dog."

"Yeah. I'm working on it."

"Chey. I'm sorry."

She looks back at him, confused.

"The night you disappeared. I was coming to check on you and I looked away for just a second. If I wouldn't have, I would have seen and you—"

"Stop it. You're here. You found me. That's all that matters."

A flash of motion catches his eye, drawing his attention away from the window. Rachel and Jason stand among the bushes waving their arms at Donovan. They don't make a sound and he's having trouble reading their lips.

"What is it?"

The dog barks and growls.

"I don't know, they're trying to tell me something."

Chey pushes her face against the opening, trying to see her brother and Rachel. It's only now that Donovan can see what the captivity has done to her. It makes him sad but rage takes over, pouring hot lava through his veins and into his temple. He's about to storm around the corner and face the beast, whatever it takes to get inside the cabin when the sound of footsteps on wood makes him freeze.

He can't see the porch but the tone of the dog changes as does the drag of the chain as the whining ensues. Donovan checks with Jason and Rachel and they're both waving at him, what appears to be a signal to run away. They drop to their stomachs as a muffled voice speaks to the dog. The sound of something heavy clanks on the porch floor.

"Don, you need to run. All of you. He's back, just go get help."

"Chey, listen to me. I'm not going anywhere, lay low and I promise I'll get you out."

Footsteps resume and he can't tell if they're moving toward his side of the cabin or the front door.

"Hold on."

Donovan ducks down and Cheyenne tries to see him through the broken pane. He moves to the back corner of the cabin where he came out of the cover of the trees. Something is holding him in place and he looks down at his shirt which is snagged on a sharp sliver of wood that juts out from the wall. He pulls at it, looking back toward the front of the cabin. The dog's chain rattles in a single, settling thud. Is it loose?

He tugs at the fabric as it rips but doesn't release. Cheyenne whispers through the opening. "Get out of here!"

"Hey, hey! Over here!" Jason's voice rings out in the clearing.

Donovan and Cheyenne look in his direction, sharing the same expression of shock. Rachel jumps up beside him lending her voice to the call.

"Yeah, you SOB, over here!" she yells.

"No…" Donovan says under his breath. "No, what are you doing?"

The growl from the dog, or the man, is haunting. Nails scrape at wood and boots stomp.

"Get 'em, girl!" a man's voice calls out.

Jason and Rachel are already running and vanish into the woods. A flash of brown flies across the clearing and into the trees in their direction. The dog is in pursuit.

Donovan manages to get his shirt free and slides behind the rear of the cabin.

"Someone else here?" the man's voice says, more of a taunt than a question. "Nowhere to run kiddo, better to make yourself known."

The voice comes from the side of the cabin. Donovan hopes Cheyenne is no longer at the window. He hustles to the other corner, nearest the old truck.

"Don't get your hopes up, little girl. Whoever the mutt doesn't get, I will."

Glass shatters and the man screams. "Ah, you fucking bitch!"

Donovan means to rush the man but a distant vehicle gives him pause. He looks in the direction of the road but can't make anything out through the trees. The hum is faint, as is the squeaking of shocks on the uneven road. He pictures Manny waving down the police back at the main road and bringing them here. *Nice work, Manny.*

He hears a curse and boots stomping off. The man must have heard the same vehicle. Donovan peers around the edge of the cabin and is relieved that the man is gone. Creeping back to the window, he retrieves his pocket knife and digs at one of the boards.

"What are you doing, I said go!" Cheyenne says.

"Someone is coming, I think it's the police. I'm getting you out."

"Don, listen to me. The man—"

"Quick, is there anything you can use to hit outward?"

Cheyenne looks around and shakes her head no.

"Try your shoulder," he says as he runs the blade around the edges of the board. "You should be able to knock them loose."

The front door of the cabin screams on its hinges and slams shut, igniting a frenzy in Donovan. He grasps the cross-section of boards on the window frame and pulls outward.

"Come on, he's inside! You gotta push!"

Cheyenne jams her shoulder into the window as Donovan puts both feet on the edge of the cabin below the opening and uses all his weight to lean back. Between the two of them, the frame shakes and loosens. A pounding on the door.

"I've wedged it shut, but it won't last long," calls Cheyenne out.

"Keep hitting it, it's almost free!"

Another slam causes a wince from Cheyenne and the frame pops out, half hanging onto the wall but leaving a gap big enough to fit through. Donovan falls to the ground on his back but is quick to his feet to help Cheyenne through the hole.

As he guides her down to the ground, he notices how light she is, her clothes baggy and her skin taut. He tries to hide any reaction to the smell, whether it's her or the room, he's not sure. Donovan looks to the door where the pounding has stopped, the thing wedged under the door brings bile to his throat.

"Is that a…hand? Human…hand?" Donovan stutters.

"We need to run!" Cheyenne is now pulling him and he's shocked by her sudden burst of strength and energy.

They make it to the trees and hide behind a stack of dead branches. He can't hear the other engine anymore, and the man is nowhere to be found. Is he still in the cabin? He looks around trying to see where they can run next. Maybe the old truck? He doubts it runs, looks like it hasn't moved in years and the tires barely qualify as inflated.

From inside, a voice yells and doors slam. They both duck further behind the pile, unable to see the cabin and hopefully out of view if he looks this way. Cheyenne fidgets next to him. She bites at her fingernails which are red and bloodstained. She seems desperate to speak, but Donovan holds a finger to his lips. Seconds drag with no sight or sound. He wills the help to hurry up. What's taking them so long?

Footsteps approach and they look at one another. He's ready to tell her to run, they'll split up and he'll buy her time. He slides his fingers over the handle of his open pocket knife. How much force does it take to penetrate the skin? Does he have the strength? Donovan gives her one last look, trying to give her confidence with his eyes. He opens his mouth to yell but Cheyenne grasps his arm before a sound comes out. A shadow is cast over them. Donovan adjusts his eyes and he draws back his hand, ready to thrust it forward. Fear is replaced with relief. It's Darren, the sheriff's deputy.

"He's inside!" is all Donovan can spit out as he points back to the cabin.

THIRTY-SEVEN

The SUV shakes and bounces as Rodney pulls up over a rise on the logging trail and slams on his brakes. He narrowly avoids slamming into the back of Darren's truck. Swearing to himself, he throws the shifter into park and eyes the surroundings before exiting his vehicle. Without thinking, Rodney has already unsnapped his holster and placed his right hand on the grip of his service weapon.

His left hand moves to his shoulder radio but he thinks better of it. Again, he looks to his phone which displays no service. Satisfied an ambush isn't waiting for him, he steps out of the SUV and closes his door with a gentle push, his hand never leaving the gun at his side. Rodney approaches the truck as he would any traffic stop when he notices a large tree across the trail that blocks the way.

"God dammit."

Rodney steps to the window of the truck and peers inside. It's tinted, but he sees nothing out of the ordinary. He can make out the shape of the vertical tube that is Darren's issued M4 rifle. This explains why the door is locked, he thinks, as he pulls on the handle.

He makes his way along the road, being sure to stay on the center grass of the road. Not that his footsteps would be followed or the noise much different, but avoiding the mud and occasional crunch of gravel keeps him on the brown, withering stalks that sprout down the middle, some reaching up to his knees.

It takes another ten minutes to reach the cabin and he's chirped his radio a few times but received no response. It's torture, not calling over it, but the thought of giving away Darren's position and putting him in harm's way, more than he already is, won't allow it. He shakes away the images that haunt his memory.

The faded black paint of an old beater truck next to the cabin catches his eye. It may even be the same one from the photo. A blue tarp covers something in the back. It sits parked, facing the same direction as the front of the cabin. Beyond both is a steep downward slope into a wilderness of trees and eventually state game land.

With quiet footsteps, he walks around the bed of the truck first and then the driver's side. He does a quick check under the tarp, which covers a few planks of wood, and then he surveys the interior from the window and notices the keys hanging from the ignition. He also notices that the tires are almost flat and the uncut grass around the base indicates it hasn't been driven in quite some time. A rusted gas can is sitting at his feet and past the bumper lies a leather tool bag. Then his focus drifts to the cabin.

The door is open. No movement. Rodney unholsters his gun and trains it on the opening as he moves to the front porch. He steps at an angle since he can't see into the cabin and doesn't want to give a nice bright target to whoever is inside. He resists the urge to call out to Darren. The element of surprise might make all the difference.

Rodney reaches to his shoulder and squelches the radio. A return squelch emits from somewhere inside, just off the door. He sweeps from right to left in front of the opening, scanning what he can of the room before entering. He ignores the reluctant voice in his head that urges caution and pushes into the cabin. Rodney does a quick sweep from right to left as he moves to the corner of the front room. Empty.

He does another squelch. The response is so loud that he thrusts his gun in its direction. On the floor next to a tipped-over chair, in what seems to be the kitchen, Darren's service belt is tangled in one of the chair's legs. The holster is empty but the radio hangs loose, its wire still looped around the belt. Rodney scans the room again and steps to the hallway. Sweat beads on his temple with the realization that Finely could be armed with Darren's weapon.

He takes a second to take in the space. Someone's instruction from long ago reminding him, "Don't run to your death." The first thing he notices is the smell. Trying to keep his weapon raised while covering his nose, he enters the hall and steps to the first door on the left. Rodney gives it a light nudge. It's cracked open but something is in the way. Two open rooms lie ahead and it's there that his attention must reside. He'll come back to the barricaded room once the cabin is clear, though he's not crazy about the possibility of being surprised from behind. The first room is clear as he steps and sweeps in a quick arc.

At the end of the hall, the door is open and he can see a mess of something on the floor. His gut tells him what to expect but he must confirm with his own eyes. Rodney comes to the shape and first scans what he can of the room from the door. At his feet, just as he thought, is a body. A moment of fear as he expects to see Darren lying before him, but it's not him. This body is decayed and the clothes are tattered and soiled.

Stepping over the remains with care, he checks the left side of the room behind the door. A stack of bodies has fallen like an avalanche out of the small closet and onto the floor. Rodney uses his non-shooting arm to push the door to get a better view. A flash of movement and he's face to face with Finely.

"Fuck. Hands! Let me see your hands!" Rodney drives his leg back trying to make room for his weapon to level a shot.

It's only now when the face he stares into doesn't so much as flinch, that he realizes he's staring at Finely's corpse. The clouded, empty eyes looking far beyond Rodney and into nowhere. The skin is a tone of gray and yellow. The jaw hangs open, showing bloodied gums and horrific teeth. The signs of decay are obvious but the temporary relief is destroyed by confusion and fear.

"It's someone else."

He panics and puts his back into a corner. Adrenaline courses through him and he's reliving Baltimore all over again. The hot pressure behind his eyes. The tunnel-vision. A defensive instinct that he's now the prey. His dilated pupils look for any source of movement, a target to release the tension with the squeeze of the trigger.

With his gun trained on the door, he pulls out his phone with his free hand. It flashes between no service and a single bar. When he swipes the screen open it's still on the text message from Janet. He's not sure what makes him do it, maybe it's the shock of seeing his prime suspect deceased, and the culmination of more than a year of utter incompetence and failure on his part, but he presses the number and hits call.

Rodney raises his phone to his ear and waits for the ring. The killer is here and if he's about to die he needs to know. He needs just one answer. A single win. When a ringing tone doesn't come, he pulls the phone away and squints at the top right where the signal has vanished. And then, with a shock that he hasn't felt since being tased during academy training, his nervous system reacts before his brain has processed what's before his eyes. A number isn't displayed on his phone any longer, but a name. The number from the text was already saved in his phone.

"Darren."

"Hey, boss."

Rodney turns to the sound of the voice. In the doorway, Darren has a gun pointed at him.

"You—"

"Shut the fuck up, Rodney." Darren emphasizes with the muzzle of the gun. "Drop it."

Raising his left hand with slow precision, Rodney contemplates surrender.

"Where is she, Darren?"

"Drop the fucking gun!"

"Okay. Okay." Rodney bends at the knees and tilts the gun sideways as if he's going to set it on the floor. "Let's just talk about this," he stalls.

His mind flashes to Melody's crime scene. Darren's truck and the cover on the truck's bed. Rodney's hand tracing the only thing separating him from the girl. The night Cheyenne went missing and Darren drove them back to the station in the same truck, the girl likely a few feet away the entire time. The visuals make him sick. Darren was there for it all and he couldn't see it. The weird interactions, the uncomfortable moments with his family, all numbed by denial at the end of a bottle.

"What about your child?" Rodney can't picture Darren as a father any longer, the two realities are impossible to reconcile.

"Not another word!"

Rodney raises his left hand as if holding his balance but he's waiting for Darren to bite. While lowering the gun toward the ground his eyes are glued on Darren's. As soon as Darren's focus shifts to the moving, open hand, Rodney twists his gun level and fires off two rounds. Everything happens in a flash. He sees Darren's shoulder flinch back and the other round smacking into the wood far above his target.

Darren retreats into the hall while returning fire, some shots hitting the door and the wall beside him. One strikes Rodney's gun, sending the remaining parts to the floor in pieces. Pain shoots through his finger and thumb. They're both still there, he thinks. He dives for cover as more shots slam into the room.

His head bounces off of the bedpost and the cabin transforms into a street. He's on one knee with a hand gripping a stained white sheet. The wetness of the pavement soaks into his pant leg. Rodney, somewhat aware that he's in danger outside of the vision, wastes no time pulling back the covering. The face underneath is young, the eyes open and looking up to the stars. Flashing lights reflect off of the damp skin. A trickle of blood has stopped just out of the corner of the mouth.

Next to the young man's shoulder, a silver and black object lies discarded. Rodney bats his eyes to focus on the shape. He knows what it is but it doesn't process clearly, like he's waiting for that part of the image to render. A firm hand on his shoulder completes the picture.

"Holy shit, Rod! He had a gun!" The man's face is no longer obscured, it's now clearly his former partner, Mike. The long nose and scattered freckles inches from his face.

Rodney looks back to the body, the gun now clear, and lets the sheet slip out of his hands as he stands to his feet. Mike uses both hands to turn Rodney's shoulders to face him. He gives him a hug and then pats him on the back several times before pushing him back to arm's length.

"Fuck. Rodney. I didn't even see him come up behind me. You saved my fucking life!"

Mike removes his cap and runs his hand through his hair. Rodney takes one last look at the body, knowing the vision is about to be over and he has places to be. "You're getting a medal for this. You're a fucking hero!"

He didn't feel like a hero. Not then and not now. No matter how many times he has to relive that night, Rodney always leaves with the same thing sickness, self-doubt. Could he have done something different? The finger was in the trigger guard and the bend of it was unmistakable, the gun could have discharged at any moment. At one time he knew that, but the years of substance abuse have made him question his memories. He pushes his mind back to the present with a renewed spirit to fight. To trust his instincts. To be who the people of Hawksboro count on him to be. The sheriff.

THIRTY-EIGHT

Barking follows their every move. Jason is running as fast as he can and Rachel is right behind him. They bought some time by jumping down a bank but the dog has caught their scent and is closing ground. Growling and snarls interrupt rabid panting as paws shuffle over leaves and fallen branches. It's difficult to locate the position of the dog so he tries to just keep the sounds at his back. He thinks they should come up on the road soon and isn't sure if that's good or bad. The dog could probably run much faster on the open ground.

Jason is driven by the sole image of his sister's hand protruding from the window pane of the dilapidated cabin. He could run forever, he thinks, on that fuel alone. He could jump the ravine and sprint back to town. Nothing will stop him from bringing help to Cheyenne. Not a dog, not a man, not the burn in his lungs and legs that spreads throughout his body as he hauls ass through the forest. He ignores his heavy breathing but can hear Rachel's with a distinct frequency that has become unmanageable. The moment he feared has arrived.

"Jason, I can't keep going!" Rachel slows and holds her knee while trying to keep pace.

Jason looks around, frantic. He stops and listens. The dog changes directions as if it knows they've stopped. It's close. Outrunning it isn't going to be possible, he realizes. He'll have to fight it somehow. He sees a tree with sprawling, low branches up ahead and he pulls Rachel along with him.

"Hurry, up there!" He locks his fingers together and leans against the trunk of the nearest tree.

Rachel limps and steps on his hands, reaching for the first branch. She pulls her legs up and loops them around. The dog emerges from the brush and skids to a stop. Its ferocious bark sounds primal and tortured. It could be a wolf if it wasn't so mangy and sick looking. More like a wolf that has been cast out of the pack for being a runt. Jason grabs a large stone and grips it tight. He dares not throw it out of fear of missing. There's no time to get up the tree and he's not turning his back on it.

The dog bares its teeth and jumps forward several times. It's contemplating its next move. Rachel screams at the dog from above, but it seems to only anger it further. After another taunt, it must have gained the confidence it needed to attack. The dog springs forward into a full sprint, its ears pinned back and saliva flying off of its fangs. Jason pulls back the rock, ready to strike the moment that it jumps.

He's willing to sacrifice his left arm to the mouth if it means landing a blow to the animal's skull. It's not fear of the pain he might endure, but fear he'll miss his one chance. The sudden courage surprises him and his fingers dig into the rock. He pictures it buried in the lifeless beast at his feet. The dog leaps from ten feet away and he can see those jaws, he offers his forearm and can see the dog's eyes shift to where it plans to bite.

A shot rings out and the dog flies sideways like it was hit by a car. It rolls across the leaves with a gasping whimper. Jason still has the rock raised, taking in the once horrific-looking dog that is now nothing more than a sad pile of fur a few feet away. He can't help but walk to its side, dropping the rock behind him as he kneels. The dog's faint panting scatters the leaves in front of its wet, black snout. It turns its eyes up to him and back to the trees as if begging for help.

In this moment he feels guilty for fearing the dog, for hating it. Jason sees it as much a victim as Cheyenne. Maybe, with the right owner, it could have been a good dog. The kind that plays fetch and enjoys belly rubs, instead of a beast. It could have brought joy, instead of fear, if only someone was there to love it. Jason places his hand on the back of its neck, it tries to flinch under his touch but can barely move its head. The dog whines once more and lets out a long, low, and final exhale.

Footsteps approach and he looks up to Rachel who holds the branch with one arm and her ear with the other. She shrugs. He turns his head to the sound of the crunching leaves. A man steps onto the top of the bank that looks down on them. At the crest of the wooded slope, the man returns a rifle to his shoulder. Manny steps out from behind him.

"Manny!" Jason screams.

He helps Rachel down and they run, as fast as she can manage, toward their saviors. Once they're close Jason realizes the man is Kenneth, Donovan's father, and his attention is on everything except the kids, scanning the trees for threats. Manny breaks away and meets them first. He grabs them both in a hug.

"Holy balls am I glad to see you two!" Manny says. "Where are the others? Did you see the deputy?"

"Wait, you saw him? Where?" Rachel grabs his shoulder.

"He passed me on the road but my dumbass was hiding."

"Thank God for that!" Jason says.

"For what, I don't get it."

"Manny, the deputy, Darren, it's him. He's the one who was keeping Cheyenne." Jason says.

Kenneth turns from the surroundings to the boy. "Jason, what do you mean it was Darren?"

Rachel answers for him. "He showed up to the cabin while Donovan was trying to get Chey out of the window. He's the one who sent the dog after us. We tried to buy Donovan some time... We had to run, I'm not sure what happened to them."

"I'm sure they're fine. Right?" asks Manny.

Kenneth unshoulders his rifle and looks at each of the kids. "I can't say one way or another. But I've gotta get you kids to safety." He checks his phone and then places it back in his pocket. "Shit. Sorry. It's going to be alright, but we need to start walking."

"Please, we need to go back to the cabin! You've got a gun," Jason pleads.

Rachel pulls on his sleeve. "Come on, if we get back to the road, I can take us there."

"And Darren's truck is there. We could wait at the road. It would be the safest and fastest way back," says Manny.

The wheels are turning and Jason can tell the idea of going anywhere near the cabin is not something Kenneth wants to consider. But neither is being stuck in the woods all night with no supplies and no way to call for help.

"Alright. You kids stay behind me and keep quiet. Do exactly what I say and if I say run, you run back in the direction of the main road and toward town. No more going into the woods. Got it?" Kenneth asks, already walking.

They nod and fall in line behind him.

"Thanks for back there," Jason says.

"I feel bad for it," adds Rachel.

"Me too, dear. Bad men rarely get to see the damage they inflict, let alone feel it themselves. I'm just glad you're both okay." Kenneth looks over his shoulder with an expression of concern.

"You walk okay, Rachel?" He nods to her knee and the limping steps.

"I can make it."

"Here, let me help," Manny says. He smacks Jason's arm who understands the intent.

They both put an arm around a shoulder and help Rachel walk, following Kenneth as he makes his way through the woods and back toward the logging road that leads to the cabin.

THIRTY-NINE

"He's inside!" Donovan shouts.

Cheyenne doesn't understand his reaction. She releases her grip on his wrist and drives her heels into the dirt, trying to push herself back into the brush. Anything to escape. Donovan looks between her and Darren, who bares his teeth, eyes darting between the two.

"It's him," she manages to spit out.

Donovan stands and she yanks at his arm back toward the ground.

"What are you doing, come on. It's safe!"

"No, it's him!" Cheyenne puts every memory of the past however many days into her expression, letting all the fear, hatred, and anger rise to the surface.

"It's okay. It's Donovan, right?" Darren says with coolness.

Another sharp tug on Donovan's arm until he looks at her with proper attention. The lights come on in his eyes. Something red hot emerges as if from the depths of his soul. Saliva collects at the corners of his mouth as he turns back to face the deputy.

Darren's face sinks and he reaches to his hip, feeling for something that's not there.

"Fuck."

In the same breath, Darren lunges toward them but Donovan is a flash. He dives shoulder first, at the deputy's legs. They collide and the man goes face-first into the pile of branches and leaves. Donovan rolls to his side and up on his knees.

"Cheyenne, run!"

She's to her feet and running parallel to the cabin. She looks back and Donovan is sprinting in the opposite direction, trying to lead him away.

Darren hesitates as he regains his footing, appearing unsure of which one to go after first. All three are stopped in place by the faint sound of a radio squelching from somewhere in the cabin. Cheyenne looks to Darren and then to Donovan who is back behind the edge of the cabin. A figure walks along the porch. It's the sheriff.

She means to scream, to call for help but Donovan waves her off, holding up his finger to maintain quiet. She looks back to Darren who is now halfway to the cabin as the sheriff enters and is out of sight. It's as if the deputy has forgotten or cares nothing about the kids now. He's laser-focused on the cabin and stomps to the door.

Cheyenne circles back, following Donovan's movements until they can regroup. Darren has vanished inside the cabin with the sheriff and no sound has come from within since.

"Are you good?" Donovan asks.

"I'm fine, why didn't you want me to call for help? It's the sheriff!"

"And Darren is the deputy. We don't know if they're working together. We can't risk it."

She thinks for a moment, trying hard to remember if there was ever anyone else at the cabin, but most of the time she was unable to see or hear anything. The times when someone was there she's almost certain it was just him. The memory makes her physically ill and she chokes back a gag of her empty stomach.

"What now?" she asks.

"We take the truck."

"How can you be sure it works?"

"Gotta try."

Cheyenne nods and they run together, crossing in front of the cabin. A shot rings out, and then another. They dive to the ground at the same time and are back on their feet just as fast. Noises come from within and the sounds of a struggle are unmistakable. Bodies hitting wood. Table overturning. Fist on bare skin. Fist on clothing that comes with a sickening grunt.

A person flies through the same window that she knocked a pane out of, sending glass outward and across the dirt yard. It's the sheriff. He rolls to his side and coughs. Cheyenne and Donovan watch as he moves to his elbows. Darren steps through the empty frame as if there weren't a door a few feet away. Shards crunch under his boots. The sheriff looks to the deputy and then to the kids.

"Get out of here, go!" he calls out between bloody teeth.

She pulls on Donovan and they make their way to the truck, just as Darren lands a kick to the sheriff's ribs. The sound is horrible and makes her cringe, even from a distance. The sheriff gasps for air and the sucking, empty call is something she won't soon forget.

Donovan takes the driver's seat and Cheyenne takes shotgun. He searches for the keys and finds them hanging from the ignition. He tries to start it but only a faint clicking responds. She reaches for the door handle but Donovan gets to his first.

"Just hold on, let me try something!"

Before she can protest, he's around the front of the truck and lifting the hood which blocks her view. She looks back to the cabin. The sheriff is on his feet but is taking punches from Darren. He throws his own, landing a couple, but the deputy grabs him by the collar and head-butts him back to the earth. The sheriff doesn't move.

"Hurry, Donovan!"

"Almost there," comes his reply.

Her eyes don't leave the sheriff, willing him to regain consciousness. Begging God, her parents, anyone out there listening, to wake him up. His hands are frozen in a clench and she can't even tell if he's breathing. He very well could be dead.

"Got it!" Donovan yells as he slams the hood and runs back to the driver's side.

Drawn by the crash of the hood, Darren's attention moves from the body at his feet to the truck. His eyes lock with hers and the bile returns. It's all she can do not to vomit all over the windshield and had she anything in her stomach she likely would have. He steps over the sheriff, who she imagines grabbing his pantleg and holding him back. No such fortune as Darren steps to the porch and picks up the chainsaw. A brief smile, something so evil she couldn't have imagined it before, initiates his sprint toward them. There is a violent rage in his howl.

Donovan cranks the ignition and the engine sputters and fires.

"Drive!" she yells.

The truck jerks forward as he shifts into gear and dirt kicks up behind them as he slams down on the gas pedal. The road slopes slightly downward and the trees jut in from the raised shoulder of the trail, leaving little room to navigate. Branches scrape along the sides of the old truck making high-pitched screams as if they know what's chasing them. Cheyenne checks the mirrors and the window. The sheriff's body shrinks in the distance but she doesn't see Darren. Desperation has her neck whipping left and right, trying to locate him.

Glass from the back window shatters into their laps and across the cracked, vinyl bench seat that was once a color of bright green but is now something faded and sad.

"Shit!" Donovan yells. "He's in the back!"

Darren has the chainsaw and is clearing the only barrier that separates himself from the kids. He clears the remaining glass with wide swings of the non-running blade. He wobbles and grasps for balance as the truck bounces. In the rearview mirror, she can see Darren trying to start the chainsaw while ducking and dodging branches.

Then the sound of the small engine firing blares from the bed. They both look back as he prepares to swing the running chainsaw.

"Down!" she screams and Donovan throws his head between his legs as the blade clears over him and smashes out the driver's side window. Sparks fly as the chain bites into the metal frame of the door. It seizes and dies, but the engine sputters just behind Donovan's head.

Darren jerks at the handle but the unsteadiness of the road sends him to the bed on top of the uneven tarp. He grasps at the side for support, somehow keeping himself from flying out.

"Cheyenne, you gotta bail!" Donovan points ahead.

The road continues on a slope and has a sharp left turn approaching. A small line of trees is in their path and she knows Donovan has no intention of slowing down to make the corner. It would be the one chance Darren needs to get proper footing. For now, he's struggling to get upright as the bed bounces with every bump.

"Not without you!"

The deputy pulls himself to his feet and his bloodied hands swat through what's left of the broken window. Donovan dodges them, keeping his head low while Cheyenne is pressed against her door. Donovan jerks the wheel back and forth keeping the grabbing fingers from finding any hold on skin or clothing.

"Just trust me, I'll be right behind you!" His eyes plead with her to listen.

With one last look at Donovan and then Darren, whose upper body now pushes into the front seats, Cheyenne forces open her door against the combative branches. She reaches over to Donovan's pant leg and retrieves his knife that's clipped to his front pocket. She flips it open and jams it into Darren's forearm and yanks down as hard as she can. The muscle and tendons fall out of his skin from elbow to wrist. He grabs the footlong wound with his good hand as the knife hits the floor of the truck. Cheyenne then throws herself out, pulling her legs in tight and away from the wheels.

She rolls in a violent tumble and the rocky bank sends pain to every part of her body, but her arm takes the brunt of a root that otherwise would have struck her head. Cheyenne comes to rest in the dirt as the truck flies past and she falls onto her back into the road behind it, somehow not being run over in the process. She can't move her hand and the taste of iron fills her mouth. Stars dance in her vision and then clear.

She squints to focus on the truck as it barrels away, toward the ninety-degree turn. The soles of Darren's boots go skyward as he pulls himself into the cab, just as it meets the trees. Cheyenne expects a violent collision but it plows through the saplings and sunlight replaces the vegetation. The truck is airborne for a second, maybe more, and then it tilts down and drops out of sight.

"Donovan, no!" she screams, the sound of her voice hollow as it bangs around her inner ear. Dizziness hits her like a wave and then recedes.

Cheyenne uses her good hand to push herself first to a knee and then to her feet. Holding her injured wrist to her stomach, she runs down the rutted path, not caring if she breaks an ankle in the process. She makes her way to the opening where the truck crashed through and looks beyond the turn. With careful steps, she walks out onto the rocky surface that transforms into a sheer cliff face.

The wind kicks up and she locks her feet in place to keep from falling forward. Hundreds of feet below, the mangled remnants of the truck smoke in a dry creek bed. Dark oil, or fuel, or something else, seeps out of the heap of rusted metal and runs down a bright, sun-washed boulder as if it was fleeing the scene to hide among the trace of water below the polished rocks of the creek. Cheyenne begins to sob.

A hand on her shoulder sends a shock of falling through her nervous system. For an instant, she feels like she's plunging to her death until she can feel her toes that are still on the hard surface of the ridge.

"It's okay, it's just me."

Donovan's soft voice is like being wrapped in the most comfortable embrace she can imagine. But her tears don't stop. Cheyenne turns to him and allows herself to cry. She pours all that she's bottled up to stay strong into his shoulder as he holds her. She can't say for how long she stands there on that cliff, feeling all alone and anything but.

A piece of her wants to take his hands in hers, say thank you, and step backward while letting go. Her eyes never leave the perfect blue sky and puffy white clouds as her body falls to meet what's left of her captor, far below. But another part of her, not so much in her mind or heart, but a voice she can't put a name to, tells her to keep holding on. In the moment, to Donovan. But in the future, to herself. Not her old self as that person died days ago, and carries on somewhere with Melody and the others. But whoever her new self has to become in order to live with what she went through.

A voice carries from up the road in the direction of the cabin. She wipes her eyes and looks over Donovan's shoulder. She can't help but laugh and is surprised that she can still find something truly funny.

"What is it?" Donovan asks as he pulls back.

She nods and he turns while still holding her.

Manny runs down the path as if he's being chased by a bear. "Don! Chey!"

Donovan laughs and helps Cheyenne away from the cliff.

"Who knew he could run that fast?"

They meet Manny a short way up the road and he nearly tackles them with a hug.

"Oh my God, you're both okay!" He's out of breath from the long sprint. "What happened, did he…splat?" Manny gestures to the chunk of trees missing from the turn in the road and the abyss beyond.

Neither answer and Manny doesn't press, just grabs the other side of Cheyenne and helps her up the road. Small engines roar as a group of four-wheelers come over the rise and make their way to the kids. Cheyenne can make out the search and rescue wording on their bright orange vests. They slide to a stop next to them and dismount, their ATVs still idling and the smell of exhaust filling her nostrils. She doesn't mind, and realizes, at least for the time being, that her tolerance for things that would otherwise bother

her, now don't.

After a brief check-up by one of the rescuers, they place her and Donovan on the back of separate four-wheelers and drive with care back toward the cabin. The other two rescuers drive down to the cliff's edge to investigate the crash site after hearing her explain what took place. Manny does his best to follow behind his friends on foot. They insisted there was room but he waved them off. He's changed too, Cheyenne thinks, as they share a smile while the ATV carries her off.

As they slow and then stop at the cabin, another set of paramedics are already on scene as are a large number of state police and fish and wildlife officers, all identified by their respective uniforms. A medic is helping the sheriff, who sits in rough shape at the edge of the cabin porch. He manages a gentle wave to Cheyenne. Police have already started taping off the entrance to the cabin with that wide yellow tape she's seen in movies and on TV.

Jason and Rachel appear from behind the rescue vehicles and rush to her side. Cheyenne and Jason don't say anything and only look at one another for a time before finally embracing in a hug. She can't remember the last time she hugged her brother and she wouldn't give it up for anything.

She hears Donovan say something as he darts off. Being a good amount taller than Jason she can see past him and watches as Donovan crashes into the arms of his dad. Cheyenne lets out a long sigh of relief as Donovan finally puts away his tough guy persona and breaks down in his father's arms. He sobs and cries like someone their age should. Her worries about what this might have done to him and the tremendous guilt that weighs on her because of it are lifted at the sight of him still being a child who needs his dad. Somehow, she knows he'll be alright.

Rachel joins the hug after giving them a moment, as does Manny, who is still out of breath from the hike back up the road. They're all sweaty and smelly and she might normally be self-conscious of her hygiene but given the circumstances, she just doesn't care. The feeling of indifference worries her, as it's such a stark contrast to how she used to feel about everything. She hopes she can control it and keep it from bleeding into things that she should care about. Her friends, her family, her future. Only time will tell and, for now, she's thankful she has that.

A helicopter buzzes the canopy and hovers overhead. The downwash kicks dirt particles into her wet, burning eyes but she holds them open.

FORTY

"We're coming back from commercial," the voice says in her ear.

The usual tension swells and she takes a deep breath as the floor manager begins counting down with fingers just off of her main camera. Erin adjusts her position in her chair and steadies her head and facial expression. She could be a photo. The red light above the camera cues her start and she and the teleprompter work in unison.

"As we close out tonight's show, I'd like to reflect on the past eighteen months. A killer is dead. His victims' families can now start processing their losses. The complicated web of deceit that allowed a predator like former sheriff's deputy Darren Harlow, or Darren Finely as we now know, to prey on a small town, and for so long from a position of power, will be a topic of investigation and discussion for years to come."

Erin pauses for effect, searching for a memory to get her to the emotional plane she's trying to reach. There, the tightening in her throat, the warmth in her eyes. Now.

"It's just so heartbreaking that those in authority, the very people who were meant to protect us, became obsessed with

James Finely as their man, completely missing the connection to his estranged son. Was Finely an innocent man? Unlikely, and it could be his own deficiencies that helped to create the monster that took the life of Melody Anderson and so many others. We're still learning the scope of his terror. We may never know the reasons or true toll. Regardless, law enforcement's singular focus on one man prevented them from seeing the snake in their own backyard. And because of those blinders, which one might even call willful negligence but that's for a court to decide, many innocent people have suffered, needlessly."

The floor manager and the voice in her ear signal to wrap it up. She can land this, she has to. So many people are watching and who knows when the next big story will fall in her lap. This is a once-in-a-career opportunity and she'll be damned if it isn't her award-winning legacy. Erin dabs her eyes, careful not to smudge her liner.

"I leave you tonight with a message of hope. A promise. I will not rest until I've exhausted every lead and held to account every person who betrayed our trust: politicians, law enforcement, and yes even news editors."

"Fucking bitch," the voice in her ear scoffs and the sound of a headset hitting the desk is unmistakable. She almost cracks a smile, but she's a professional. Only sincere stoicism is on display for her viewers. Her fans. All of those tuning in to see her hand them their opinion.

"Join me next week in my new time slot with my brand-new show: 'Truth to Power' that you can't afford to miss it. I'm Erin Heart. Goodnight."

With lackluster enthusiasm, the floor manager gives the all-clear as the red light goes dark. The studio lights switch to house lights as Erin stands and unclips her mic. She dismisses the crew that approaches and waves off her assistant.

"Clock out and go home. I'll be here awhile."

It takes no more than five minutes for Erin to make her way to the fifth floor. Marcus' door is cracked and she doesn't even knock. A single light in the corner of the office illuminates his silhouette. There's a stack of something on his desk next to a glass of brown liquor. The bottle sits uncapped with a good amount missing. That can't be a good sign.

"I figured you'd want to chat," says Erin in lieu of a knock.

"Jesus, Erin. I can't pretend I didn't see these. We are so fucked. Does anyone else know about this? And who the fuck gave you the green light on your show pitch? I shut that down weeks ago and you're on the air announcing it. We didn't even have CG!"

Erin is cool as can be and pours herself a glass of whatever he's having.

"Yeah, help yourself." Marcus downs what's left of his and slams the cup on the desk. "You really don't give a fuck that I'll likely be fired for this?"

She doesn't so much as flinch or spill a drop. As she sits across from him and takes a long, smooth sip her eyes roam over the stack of open envelopes in front of him. For once, he's observant, apparently.

"Erin. This may be criminal. If Finely had anything to do with those murders, abductions, who the fuck knows what else, you're complicit. Which means we're complicit!" Marcus gestures to the building around them.

Her glass touches down on the edge of the desk without a sound. Erin leans back in her chair and locks eyes with the man she used to let fuck her. Now it's her turn to do the fucking. And she's got a bigger dick.

"What? Some love letters from a fan? That's as common as Adderall in this business."

"Don't. None of your cutesy, intellectual games you like to play. Do you realize we could all be subpoenaed? I read them. All of them. Jesus, some of them came from prison, so you know there's a record! I mean, what the fuck, did you help him skip parole?" It doesn't sound like a question which is fine because it's too stupid to answer.

"Are you getting to your point or is this going to be as dull as having you inside me, because I've got places to be and a new show to prep for."

The color drains from his face. Good.

"I have no choice but to fire you, Erin. Call your lawyer, or whatever it is your ilk do when they're caught, but you're a cancer and I'm not letting you bring this whole thing down because of your ego. Or trauma. Maybe you're just unwell." He holds out both arms, going from angry to exhausted. "Regardless, you're done. Hand in your key card."

Checkmate. Erin allows a smile to slip, throwing gas onto whatever coals are smoldering underneath his distraught composure. She lifts her phone and presses send. A moment later his phone chimes. He looks down at the device, then back to her.

"The fuck is this?"

After she doesn't respond, he swipes open his phone and begins scrolling.

"This is extortion—"

"You see, Marcus. I'm not fired. You're going to resign. I've saved everything, and I mean everything. Every nasty text, email, sad little dick-pic you've sent me since I started here. And unless you want to be the lead story on my new show, I think you'd best find a new desk to sit behind."

"You fu—"

"Ah, ah. Before you blow prematurely, you might be thinking you'll take me with you. Maybe. But consider this, the conversation is already on my side. Anything you say in rebuttal will be seen as victim shaming, and if you have the balls to bring the Finely story into it, you know you'll be steamrolled by all of the keyboard warriors out there. Have you not been keeping tabs on my current follower count?"

Marcus stares back at her, water filling the corner of his eyes. She envies it, not having to go someplace dark to bring them out. With a sigh, Erin drinks the remainder of her glass, collects the stack of envelopes, and makes her way to the door before turning back. The tough-guy shell has crumbled and Marcus sits flaccid in his chair.

"Send out a resignation email and I'll endorse and sing your praises, but I expect your office, er—*my* office, to be empty come Monday. Open or closed?" She gestures to the door and when he doesn't respond she shrugs and closes it behind her. A flutter fills her stomach and a warmth flows south as she hears sobbing from within. She walks away, clutching the stack of envelopes close to her chest.

FORTY-ONE

The three weeks laid up in the hospital were worse than the beating he took at the cabin. Broken ribs and the deep lacerations from flying through one-hundred-year-old glass were among the worst of his injuries. A mild concussion was a walk in the park, in comparison. Two days of heavy painkillers did the trick and he missed them once they were gone.

Then, the infection set in. With a heavy dose of antibiotics, the fever came down, just in time for a fit of withdrawal. He hadn't had a drink in eight days and his body was treating him worse than any deranged killer could. The only silver lining was not having to conduct the closing case interviews, though he had several directed at him from different bedside agencies. The thought of himself questioning Carla while she soothed her now fatherless baby was enough to cement his decision, well before he was discharged from the hospital.

Now sitting on the edge of the Hawksboro cemetery in the comfort of his police SUV while frost clings to the dried grass, Rodney observes the memorial from a safe distance. Safe from forced gratitude and well-wishes, accolades of heroism and duty, all received with the aftertaste of bitter guilt. Unavoidable disappointment with the stark reminder right in front of them, now no more than vertical stones of masonry art.

Closest to the new gravestone in a bundled semi-circle, are Melody's friends and family. Simone stands front and center, her father's hands placed on both of her shoulders. She cries, staring at the fresh mound of dirt at her feet. The brave group of children that Rodney found at the cabin stand not far off in a huddle. Cheyenne, who Rodney admires more than he could ever vocalize and has no intention of trying, is also centered among her friends. Rodney's surprised, but even her grandparents have braved the cold front and are paying their respects. Kenneth and Miguel stand a short distance behind their sons.

Rodney's breath flows as a cloud into the air out of the open window and vanishes in the light breeze. His arm rests on the door frame and his bare, scab-covered fingers ignore the freezing bite. Footsteps crunch and he instinctively reaches to his empty hip. In the side mirror a light brown business coat fills the reflection. The mayor places a leather-gloved hand on Rodney's forearm, blocking the view of the memorial. He has no choice but to give him his attention as there's nowhere else to look.

"Mayor," Rodney's greeting is as cold as the day.

"Sheriff, glad to see you out and about. We've been worried about you."

The mayor looks over his shoulder at the gathering and then back to Rodney.

"That so? I'm doing just fine."

Fingers squeeze his forearm.

"I've been meaning to speak with you, but you haven't returned my calls."

"Yeah, you know I've just been getting myself situated. A lot of loose ends."

"Interim Sheriff Peterson has been doing a fine job keeping pressure off the department and the town, I'm sure you can imagine our own deputy's involvement in such a travesty has led some to point fingers. Ugly, nasty accusations, really."

"I've only heard great things about Peterson, I'm sure she'll do great."

The sound of the mayor's exhale as he leans down to eye level is excruciating, as is the breath that fills the driver's window. Coffee, maybe an everything bagel with cream cheese. It's all Rodney can do to keep from gagging like a cat on a hairball. If he ever needs a reminder as to why he drank, it's never far away, just has to wait a minute and one is sure to pop up.

"I think we can still turn things around. Return to your post and be the face of accountability. Show everyone that Hawksboro is a place of resilience. Defiance in the face of evil." The mayor makes a fist with his free hand to sell the point.

Rodney uses his right hand to point past the mayor's head, his finger just missing the thick-rimmed glasses and causing a small flinch, as intended.

"Look at that girl over there." The mayor squints and Rodney nods with his chin. "Go on, look at her."

The mayor turns his head and has to crane his neck to swing his nose past Rodney's finger. The group that has gathered at the gravesite has begun dispersing. Simone hangs back and Cheyenne breaks away from her friends. It's only the two girls standing side by side next to the dark earth of Melody's grave. A small pile of soil acts as a wall surrounding the disturbed ground, signifying the break between life and death. It's crazy how his mind thinks when it's not constantly being dulled by substance.

"Cheyenne. The girl we failed."

"What about her? She seems to be doing fine to me. A

real trooper."

Before the mayor can turn his attention away, Rodney grabs the coat collar and rolls his restrained arm free from the grasp, flipping positions and securing the gloved hand to the SUV.

"Watch."

Simone stands with her head down, staring at the brand-new marble slab with ornate writing and dates not yet faded by the wash of time. Cheyenne inches closer until she's within reach. A moment passes and Rodney can feel the mayor move against his grip, but he holds firm. Cheyenne reaches a hand and places it on Simone's shoulder who begins balling, heavy heaves raising and sinking her shoulders. Then Cheyenne retrieves something from her pocket with a free hand. Rodney can't see what it is so he pushes the mayor to the side but doesn't let go. He strains his eyes, but they see clearer than they have in years.

Cheyenne extends a clenched and bare hand in front of Simone who opens both of her black-gloved palms to accept the offering. A flicker of light catches the object as what appears to be a necklace falls from Cheyenne's hand to Simone's. It catches by the chain before it crashes and is lowered with gentle ease into the cupped hands.

Rodney can feel the water filling his eyes, the choke in his Adam's apple restricting his throat. He wills it away so the mayor won't see. Simone looks at her open hands before clutching them shut as if she'll never let go. She pulls her hands to her chest as Cheyenne slides her consoling touch off of Simone's shoulder. Before Cheyenne can turn away Simone throws open both arms and envelopes Cheyenne in a hug. He can't hear what she's saying through her tears but the embrace is returned and both girls stand as one next to Melody's place of rest.

The feeling in Rodney's fingers has gone, either from the cold or the death grip on the mayor's coat, and he releases both hands from the restraint. The mayor stands and straightens himself before looking at Rodney with a blank, uncaring gaze.

"You see, mayor. Cheyenne already represents the best of this town. People like you, and me, only stand to tarnish it further. It's time for us to get out of the way."

"If you think I'm resigning over thi—"

"With all due respect, I find it more likely you'll be recalled. I made sure Sheriff Peterson has access to the whole file, with implicit instructions to share publicly the failures in this case. From the top down."

"Who do you think you are you son of a bitch?"

"Just a civilian, mayor. Just an ordinary citizen."

The mayor's look suggests he didn't see that coming. Rodney retrieves the service belt and badge on the passenger seat from atop a shiny folder. He thrusts the empty weapon and credentials into the stomach of the mayor who has no choice but to hold them lest they fall to his wet feet.

"If you think this—"

Rodney has already started rolling up his window and feigns not being able to hear by pointing to his ear. He shifts into drive and eases down the cemetery road, headed for one last stop to drop off the SUV with Sheriff Peterson at the station. Bystanders cross the path between the disheveled mayor and his view in the mirror. None so much as look in his direction as he leaves, just as he would have it. Rodney's eyes move from the cemetery to the road ahead and then down to the passenger seat. The folder rattles with the vibrations of the rough gravel, threatening to slide to the floor, so he pushes it back away from the edge. The shiny cover of the Canopy Rehab Clinic welcome packet catches the sun's rays and casts a brilliant, colorful reflection across the dash.

FORTY-TWO

"**D**on't forget your jacket," says Gram.

Cheyenne is already pulling on the puffy sleeves. "How could I? It's like thirty degrees outside." It sounds more sarcastic than she intends, but she can't help how some things come out now. It's as if her heart and brain have a strained relationship and aren't on speaking terms.

She feels bad, purposely avoiding Gram's look in case any signs of hurt manifest across those tired wrinkles, but an apology won't come either. Whatever mechanism produces the will to ask for forgiveness is broken, along with who knows what else. It's not that she isn't sorry, just that the will to speak it, to hear her voice say the words and await a response, is gone. It's as if she feels like she's paid her dues for life and the requirements of etiquette shouldn't apply to her, but again her mind and heart are at odds.

"Just don't want you to catch a cold is all. Here, I packed your lunch." Gram rushes to the counter to retrieve the brown paper sack.

"I know Gram, thank you." Cheyenne hugs her as she turns to hand over the lunch.

Grampa enters the kitchen with a newspaper in hand. "Gonna be a cold one," he adds without looking up.

Gram and Cheyenne share a smile but it quickly fades. As Grampa sits at the table, Jason bounces into the kitchen already dressed to leave the house. His hair is combed neat and while it's been months since she's been back home, he suddenly looks older. Not like her little brother, but equal or older to her. She might think back later that this was the moment when he was no longer under her care, even if it was never official, the weight of it lifts and evaporates so fast that she's not even sure it was a real feeling at all. Her memory provides no reassurance that it had ever been any other way than how it is now.

"I'm buying lunch today, Gram," he says as he looks through the fridge for who knows what.

"Alright sweetie, but you take this just in case you change your mind."

She hands him a brown bag of his own and he accepts it without skipping a beat.

"Ready, dork?" Jason asks as he closes the fridge empty-handed. A grin follows and he turns to the door.

"Ready, dweeb," Cheyenne says as if going through the motions of what the banter is supposed to be between them.

"You two keep an eye out for each other," Grampa calls out from behind his paper.

"We will," they say in unison.

"Cheyenne, you sure you're ready to go back? It's been a while—"

"Hun…" Grampa says while folding the corner below his eyes.

"I know, I know. You've been home all winter break, is all."

"It's okay, Gram. I'll be fine. I can't stay cooped up in this house forever."

Grampa returns to his reading. Gram nods and gives a wave.

"Have a good day sweetheart. You call us if you need anything at all. Grampa can come pick you up. There's no shame in easing back into a routine."

The word routine almost makes her laugh, not in the way a funny video or joke would, but from it being an absurd notion that something could be normal enough to feel routine again. She holds it back, daring not to risk hurting Gram's feelings any more than she already has this morning, by the fault of her new, dark sense of humor that is undoubtedly unshared.

She leaves her jacket unzipped as they descend the slick porch steps and onto the sidewalk. A light snow covers everything and the air is bitter. The salt Grampa had put on the stairs and landing the night before had done its job and just the shine of the melt remains on the cracked and dirty concrete.

It's frigid, but Cheyenne drinks it in. She allows the chill to seep through her bones, the dull pain a welcome visitor like an undeniable truth coursing through her nerves. A reminder she's alive and present. Jason walks next to her on the sidewalk, already playing on the phone. He scrolls and taps away. He must have felt her watching as he looks up and turns off the screen.

"You sure you don't want it, now that you're going back to school?" Jason asks as he gestures the device toward her.

"I'm sure. It's yours now."

"Good. I mean I would have, but I'd have to delete all my settings and tell all my girlfriends to stop messaging me. Would have been a whole thing."

Cheyenne musters a laugh. "Does Rachel know about these girlfriends?"

"I'm kidding! Don't tell her I said that."

They walk in silence a few blocks until they reach Main Street.

Other kids, also bundled for the walk outside, are staggered on each side of the street, all headed in the same direction of Hawksboro High School.

"Hey, over there!" Jason points to the other side of the crosswalk.

Rachel, Donovan, and Manny walk down the opposite side of the street, stopping at the intersection. They notice each other and wave. Donovan gives a head nod and Cheyenne does her best to return it in kind.

Once traffic passes, they cross to meet the others. Donovan and Manny both fist bump Jason who gravitates to Rachel, his phone suddenly out of sight.

"Hey, Chey," Rachel says, a polite softness to her voice.

Cheyenne puts on her first smile of the day, but she's cringing at the thought that this is how everyone will be around her. Maybe she will take an early day to save her face muscles from revolting against the continuous commands to perform.

"Hi, Rachel. You look nice today. I like your hat," says Cheyenne, trying to move the group forward from standing still. Anxiety has crept into her subconscious where stillness feels akin to vulnerability, and only fidgeting, movement, progress, bring temporary relief.

"What up homie!" Manny says as he devours her in a bear hug. She doesn't hate it. At least he's being himself around her and not putting on kiddie gloves. She hates that.

"Good to see you, Manny."

"Holidays were good to you, I see," adds Jason.

Everyone but Chey and Manny laugh as he grabs his stomach. "Hey, what's that supposed to mean?"

Donovan shoves him out of the way and Manny laughs it off. They finally walk forward and Donovan and Cheyenne follow close behind.

"Hey," he says.

"Hey."

He blows out air into the cold, filling the void it would seem with a classic cloud of vapor that seems a requirement under such weather. Cheyenne doesn't have the motivation to try to think of anything to say. She hopes the silence is good enough and hates to think that if it's not, she just doesn't care enough to fake otherwise.

As they approach the turn into the school, pattering footsteps race up from behind them. They startle Cheyenne as she has a flashback of being grabbed off of the bench. It's not a vision, more like muscle memory, a sound forever associated with an experience. Her eyes tighten and her body stiffens, her feet glued to the sidewalk. Donovan's hand finds hers. Thank God, as she couldn't move to find his if she wanted to, a night terror in the broad, morning sun.

"Wait up," a voice calls out.

A girl, maybe a grade younger with thick glasses and a bright pink stocking hat, catches up to the group. Donovan releases his grasp and Cheyenne's hand falls to her side.

"Sorry, is it okay if I walk with you?" she asks nobody in particular.

They all look to one another but no one answers for the group.

"It's just, I'm new. And some kids have already been on me about my glasses. I won't bother you or say anything at all, I promise. I just don't want to walk alone."

The girl looks at her feet, her body language suggesting she expects them to laugh or walk away. Maybe even grab her glasses and smash them on the ground. Cheyenne shakes off the vision, or what she's come to call "The Visitor." In seemingly random but frequent social situations, her mind conjures the worst thing that could be said or done to someone. It makes her feel evil, even thinking it, but she's reconciled that it's not an impulse to do it, the way a sociopath would, but a defensive measure. She can't be surprised by her worst feelings if she's already played them out before they happen.

"You said you're new?" Manny speaks up, louder than he probably intended. It comes out as eager and pitchy.

She nods.

"Picked a hell of a time to move here!" He guffaws at his joke. "Name's Manny!" He thrusts his hand out which makes the girl jump back. "This is Jason, Rachel, Don, and Chey," he points with his outstretched hand.

The girl finally takes it and shakes it for a brief moment before withdrawing it to the safety of her coat pocket.

"I'm Willow."

The poor girl couldn't make eye contact to save her life, Cheyenne thinks.

Manny steps toward her and gestures for her to join him at the front of the group.

"Well then, I *Willow* you to walk with us," Manny says with theatrics.

"Jesus, Manny." Donovan slams his hand to his brow.

Willow steps past Cheyenne and Donovan with a polite smile and walks up front. Manny walks next to her as Jason slaps his arm from behind. "That was awful, dude. Seriously."

Manny pops a middle finger in his direction but is quick to cover it with a smile as Willow looks at him. Cheyenne can hear Donovan giggling to himself. She knows he's trying to stifle his amusement for her sake.

She starts laughing out loud, hoping the others will feel at ease. As the jovial sounds taper, Cheyenne reaches over to

Donovan, her numb fingers finding his own once again. They interlock but nothing is said. Nothing needs to be said, she hopes.

A truck's engine roars somewhere along the street of the school zone where crossing guards wave behind tightly buttoned and reflective parkas. Their faces are hidden behind sinister scarves that obscure their identities. They could be anyone. They could be him. The truck is his truck and the guard is a tall deputy waiting for the right moment. She can't help but clench Donovan's hand even tighter and tries to sense if it causes him pain. As it passes at the mandated 15 miles per hour, it's not his truck at all. It's not even a pickup truck, but a delivery driver and the guard isn't tall or even a man. It's Marianne, the kind, older Hispanic woman who's been at the same crosswalk for as long as Cheyenne has trekked to school.

The tension passes as it drives away, her anxiety fading with the noise. Cheyenne has a moment of reconsideration. Panic that she can't handle whatever her life is now. That all of these new quirks that plague her mind are somehow visible to everyone that she encounters. She's certain they can see that she is buried beneath a stack of crazed animals, beating and pounding on her head, commanding her every move, and operating her hair like the strings of a puppet.

And then she takes a deep breath, letting it flow from her lips as slow and silent as her burning lungs will allow. Cheyenne pictures the suffocating feelings riding away on the cloud of vapor into the air, while not missing a single stride in lockstep with her friends.

FORTY-THREE

Melt runs down the large street-facing windows of the Manhattan coffee shop. Outside, stacks of snow plowed to the curb, line both sidewalks where pedestrians move, undaunted by the weather. The line from the cash register extends out of the door and those inside shiver as a new patron opens, holds, and then finally closes the door to wait for their turn to order.

The aroma is rich and warm. When asked where she could take a meeting, she was quick to Google the trendiest but least tourist-frequented coffee shop on the Lower East Side. This place did not disappoint though the lukewarm reaction from the woman across the table when she arrived made her second guess the choice. Erin looks at the other people sitting and chatting and decides she's overthinking it. She fits in. This is where she belongs.

"No bullshit?" the woman across from her asks while flipping through a thick, brad-bound stack of papers.

"Linda, I've poured my heart and soul into this manuscript. The past two years of my life have been consumed with this story and the public deserves a tell-all." Erin takes a long, dramatic sip of her latte, careful to wipe any foam away before it can cling to her upper lip.

After flipping through the last few pages, Linda closes the manuscript and slides it off to the side to make room for her own steaming cup. Erin watches the papers move and turns her eyes back to Linda to get a read on where she stands.

"You know, when you first sent this to me, I wasn't sure. But I gave it a read and was quite shocked. After my editor pushed back on some of the details, we were going to pass. But your persistence, shall we say, was cause to reconsider."

"Look, I understand. It's unbelievable, I'll be the first to admit it. But that's more of a reason that you should be the one to help me tell it. Picture it, out there." Erin waves to the sidewalk. "People walking to work, on the subway, book in hand. Listening to the audio version while their earbuds give them every jaw-dropping and gruesome detail."

Linda follows along looking around the coffee shop before returning her consideration back to Erin. "Did you bring them?" Linda says, finally.

"Skip the foreplay, I get it." Erin smirks and pulls out the stack of envelopes bound by a thick red rubber band. She places them with a thud that causes a small drip of coffee to spill over Linda's cup and onto the distressed wood table.

"Oops."

The joy that falls over Linda's face suggests she didn't even notice the spill.

"May I?" She's terrible at hiding her greed.

"Take your time."

Erin sits back in her chair pretending not to watch the woman fawn over the contents of the Finely letters. She fantasizes about making this place her regular spot, fans stopping her for a photo, sitting quietly in the corner pretending to work while watching others go about their days.

She loses track of time in her fantasy until Linda places the current letter down and stares with her mouth agape.

"So, this bastard covered for his deranged son the whole time? And as a thank you he gets whacked in a bout of patricide, but not before spilling his metaphorical guts to you in this letter?"

A humble nod seems appropriate. "Sounds about right."

"The date on this letter, the last one, is a few months before that last girl was taken. You realize if you put this out in public, they could come for you, especially as a journalist. Say what you will, but *they* believe you have an obligation to report this. They could rightly say you were in a position to have prevented the second girl from being abducted altogether."

Fuck, I'm losing her, she thinks. If anything will give her cold feet it's the risk of representing a tarnished name.

"You're right, the date is the summer prior, and had it been in my possession then I would have been the first to turn it in to the authorities."

Linda seems a bit more at ease.

"Unfortunately, it didn't find my desk until after the incident with the sheriff and the death of the perpetrator. Because of that failure, the head of the mailroom has been let go. What you see as a loose end is now a pretty little bow."

"Let me ask you though, why you? What did Finely see in you that he trusted you with all of these admissions? He could have cleared his name if he really was having second thoughts on being the scapegoat for his son."

"I wish I knew. Ever since that first meeting at his parole hearing he took a liking to me. I ignored the first few letters, but they kept coming. Then once I heard he fell off the map, I thought I should crack into them, maybe see if I could help. But I'd be lying if I said it wasn't out of fear that he might be coming for me. Safest place was in the know, I thought."

"You turned these over to the police? How on earth did you get them back?"

"Not exactly. As you've read, nothing in the early letters suggested anything criminal. Just the ramblings of a crazy man. He didn't mention his whereabouts or anything time specific, all history and philosophy from a demented mind. It wasn't until later that he started opening up about his supposed innocence and slowly letting on that he had a son."

"Who happened to be a sheriff's deputy in the very tow—"

"Which you'll notice he also never mentioned. Had I known any details it would have been my duty to deliver it to the proper authorities. And they were the ones being tight-lipped on the investigation."

Linda looks over the table in front of her. She places a hand on the manuscript then stacks the envelopes back in a neat pile and slides them back in front of Erin.

She's quick to take them, reapplying the rubber band and placing them in her bag.

As Linda lifts a folder from her lap and places it in the center, she clicks a pen between her thumb and finger. "Now, I'll still need to run this by the editor and then legal once more, but if it's all true then I think we'll have quite the hot item on our hands. Might even get your book on a board in Times Square."

Erin can't contain the beaming smile that follows. She pictures the cover, yet to be designed, on a digital display high above the world-famous plaza, seen by millions. Her name in bright letters with a blurb from an author of note. Linda pushes the folder and the pen closer to Erin, indicating it's now her decision to make.

"It is all true, isn't it?" Linda asks with a laugh.

Grabbing the pen with more eagerness than she should, Erin flips open the folder to the first page of her contract and looks up before signing.

"Well Linda, you know what they say. Truth belongs to the storytellers."

She scribbles her name in a wide sweeping motion and flips to the next page.

ACKNOWLEDGEMENTS

Thank you to the many mentors who made this book possible. Writing can be a lonely business but everything that comes after the first draft is anything but a solo effort. Grinding through the real work is made that much easier with talented and generous professionals in your corner. Scott Blackburn, one of the most pay-it-forward authors out there. Thank you for your kind words and support. I'm punching above my weight because of it. Coy Hall, your deep knowledge of horror and history are inspirational and one of those reminders that one can always do more research. I appreciate your feedback. Alexander Nader, thank you for being one of the first authors to take on my manuscript and the cool blurb. Keep your foot on the gas. C.W. Blackwell, thank you for fitting my work into your schedule and providing a phenomenal blurb. Brett Allen and Travis Klempan, thanks for providing a sort of writers' therapy group. It's nice to complain where it's not encapsulated for all of time.

Those who read my book early and in a very rough form, thank you for braving the errors and providing your valuable story feedback. To Dianne Stevens, your excitement and positive notes gave me fuel right when I needed it. Thank you, thank you,

ACKNOWLEDGEMENTS

thank you. Linda Walker, gaining a reader's perspective early on is crucial to the revising process. Thank you for your thoughts and I'll keep sending you my early stories for as long as you'd like. Will Pittman and Marie Sinadjan, your attention to detail is baffling and a commodity that, lucky for me, is worth far more than what you charge. Thank you both in all sincerity.

To my wife, Jessica, for agreeing to read this one in its first form and helping to identify errors. Thank you for at least pretending you don't see me differently after reading what comes out of my crazy mind. You're the best mom ever.

And to my daughter, who better not be reading this for at least another 15 or 16 years. You're the reason I do everything. May I never fail to keep the real monsters at bay.

Verba volant, scripta manent.

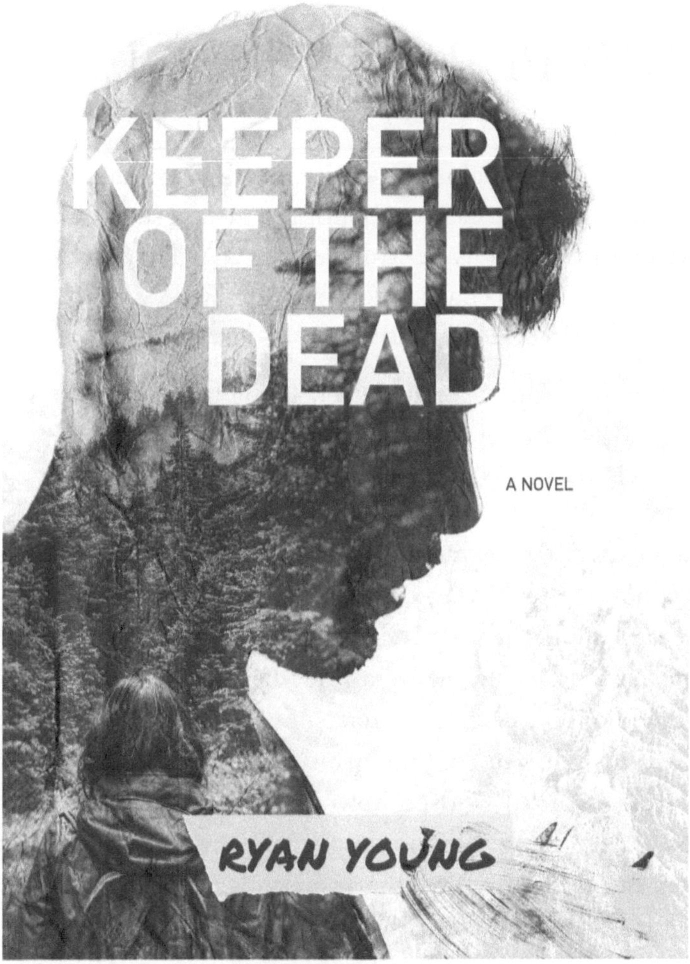

ABOUT THE AUTHOR

Ryan Young is a writer and video producer with nearly twenty years of experience in the creative industry. After graduating from the inaugural Film Bachelor's program at Full Sail University, he fell in love with writing, producing, directing, and editing. Ryan lives in Orlando, Florida with his wife and daughter. When he's not writing or filming, he enjoys cooking, working out, and traveling to places with some elevation. His debut novel, KEEPER OF THE DEAD, was released in September of 2022 in paperback and an audiobook is forthcoming.

www.theryanyoung.com
Instagram @ryanyoungwriter
Twitter @ryanyoungwriter